INSIDE CUT

A C.T. FERGUSON CRIME NOVEL (#7)

TOM FOWLER

WIDENINGGYREMEDIA

Published by Widening Gyre Media.

Cover Design: 100 Covers

Editing: Chase Nottingham

For Lisa and Isabel.

And for my grandfather Bill, who helped instill in me a lifelong love of words.

CHAPTER 1

THE ARRIVAL OF SPRING MEANS MANY THINGS TO MANY people. For several of my college friends and me, it meant the start of a new lacrosse season. We enjoyed a good run at Loyola, even winning it all my last year of eligibility. As we got older, some guys moved away, others married off, and it became harder to get the band back together.

Tonight, I'd tossed back a few brews with five of my former teammates. One had a six-year run as a pro lacrosse player before injuries got the better of him. All of us were doing well. I was still the only one with an interesting job, though the fact I still held it provided some surprise to my fellow revelers. And maybe a little to me, too.

A couple of the fellows had families to get home to, so we called it a night just after nine. I'd turned thirty the previous November, and I never felt older than I did in this moment. Leaving a bar shortly past nine? Didn't we stay up all night in college? How often did we woo coeds until the wee hours and then arrive on time for eight AM classes? I reminded the family men they should each get a glass of prune juice for the road. They responded with a common gesture telling me I was number one.

I exited onto the mean streets of Towson. Pubs and restaurants dominated both sides of the road with a few retail stores mixed in for good measure. I walked down York Road to the garage where I left my car when parking—as it often did in the area—proved dicey.

Before I made it half a block, I saw two men toss another guy onto the sidewalk. They were too small to be bouncers and too unsteady to be sober. The fellow on the ground stared back up with wide eyes, which he cast to me when he noticed my approach.

"You take it back, you damn Ay-rab!" one of the men said. I figured he pronounced "Arab" the way he did because he was a cretin, and being at least two sheets to the wind didn't help.

"Go back home and speak Ay-rab!" the other added. They both loomed over the third man, who remained on the ground. He wore jeans and a white sports team jacket, and as I drew closer, I noticed the green, white, and red bars on the left breast.

I stopped a couple paces short of the scene. A few other people walked by, some stopping to snap a picture as they did. Never mind there might be an assault happening; Instagram needed to get the scoop. "Ease off, guys," I said, eyeing the angry duo. "You're both drunk." Each man stood about six feet, giving me two inches on them. They weren't particularly big—both were built like they peaked in high school and spent the next two decades sliding downhill.

"He's an Ay-rab," the first one said. Gray chased away the black hair on his head. His beady eyes darted between me and the frightened fellow on the concrete.

"Arab."

"Huh?"

"The word is 'Arab,' and I don't think this guy is one."

"How you mean?" the other one said. Breath reeking of whiskey and old tobacco blew into my face. His blond hair remained untouched by gray, though pockmarks dotted his face.

"See the flag on his jacket?" They both looked down and then nodded a second later. "It's the flag of Iran." Below it was script I couldn't read.

"So?" the gray-haired one said.

"So it means he's most likely an ethnic Persian." The man on the sidewalk bobbed his head in assent. "Not an Arab."

"We don't much like Iran, neither," the blond one said.

"Guys, move along. You're drunk."

The fair-haired one stared at me. "Who the hell are you?" He gave me an ineffectual shove to the shoulder.

I answered with a hard punch to his solar plexus. He stumbled back a step, sucked wind, and leaned on a street-lamp for support. The other one scowled. "Plenty more where that came from," I told him. He glowered a bit more, collected his buddy, and they walked away. I was about to offer my hand to the guy on the sidewalk when he got to his feet.

"Thanks," he said, running a hand through wavy black hair. "Buy you a drink?"

"Sure."

* * *

"WHAT DO YOU DO?"

It's a question I've gotten a lot. Most men in fact hear it any time they're talking to another man at a social gathering of any sort. Ages ago, we might have compared spears or pelts. Now careers were the measure we took of one another. Once names and how everyone is doing get sorted out, the occupation query inevitably comes next. Sometimes, it's posed out of genuine curiosity and others as a form of one-upmanship. I took it in the former sense. "Private investigator."

Arash—we established names right away—showed wide eyes and then offered a slow nod. "Seems like you can handle yourself." He looked around the pub, and I did, too. We sat at a table near the bar. The place was at about half capacity. The menu and decor would not help it stand apart in any way; I didn't even catch the name as we walked in.

"I do all right," I said. "A pair of drunks like those two makes it easy." Arash sipped his amber lager. I nursed a ginger ale, having already downed three beers earlier. "What about you?"

He thought about it, frowning a few times, then opening and closing his mouth before answering. "Sports analytics."

I glanced to the Iranian flag on his jacket and the foreign script beneath it. "You a soccer player?"

His eyes brightened. "Yes. How did you know?"

"I figure you don't play a lot of hockey in the desert."

Arash chuckled. "No, we do not." He paused. "America does not care much about soccer, so I've focused on other sports. Baseball has already seen a . . . statistical revolution, I believe it's called. I work mostly on football and basketball."

"You working on new stats?"

He answered with another pause, this time for another swig of beer. "Sort of. I try to stick more to . . . predictive modeling. Are you familiar with statistics?"

I nodded. "Computer science degree."

"How did you end up as a private investigator?"

I never had a good answer for this. It was a complicated

journey with a long stop in Hong Kong, an arrest by the Chinese police, my eventual return to the States, and my parents funding my *pro bono* cases. Rather than spill this considerable cup of beans, I said, "It lets me do some things I'm good at."

"This is what my job does, too."

"You trying to catch on with a pro team?"

Arash didn't answer right away. Maybe he simply liked to consider what he said, especially after two inebriated idiots almost beat him up over his words. English was probably his third language, though he spoke it well and with only a light accent. "I guess it would be good. I am still establishing myself, though. Maybe later."

I didn't think there was much more ground to cover. A chance encounter spurred this conversation, but I thought it ran its course. "I should get going," I said, gulping down the rest of my soda and tasting its gingery bite.

Arash held out his hand, and I shook it. "Thank you, C.T. I have a feeling my night would not have gone very well without your help."

"If I get home in time, maybe I can make someone else's night, too." I walked out into the chilly Towson night air. After a couple blocks, I arrived at my car. It was an Audi S4, the last year of the prior generation and thus the final one to come with a manual transmission. I put it in gear and started my drive back to Baltimore.

* * *

I PULLED onto the concrete pad behind my house in Federal Hill. Thanks to a surge of revelers on weekends, leaving cars on the streets became dicey even with the parking pass issued to all residents. I shut off the car and entered my house through the back. I owned an end-unit rowhouse, and the rear door opened into the kitchen. When I walked into the living room, I smiled when I saw Gloria Reading on the couch waiting for me.

We met more than two years ago during my first case. Our relationship was one of fun and convenience for a while before we both discovered we wanted more. Gloria didn't live with me—her house was three of mine, so why would she?— but she stayed over most nights. The room seemed to brighten as she beamed, stood from the couch, and kissed me. "How was it?"

"Not bad," I said, keeping my arms around her. "The crew seems to get smaller every year."

"Probably harder to get everyone together now that you're all so old," she said. "Some of your teammates might even be over thirty."

I'd hit the big three-oh a few months ago. The late birthday meant I was usually the youngest person on the team. This got balanced out by our club winning the championship during my first year of graduate school. One of the fellows I hoisted brews with tonight was thirty-one, but the rest were my age or younger. "Just wait a couple years," I told Gloria. "When you hit thirty, I'll never let you forget it."

"I'm going to be twenty-nine forever."

"I'm pretty sure numbers don't work the way you want."

"I'll make them work that way," she insisted.

"Let me know how it goes. Meanwhile, you'll have a big three and a big zero on your cake before long."

"Will you still love me when I'm an old woman of thirty?" I shrugged. Gloria put on her best shocked face and slapped me on the shoulder. "Afraid I'll be past my prime?"

"Not really," I said. "I do OK for a man of such advanced age."

"You're not bad." Gloria pressed herself against me, and we kissed. In a cosmic display of bad timing, my cell phone buzzed in my pocket. "Ignore it," Gloria said in a breathy voice. She pulled my quarter-zip sweater over my head. The phone quieted.

Then it buzzed again.

Gloria frowned. I pulled the blasted thing out of my pocket and declined the call. When I checked the log, I saw the same number had tried me twice. Make it three times as the same digits flashed across the screen again. "I guess I should answer it," I said. I leaned in and kissed Gloria one more time. "Won't be long."

"You'd better not be." She headed upstairs.

"Hello?" I said to the person harshing my groove.

"Are you C.T. Ferguson?" A woman's voice, and it sounded kind of weak and tired.

"I am."

"I think I need your help . . . my son needs your help."

"What's the problem?"

"He's in trouble, and I'm not sure how he's going to get out of it."

"Have you been to the police?"

She sighed, and it hit my ear like the hiss of a dying snake. "We can't go to the police."

I expected more explanation there, but none was forthcoming. Extracting information from reticent potential clients was probably my least favorite part of the job. "Why not?"

"It's something I think I should tell you in person," she said.

I glanced upstairs. Gloria would be in bed waiting for me by now, and I didn't plan on disappointing her. Or myself. "Can we talk about it tomorrow morning?"

She hesitated but eventually said, "That should be fine." We confirmed the address of my office, and I talked her out of the beastly hour of eight AM for the more reasonable ten o'clock. She ended the call.

I bounded up the stairs two at a time.

CHAPTER 2

I NEVER ARRIVE EARLY. NO MATTER THE OCCASION, I CAN
be counted on to show up at least a few minutes late. Most
people who know me take this into account and adjust their
expectations. Potential clients, however, usually seethe as the
minute hand advances.

At six minutes past ten, I exited the elevator and walked
down the hall to my office. I'd rented this space in the Care-
First building for about a year after running the business out
of my house grew too dangerous. The corridor carpet got
stained with blood—not mine—once, and the management
company sounded frosty most of the time I heard from them.
My good publicity was ultimately a boon for the building, but
if I hit a patch of bad luck, I think their calculus would work
against me.

A slender black woman in a baseball cap stood outside
my door. As I drew closer, I realized she was thin to the point
of being unhealthy, exemplified by the wispy and patchy hair
under the cap. I offered her a smile as I unlocked. She didn't
return it.

We both entered, and I keyed into the inner part of the
office. My desk and computer equipment sat in there, while

the rest served as a no-frills reading room. The only maga-
zines I scattered about were outdated ones I swiped from
doctors' offices. The place had room for a secretary, but my
caseload didn't justify such an expense, which was entirely
by design.

"Coffee?" I said as the serious woman sat in a chair. She
nodded. I'd already wolfed down two cups in my mad dash
out of the house this morning, but one more wouldn't hurt. I
don't think it's possible to drink too much coffee in a day. The
Keurig formerly in my home kitchen now plied its trade here.
I brewed two single cups. "How do you take it?"

"Black." She sounded tired.

I carried the cups to my desk, placed my prospective
client's in front of her, and sat in my leather executive chair.
"What can I do for you?"

She didn't answer right away. Instead, she made a show
of sniffing the coffee a few times, offering a faint nod of
approval, and taking a small sip. Once she seemed happy
with the quality of my java, she spoke. "It's my son. I think
he's in trouble."

I glanced at her hat, which read J-H-C in block letters.
John Hanson College, unless I missed my guess. "At school?"

"Yes."

I expected her to elaborate, but she said nothing else.
Rather than roll my eyes and sigh, I took a sip of coffee.
"What kind of trouble?"

"I'm speculating," she said. "It's all based on a phone
conversation."

Again, nothing else was forthcoming. I wondered why
this never happened to detectives in the books I read. They
either got a man who wouldn't shut up or a woman whose
legs never ended. "I need details if I'm going to help you.
Being coy doesn't work for anyone here."

She bucked herself up with a drink from her mug. "I heard my son talking on his phone. He kept saying he didn't want to do something. Told whoever it was a bunch of times. Eventually, he sighed and gave in. I don't know what it was about."

"Who's your son?"

"Calvin Murray."

I blinked a few times. "The point guard?"

"Yes."

"He's a really good player," I said. "If he comes out this year, he should go in the NBA lottery."

My prospective client showed me a thin smile. "I know. I've been hearing about his draft prospects and pro career for years now. Ever since he was in high school. If he could've gone directly to the NBA then, I think he would've."

"You don't know what the conversation was about?" She shook her head. "Or who he was talking to?" Another shake. "They play soon, don't they?"

"Yes. First round of the conference tournament. They're expected to win."

I didn't follow college hoops much except when the tournaments began. Then things got interesting. JHC played in the Colonial Athletic Association. It wasn't a big or prestigious conference, but whoever won received an automatic bid to March Madness. As they were last year, JHC was favored to win the CAA and advance to the big tournament. Calvin Murray, one of the top point guards in the country, was the main reason for their success. "Could he have been talking to a coach?"

"I doubt it. They usually text."

"Potential pro agent?" I said.

"No. We haven't decided on any of that yet."

"I don't have a lot to go on here," I said. "He could have been talking to a friend about—"

"No," she broke in. "He wasn't talking to someone he liked. I could tell." She paused. "I got cancer."

I figured this to be the case. "I'm sorry."

She waved a thin hand. "It's not so bad. I'm doing pretty well. Got into some clinical trial a few months ago, and now my medication's getting paid for."

"Great news."

"It is . . . except I think my son had something to do with it."

"Is he pre-med?"

"No."

I frowned in thought. College athletes were amateurs. They could hardly get a donut from someone without being suspended for it. Open payouts were highly unlikely. There were ways to funnel money to a college athlete, however. The kind of money needed to buy cancer medication probably required something significant in return. People in position to hand cash to a basketball player probably had specific favors in mind. An idea formed in my head. "Like I said, there's not a lot to go on here, but I can look around."

This got me my first smile. "Thank you."

"No promises, though. If it turns out this was just some college bullshit, I'm going to leave you to have a conversation with your son."

"I understand," she said.

We went over a few more details—including my client's name, which was Denise—and then she left me to ponder the matter.

I came up with an idea, and it wasn't good . . . especially not for Denise Murray.

* * *

BEFORE I COULD DELVE TOO FAR into my idea, I heard the
familiar ding of the elevator. A few other businesses shared
the floor with me, but they rarely got much foot traffic. Sure
enough, the footsteps headed in my direction, and I thought
the cadence sounded familiar. A few seconds later, Gloria
poked her head in the door.

She smiled when she saw me behind my desk in the inner
office. I spied the brown bag in her hand. A glance at my
watch told me it was almost one o'clock. It appeared I'd be
having lunch at my desk today. "Want some company?"
Gloria said as she walked in and sat in one of my guest chairs
—the same one Denise Murray occupied not long ago.

"If it's yours, always."

Gloria opened the bag and removed a few paper-
wrapped sandwiches. "Shrimp salad," she said, dropping one
in front of me. It landed with a thud not unlike that of a brick.
An entire school of prawns—or whatever the hell of a group
of shrimp is called—gave their lives for this sandwich, and I
intended to honor them.

I unwrapped the monster meal as Gloria extracted two
cups of coleslaw, a couple cheap plastic sporks, and a small
stack of napkins from the bag. The sandwich featured a
kaiser roll packed with more filling than its bakers intended it
to hold. I inhaled the aromas of seafood, Old Bay seasoning,
mayo, onion, and a few random spices. "Thanks for lunch."

Gloria gave me a thumbs-up with her left hand as her
own hoagie dominated the right one. We each ate for a few
minutes before she said, "You busy?"

"Just met with a client not long before you walked in."
Gloria usually asked about my cases, but I couldn't recall her
asking if I were busy. Her opening smile faded to a more

serious look. Some of it could be attributed to eating, but I got the feeling she wanted to tell me something. "What's up?"

"Davenport's having a fundraiser soon." Vincent Davenport, local business mogul and asshole of the first division, was the first person to work with Gloria as she began organizing charitable soirées. He's also the father of Melinda, a former prostitute and current friend of mine, and their reunion was a hundred percent attributable to my hard work. Melinda heads up the Nightlight Foundation, trying to save other young girls from the life which derailed her for years. Normally, Gloria would be upbeat about a Davenport-helmed fundraiser.

"Isn't this a good thing?"

"Usually," she said. "He didn't reserve me any seats this time."

It may have seemed like a small slight, but I knew this was unusual. Gloria has worked on a bunch of fundraisers, and she always gets offered a pair of tickets. "Why the hell not?"

She shook her head and blew out a snort. "He says it was an oversight. The event's sold out now, of course."

"Sounds like it's one you want to attend."

"I do. You know we don't go to a lot of these." I nodded. "I often decline the tickets and let the organizers sell them and raise a little more money. Davenport puts on a good show, though, and it's not like the price of two seats is going to break him."

"I told you he's an asshole," I said.

Gloria smiled gently. "I know you don't like him."

"Not liking him is an understatement."

"For what happened with Melinda?"

"Mostly. Plus, his general demeanor. If he told me the sky was blue, I'd run outside to double-check."

"I'm just frustrated, is all." Gloria absently stirred her remaining slaw with the spork.

"Try not to worry about it. I'm sure you'll have something else coming up." Her head bobbed as she continued to look at the small container on the desk. "The next time Davenport calls, tell him to fuck off."

"I could never say that to him," she said, though the grin playing on her lips told me she'd considered it before.

"Fine," I said. "Pass the phone to me, and I'll tell him."

"I know you would."

We finished eating, but Gloria didn't go after the rest of her meal with much enthusiasm. About a quarter of her sandwich remained, which I gladly wrapped up and put in the fridge. I hoped I'd remember it before the shrimp turned green. We kissed goodbye, and Gloria left. I watched her walk down the hall, and she gave a small wave as she got on the elevator.

This was her first taste of disappointment. I was proud of her for working with charities and using her money and connections to open doors for them which may have otherwise remained closed. Over time, she'd learn to deal with situations like this.

After all, my job disappointed me all the time.

* * *

JOHN HANSON COLLEGE was named for a long-dead Maryland man who served as President of the United States under the Articles of Confederation. Some local historians insist Hanson was the first president elected under the Articles, but this does not withstand scrutiny. Still, Hanson has been something of a celebrity in Maryland for his work in the late eighteenth century. We don't get a ton of famous people, so we tend to cling to the ones we have.

The college bearing his name—and his mascot, the Presidents—stood on a campus in Cockeysville. It sat about a mile from the state fairgrounds in Baltimore County. JHC was smaller than similar schools like Towson but enjoyed a sports resurgence in the last few years. The apex of this was recruiting Calvin Murray to play point guard. He was easily the best player in the state and the conference, and probably top five in the country.

Being the runaway best player on an otherwise so-so team afforded Murray a great deal of control over the outcomes of games. From what I saw, JHC ran a modern offense with lots of motion, picks and rolls, and quick guards darting and cutting through opposing defenses. Lacking elite size, they often deployed a three-guard lineup and beat other schools with speed, motion, and good shooting.

I scanned their results. The Presidents led the conference and were expected to win its tournament. They'd seen a few close games along the way, however. In December at home against Drexel, they squeaked out a three-point win. A quick search of gambling lines showed JHC favored by nine going into the game.

One event did not a pattern make, of course. I cross-referenced JHC basketball results with posted lines. I found eight games where the Presidents were favored by eight or more points. They lost one outright and won the other seven. In only one of those seven wins did they cover the spread, winning by an even dozen. The other six saw them eke out close wins. There were a couple other games where they were favored by four or five and lost.

None of this constituted a smoking gun. However, it looked an awful lot like point shaving. At least one player on the team—and Calvin Murray would be the logical target—needed to be involved, playing worse than normal to influence the outcome. Officials could also be involved.

For any of this to work, some heavy-stakes gamblers or bookies needed to pull the strings. The Colonial Athletic Association enjoyed a fair bit of local prestige, but it wasn't a big deal nationally. This could work in the favor of whomever ran the operation. Fewer people would be sniffing around a smaller conference's games.

My first case saw me bust a local bookie and budding loan shark, my old friend Vinnie Serrano. He was busy making license plates somewhere. If a local person were involved, someone probably gathered up the rubble of Vinnie's empire and rebuilt.

I didn't like where this was headed.

CHAPTER 3

A LITTLE LATER, I DROVE INTO LITTLE ITALY. IT'S ONE OF Baltimore's iconic neighborhoods. While many of the old-guard Italian residents died or moved away, some still remained as did the restaurants. Today, I parked near *Il Buon Cibo*, which was well-known for its cuisine and little-known for being owned by the head of organized crime in the city.

My parents had long been friends with Tony Rizzo, which meant I'd known him most of my life. We got along well, though things became a little frosty when I came back from Hong Kong and told him I was a PI. I walked into the restaurant and surveyed the lunch crowd. The dining room was filled to about two-thirds capacity.

As usual, Tony sat at his spot near the fireplace. No other tables were positioned close to his. When the man needed to discuss business, the diners wouldn't overhear. As I drew closer, I saw Tony lost had even more weight. Before I went overseas, he was a man of good appetite. When I came back, he looked like he'd dropped at least sixty pounds. Subtract another twenty. He looked unhealthy now, and his skin appeared thin over bones which were never more prominent.

Tony showed a tired smile as I approached. I must have

looked concerned. "I'm fine," he said before I could ask. "Caught the flu around the holidays, then got pneumonia right after."

"Jesus."

"Yeah. Health has been kicking my ass this year. I'm doing OK, all things considered." He gestured to the chair opposite his, and I sat.

"Glad to hear it," I said.

Tony snapped his fingers, and an eager young waitress appeared. If I were a college classmate of hers, her dark hair, Italian complexion, and beach-ready body would distract me from the subject at hand. The comely combination almost kept me from ordering, but I put in my request with minimal delay. I watched the waitress return to the kitchen and noticed Tony did the same. "Bruno's daughter," he said.

Bruno was Tony's consigliere and a prick of the highest order. "Her mother must contribute all the looks and personality," I said.

"He ain't so bad." Tony sipped water and muffled a cough. "I don't think you came here to talk about my human resources department, though."

"Not exactly." I fidgeted in my seat and paused as the waitress dropped off my unsweetened iced tea. "Is there a lot of local action on college hoops?"

Tony frowned and regarded me for a moment. "You thinking of opening a book?"

"I have enough problems," I said.

"I'm sure you do. There's . . . some interest in college basketball, yeah. Why?"

"A lot of interest?"

"Enough to make me a decent chunk of change this time of year. You got something in mind?"

I bobbed my head. "I'm not sure I have it right yet. It's

more of a guess at the moment." I paused for a breath, hoping this idea didn't come off as absurd. "Anyone involved in point shaving?"

"Christ." Tony leaned back as far as the chair would allow. "A little old-fashioned, isn't it?" I didn't say anything. "There was the thing in the NBA with the referee, but it was . . . what . . . fifteen years ago?"

"Close to it."

"Maybe even before. I think you're looking at something in the 'seventies or 'eighties."

"So no one's doing it today?"

"I'd be surprised."

I wouldn't be, but I hid my opinion behind the massive plate of food set in front of me. An entire henhouse went into the massive piece of chicken parmesan. It consumed so much of the real estate I didn't end up with as much pasta, which was fine with me. I cut some of the chicken to let it cool. Enticing aromas rose with the steam. "Old-fashioned doesn't mean no one's doing it," I said. "Maybe it helps, actually. If people aren't expecting something, it's easier to get away with."

"Maybe. The law seems to be a little more favorable to gambling these days . . . online, at least." Tony narrowed his eyes. "You know who's running this?"

"I don't even know if it's happening," I said. "At the moment, it's my best guess." I didn't elaborate. Calvin Murray and his mother didn't need to wind up on Tony's radar. Still, I needed some more specifics. "What about JHC?"

"Hanson?"

"Yeah. Any more action than usual there?"

I ate more chicken as Tony pondered his answer. "There's action on pretty much everything. Every July

Fourth, people bet on who'll eat more fucking hot dogs in that stupid contest. College sports have gotten more popular over the years." Tony grinned. "I made money on your lacrosse championship."

"At least one of us did."

"Look, I don't get involved in the actual wagers. I might know which games are big and who's got a lot riding on them, but I ain't digging too deep. As long as my cut is right, I don't ask a lotta questions."

It made sense. Still, something tugged at me. I hoped I didn't move JHC games—and Calvin in particular—up Tony's priority list. He probably didn't follow the games, but at least one person who worked for him would. "All right," I said. "I guess I'll poke around and see what happens."

"Keep me posted," said Tony. "If somebody's doing it and ain't paying their share, I want to hear about it."

I knew what would happen if I did this. Tony treated me well because we enjoyed a pretty long history. I'd never gotten on the bad side of his ledger. I didn't envy those who did. Tony's men were typical enforcers, and they'd probably enjoy working over whomever hatched the point-shaving scheme before eventually killing them. Still, I couldn't do something as stupid as to refuse the man in his own restaurant. Around a bite of pasta, I said, "Sure."

Tony drank some more water and chuckled. "Point shaving. Christ Almighty. I guess everything old really is new again."

I looked across the table at my host. Tony must've been seventy if not more. He'd suffered a run of bad luck with his health, but I thought he started looking thin before. I felt concerned for him. "Here's hoping," I said.

* * *

AFTER MY LUNCH chat with Tony, I chose between going home or driving to my office. I opted for the latter. It turned out to be a wise decision when Denise Murray walked in a short while later. I summoned a smile for her, but I really hoped she wouldn't keep dropping in on me. I didn't like it when clients asked for frequent updates. To me, working mostly update-free came with the territory of taking my cases *pro bono.*

Denise eased herself into one of my guest chairs. She cast her eyes up, and relief spread across her face. I wondered if she still underwent any treatment for the cancer. Denise thought Calvin paid for her trial and medicine. If so, he needed to be raking in a lot of money from the point-shaving scheme, and whoever organized it must've been collecting even more.

"What can I do for you?" I said.

Her hands gripped the edge of my desk as if she needed to steady them. "I was wondering if you had any thoughts."

"My brain goes a mile a minute. I always have thoughts."

Denise showed a weak grin. "I mean about Calvin and what we talked about."

I wondered how to frame my answer. *I think your son's probably in league with a bookie or a gangster and is fixing basketball games.* This would not lead to a productive conversation. After a moment of deliberation, I came up with, "Have you ever heard of point shaving?"

She shook her head. "What is it?"

This would be easier if she'd been even a little familiar with the idea. "You know all college basketball games see betting action, right?" Denise nodded. "As part of this, bookmakers put out a point spread for the game. You know what a point spread is?" Her head bobbed again. "Your son's a great player, and JHC doesn't compete in a strong conference. They're favored to win most of their games."

"They've had a really good season," Denise said.

"They have. Let's say they're a ten-point favorite in a certain game. Some bookies or big bettors will bet big on the underdog. Then a player—or more than one—on the favored team will make a few misplays, take some bad shots . . . those sorts of things. Enough so the favorite still wins, but they only pull it out by a few points. Under ten."

Denise frowned in thought. "And all those people who bet on the underdog win?"

"Against the spread, yes."

"Do they give money to whoever on the better team helped them?" she asked.

"Usually, though I imagine it depends how much they made on a given day."

"So my son's on the take?"

"I don't know this is what's going on," I said. "So far, it's my best guess." To be honest, my only guess—which made it my best by default—but Denise didn't need to know this.

"The money he made . . ." She trailed off and took a deep breath. I saw her eyes moisten, and I nudged a box of tissues across the desk. "I think he's the one who paid for my cancer treatments."

"What makes you think so?"

"When I got sick, we didn't know what we would do. I have a job and insurance, but it only covers so much. Not to mention the time I'd need to be off." I had a feeling I knew where this was headed, but I let her keep going. "Calvin took it hard. He's my only child. His father . . ." She snorted. "Well, he's sniffing around again now that his son's probably going to the NBA. He left when Calvin was young, though, and ain't been involved.

"Maybe a week after I told Calvin my diagnosis, he said he felt it would all be taken care of. I didn't know what he meant. When I went to my doctor a few days later, she told me my treatment and medicine was all paid for. I didn't know what to say. She wouldn't tell me who set it all up."

"Seems pretty apparent Calvin arranged it," I said.

"No one else could've. You think he got the money from this point-shaving thing?"

"I don't know how much cancer treatment costs, but I imagine it's expensive. Seems like a lot of money to have at once. My understanding is players are paid after the games they affect."

"This was a few months ago . . . early in the season. I don't think he could've done much for them by that point."

I wondered if he got paid an advance. Someone fronted Calvin the money in exchange for him affecting the outcomes of a bunch of games later. This would probably prove an onerous thumb to escape from under. There were always more games, more bets, and more dollars. "Have you seen any strangers around him?"

"No. Until the phone call recently, I never saw or heard him have an argument with anyone."

"I'll need to know more about Calvin," I said. "What can you tell me about him?"

"He has a daughter."

I started to reply but stopped. This fact changed a lot. "Might as well lead off with the good stuff."

"She's terrific," Denise said, beaming. "She just turned a year old a couple months ago. Iris is her name."

"Is Calvin still with the mother?"

"They ain't married, but they're together." Her eyes widened suddenly. "Do you think Iris is in danger?"

"I'll put it this way," I said. "If I'm right, Calvin's cast his lot with at least one shady character. When people like this don't get their way, they lash out. They can't hurt Calvin because he's the one who makes the scheme work. But if they need to exert a lot of pressure on him—"

"Iris," she broke in.

"Or you."

"Shit." She stared at my desk for a moment. A tear slid down her cheek, so she snatched a tissue from the box. "What are we going to do?"

"I need to figure out what's going on," I said. "The conference tournament and March Madness would be the best time for people to make money."

"What will you do when you know?"

"I'll try to get Calvin out of whatever mess he's landed in."

"You think you can?"

"I'm pretty good at what I do."

"You'll need to be at your best . . . for Iris."

I nodded my concurrence. "And for you."

As dusk settled, I sat in my car, waiting for someone to return home. My first case, where I busted Vinnie Serrano, brought me into contact with one of his employees. Margaret Madison was a pretty woman in an ugly business, taking bets and roughing up the marks when the situation called for it.

I used the Baltimore Police Department to confirm she still worked in much the same job. During the aforementioned first case, my cousin Rich, then a uniformed sergeant, left me alone with his unattended computer. I quickly snagged his addressing information, used this to fingerprint the BPD's network, and have enjoyed access ever since.

Margaret Madison popped up in some vice investigations, but nothing ultimately came of them.

In the two years or so since Vinnie went down, Margaret moved up in the world. She basically took over Vinnie's books, added some clients, and did well for herself. Living and working in the city, I knew she paid her tithe to Tony Rizzo. Vinnie would've taught her as much. In Canton, another historic Baltimore neighborhood, Margaret lived in an end-unit rowhouse. Gentrification came to Canton several years ago, bringing new construction, higher home prices, and younger buyers. I sat across the street about a hundred feet away.

While I waited for Margaret, I used my phone to open a secure connection back to my office computer. JHC would play a game tomorrow night, the first of their expected run through the conference tournament. The Presidents currently sat as a twelve-point favorite over Delaware. I wondered if Margaret set different lines than Vegas.

Still no sign of my quarry. I used the connection to my office PC to track her phone. It pinged a nearby cell tower, and as far as I could tell from one data point, she moved in this direction. I went back onto the BPD's network and looked for other people who'd been arrested for offenses like bookmaking. There were a few, but they constituted small potatoes. Margaret ran a professional operation.

A few minutes later, she walked down the street from the opposite end. She wore jeans and boots coming halfway up her calf, and her hands were shoved into the pockets of a black overcoat. Margaret ascended the three steps to her front door, glanced in both directions, and went into her house.

I got out of my car and dashed across the street.

CHAPTER 4

I RAPPED ON THE DOOR AND MOVED OFF TO THE SIDE. IT had been a couple years since I was here last. Margaret wasn't happy to see me then, and I doubted she'd be doing cartwheels upon finding me on her doorstep tonight. Two locks disengaged, and the door swung in. I moved to stand in line with the opening.

Margaret got a haircut since the last time I saw her, now wearing her blonde hair in a short bob. She remained a pretty woman by any measure with striking blue eyes and classic features. She looked at me for a second before recognition flashed in her eyes. Her brows pulled down.

"Hello, Margaret."

Her answer came in the form of a quick right jab. I leaned away, but she pulled her arm back and shoved the door. Before it shut, I jammed my foot in at the bottom. Note to self: wear steel-toed shoes next time. My Nike cross-trainers were ill-suited to this task. Margaret leaned her weight into the door. My foot throbbed. I rocked back, then threw my body forward.

The door burst in. Margaret staggered rearward a couple

steps. I crossed the threshold. She glared daggers at me. I put up my hands. "I came to talk."

Miss Madison acted on a different idea. She fired off two quick punches, then snapped off a nice side kick. I turned all three aside. "Get out of my house!" I blunted a few more attacks. I didn't want to fight Margaret, but I also couldn't stand here and let her whale away at me until she grew tired. "Haven't you done enough?"

"You've been quite successful these last couple years," I said. Pointing this out did not improve her mood. Her foyer afforded barely enough room for our little scrum. She threw another hard right. This time, I evaded it and caught her wrist. When she tried to pull it back, I maintained my grip. "I might need your help."

"Why would I help you?"

"Don't do it for me," I said. "Do it for the one-year-old girl and woman with cancer who might soon be in the crosshairs."

Her arm went slack, so I released it. Margaret still glared at me, but the expression softened to one of mild distaste. I could live with it. "You want some decaf?" she said.

"Sure," I said.

* * *

As unleaded coffee went, it wasn't bad. I'd sampled plenty worse. We occupied two of the four chairs at Margaret's dining room table. Nothing sat atop it except dust in a few spots, and the china cabinet in the corner held about four dishes. I got the distinct impression Margaret didn't use this room often. We detectives often possess piercing insight. I congratulated myself for my smarts with another sip of hot java.

"You said you might need my help," Margaret said.

"Information more than anything."

"I helped you with Vinnie."

I nodded my acknowledgement. "He was off the rails. I get the fact your business is tough, and you need to be, too. I also get not wanting to go along with kidnapping and murder."

"It was hard. It didn't get any easier when he went away, either."

"You seem to have landed on your feet," I said.

A smile slowly spread across Margaret's face. It was a good one. "It took me a little while. I was always smarter than Vinnie gave me credit for."

"Now, I hope you're smart enough to help again."

"What do you need?"

"You know anyone involved in point shaving?"

Margaret's smile turned into a laugh. "Seriously?"

"I have a theory," I said, "but I think it's pretty sound."

"I have a theory, too. Anyone who's shaving points is about a hundred years old."

"I know no one's heard of it being a thing for quite a while." I raised my hand to preempt her objection. "Hear me out. In the old days, guys who were known to be gamblers or crime figures needed to place bets in person. Plenty of people could get eyes on them. Today, it's different. They could do it online at some offshore casino. It could be local through someone like you. No one needs to go to Caesar's anymore and get seen by half of Vegas placing a bet."

Margaret sipped coffee and pondered what I said, her eyebrows raised. "That makes some sense," she said after a moment. "It's inevitable someone will see a pattern in big bets and game results. Visibility becomes the killer."

"But when the process is anonymous, no one knows who's doing it."

"All right. I guess this could make sense. I can't say I know anyone who's involved in it, though. Like you say, there's a lot of anonymity today. Way too many offline places taking bets."

"You live and work in the city," I said. "I know you're giving Tony his percentage." Margaret didn't confirm this in any way, choosing to sit there and look at me over the rim of her cup. I pushed on. "Whoever's doing this probably isn't paying the tithe."

"If Tony knows about it, he'd be pissed. I'm not sure how he could figure anything out, though."

"True. This involves JHC."

"Hanson?" said Margaret.

"Yes. I think one of their players is involved. He has a very young daughter and a sick mother whose treatment got paid for out of the blue."

"Wow." Margaret set her cup down and smirked at me. "You probably should've led off with that."

"My lack of journalism classes is showing."

"I've heard rumors of someone working in the county," she said. "Don't know who. He's supposed to be running a book, though."

"Nothing else? No loan sharking or anything?"

"Not that I've heard."

"And you don't know this guy's name?"

She shook her head a little too quickly. "No."

I let it go. Even if she knew, Margaret wasn't going to tell me. Maybe she was still salty about the whole Vinnie thing, even though she ended up doing very well in the fallout of his arrest. "If you think of anything, let me know." I dropped a business card on her table. "The player's an adult, but I'm worried about the young daughter and his mother."

"I'll call you if I hear anything."

I didn't believe her but also didn't see the point of arguing. It would only cement her decision to shut me out. I downed the rest of my now-tepid coffee in a single gulp. "Thanks for talking to me and for the coffee. You throw a pretty good side kick, too."

Margaret grinned. "I bet you say that to all the girl bookies."

I didn't, but maybe I should start.

* * *

MY OFFICE WAS CLOSER than my house driving from Margaret's, so I went there. She told me someone operated in the county. I flashed back to Alberto Esposito, one of my big early cases. He worked in the county, too, and he tried to amass an empire to usurp Tony Rizzo in Baltimore. His quest ended with a bullet to the head.

I'd been standing next to him when it happened.

A shudder ran down my spine as I searched for someone who might end up being the next Esposito. While I enjoyed unfettered access to the Baltimore Police Department's records, I'd never tapped into their county counterpart's network. Rich gave me an easy way in. My usual contact with the BCPD, Detective Sergeant Gonzalez, hadn't committed such a technological *faux pas* yet. I could probably get in anyway without them being any the wiser. It would take time, however, and I could spend those minutes—and potentially hours—doing research.

I opted for the less invasive track. News articles made little mention of any organized gambling in the county, and no one talked up point shaving. Maybe Margaret was right: it was an old-fashioned notion in today's era of placing bets with random offshore companies. I still thought this made it ripe for exploiting today. So far, I couldn't find anyone who shared my sentiment.

Searching Baltimore County-focused Facebook groups, forums, and subreddits didn't unearth a lot more. The occasional person complained about a couple of JHC's close wins when they were sizable favorites, but no one connected the games to anything sinister. It took quite a few more minutes of searching and unscrambling coded language, but I finally found two mentions of locals placing a bet with someone.

They referred to the mystery person only as Eddie. It was a common enough name to yield tons of results whenever I executed a broad search and no results when I narrowed the focus to gambling. Pairing the name with sports turned up too many athletes named Eddie, none of whom would be bookmakers in Baltimore County. I used my Google-fu until I became convinced I wouldn't find anything else.

When I first began doing this job, I told my parents I could solve most of my cases while sitting behind my keyboard. Most of my work pointed out how wrong this sentiment had been. I called Gonzalez to get a line on what the BCPD knew. "What now?" he said.

"Hard at work again."

He snorted. "I know you better. Sometimes, I wish I didn't, but I do."

"Remind me not to use you as a character reference," I said.

"My shift's about over. What can I do for you?"

"I have an idea and a couple questions."

"Christ, now I know I'm in trouble," he said.

"Buy you a beer?"

"I might need something stronger." We agreed on a place, and Gonzalez hung up.

Depending on what he could tell me, I might wind up needing something stronger, too.

* * *

I PARKED my Audi S4 in the lot of Glory Days Grill in Towson. The old Bruce Springsteen song played in my head —I figured they gave everyone this earworm on purpose—as I walked in. Glory Days sat on East Joppa Road a short drive from BCPD headquarters. There were plenty of closer places to grab a brew, and I guessed Gonzalez picked this one so his coworkers wouldn't see him slumming with a PI.

The interior, like many sports bars, consisted of wood to the max. It looked like someone felled a forest of trees, and this place was the result. From the floors to the walls to the bar and the paneling, wood covered basically every surface. I wondered if the men's room would feature urinals carved from old cedars. It might improve the smell.

Gonzalez sat at a two-top table not far from the bar. He was about forty and wore his black hair short enough to do a good job masking the bits of gray. A beer sat on the table in front of him as did a basket of onion rings. I slid onto the chair and snagged a ring. Nonplussed by my thievery, Gonzalez enjoyed a drink of his amber brew.

A college-aged waiter walked up a moment later. I requested a draft IPA, and Gonzalez ordered dinner in the form of a cheeseburger and fries. When the waiter went away, I said, "You and I define getting a beer differently."

"A humble public servant like me has to take free meals when he can."

I responded by helping myself to more of his appetizer. I was paying for it, anyway. The waiter dropped off my beer, which was much darker than Gonzalez's. I sampled it and approved of the flavor and bitterness. "You working at head-quarters?"

"I was today," he said.

"Didn't want to be seen so close to base with someone like me?"

He raised his glass. "You got it."

"I could only improve your reputation. Especially with the ladies."

Gonzalez rolled his eyes. "I presume we're not here so you can dispense dating advice."

"I need some information," I said. "I have a theory, and I'm trying to confirm it."

"I thought you were good at getting information."

"Leave me alone with your computer for a few minutes, and my success rate will go up."

A snort served as the only reply. Gonzalez munched on a breaded onion before saying anything. "What do you wanna know?"

"Anyone running any big sports books in the county?"

He frowned. "Gambling?"

"I can see why you're a detective sergeant."

He ignored the barb. "Probably a few pricks here and there," he said. "No one jumps out at me right now."

"Can you ask around?"

"Can you tell me why I should?"

I laid out my theory. I told Gonzalez what I knew, what I suspected, and why I reached the conclusion I did. For extra credit, I mentioned my conversation with Margaret Madison, though I kept her name out of it. The chat with Margaret left me feeling pretty good about my supposition.

Gonzalez laughed when I finished talking. Feeling now: less good. "What?" I said when his amusement died down to a mere chortle.

"Point shaving? What is this, nineteen eighty-nine?"

"It'a a valid theory."

"Sure . . . as long as the perp is about eighty years old. Tell you what—we'll start asking around the old-age homes and see if anyone's running a cutthroat tournament pool."

"I understand it's an old idea," I said. "Think about it, though. What brought these schemes down before was people placing bets in person. Wiseguys got recognized. Not the case anymore. No one has to walk into a seedy backroom somewhere."

"Because it's all online," Gonzalez said. If any more skepticism dripped from his words, he'd need to wipe the table.

"Exactly. There are a ton of offshore casinos making lines and taking bets. You just need someone local to manage the scheme."

"No, *you* need someone local to manage it. I don't need anything . . . except dinner. Where the hell is the waiter?"

"You're dismissing my idea."

"Yeah. Happens to me all the time."

"Maybe my ideas are better than yours," I said. "Remember, I can only improve your reputation."

"Whatever." Before Gonzalez could say anything else, the server brought his burger and fries. Gonzalez ordered another beer, and I opted for an unsweetened iced tea. Once we each held our second round of drinks, he continued. "Look, if this turns into anything, let me know."

"Why should I? You laugh when I tell you my theory, but if it turns out I'm right, then you want to be involved?"

He nodded around a bite of his cheeseburger. "Pretty much."

"Is having your cake and eating it, too, part of the police handbook?" I said.

"It's in the appendix." I took out my money clip, peeled a

twenty and a ten off, and dropped them on the table. "Ain't enough to cover it."

"Read the appendix again," I said as I stood. "I'm sure there's something in there about accepting meals from people like me."

* * *

WHEN I GOT HOME, I slammed the back door louder than usual. Gloria walked into the kitchen from the living room frowning at me. I spiked my keys into their usual wooden bowl. "Bad day at the office?" she said, putting a hand on my shoulder.

"An annoying chat with Gonzalez," I said. I filled her in on the details as we walked back to the front of the house and plopped down onto the couch.

"I thought the police were supposed to be receptive to ideas," she said.

"Once they have an investigation going, yeah. Before then, I guess they can afford to be selective."

"You're going to stick with your theory?"

I nodded. "Until a better one emerges."

"What's your next move, then?" asked Gloria.

I appreciated the growing interest she took in my cases over time. Initially, talk of work repulsed her. Gloria didn't need to work a day in her life, and when we first met, I think she'd committed herself to it. Before long, she saw people helped by my investigations and began looking for her own meaningful work, eventually landing in the fundraising arena. She also served as a useful sounding board for my ideas, some of which were admittedly hare-brained.

This one, however, was not. I knew it had merit. I only needed to prove it. How could I figure out if someone sank his (or her) hooks in Calvin Murray? His mother was concerned. I wondered how the young man himself dealt with everything. An idea formed in my head. There was an easy way to find out. "I think I'm going to go back to college," I said.

CHAPTER 5

Social media is a wonderful thing, especially to people like me. I could've broken into John Hanson College's records and obtained Calvin Murray's schedule. The odds of getting caught were minimal, and the only real expense would be time. However, Calvin posted a photo of the current semester's schedule to his Instagram account back in January. The hashtags he chose suggested he was not a fan of the early start.

Neither was I, but I arose at the dreadful hour of seven, left a sleeping Gloria in bed, and snuck downstairs for coffee and breakfast. With my caffeine and food levels acceptable for the morning, I padded back up and got dressed. Gloria remained in dreamland. She'd rolled onto her other side since I went downstairs, and one of her shapely legs stuck out from under the blanket. I took a deep breath to steel my resolve and left the house.

Calvin Murray's first class began at eight. This presumed he went, of course. The athlete who doesn't go to class is something of a stereotype, but it's one I witnessed firsthand during my time at Loyola. If Calvin didn't make his appointed rounds, I'd be left with trying to find him on a college campus. It could be done, but I'd be relieved if I found him in the lecture hall.

After parking and traipsing from the lot, I hit the building at eight-ten. Calvin's chemistry lecture would've already started. The good thing about a large class like this would be the anonymity of sitting in a large room. Walking in late would draw eyes to me, and a few people would wonder who I was. But in a room with two hundred students crammed in, being one of the crowd would prevail.

I opened the door and, sure enough, more than a hundred heads pivoted to the noise. The professor, a middle-aged man who spoke with an Italian accent, paused as I found a seat in the last row. I chose the center so I could survey the hall. The professor resumed, and my intrusion was forgotten. No one challenged me. To play the part of a college student, I brought a spiral notebook and a pen.

A few years passed since I studied chemistry. Probably about eleven, a thought which made me feel older than my thirty years. Based on what I saw in the PowerPoint, this was the 101 course. I tuned out the instructor and scanned the rows of students in front of me. While I knew what Calvin looked like, all the pictures I saw were obviously from the front.

He was tall, though—the college listed him as six-seven. Unless he slouched very low, he'd be among the highest head-and-shoulders in the hall even while seated. My scan yielded a couple possible hits. Both were to my left and near the front. I couldn't tell which (if either) was Calvin from where I sat, however. This meant enduring the rest of the chemistry lecture.

The things I did for this job.

At eight-fifty, it mercifully ended. Everyone rose and filed out at the nearest exit. I bucked the tide leaving at the top, instead scooting down the steps. My two prospects turned the corner, allowing me to see them. One was Calvin Murray. His next class was in a much smaller setting. I couldn't just slip in the back and pass it off. I needed to get closer.

A flock of other students were in my way as we all exited the building. If I knew the campus layout—and my grip on it was tenuous—we'd have about a five-minute walk to our next destination. Once outside, I used the ample free space to bypass the stragglers and slow walkers. I fell in a couple paces behind Calvin, whose longer strides forced me to walk quickly. Many of his fellow students wished him good luck or offered high-fives as he passed. To his credit, the young man obliged them all.

I dug my phone out of my front pocket and launched a Bluetooth attack on Calvin's. It connected immediately, quickly cracked the feeble security protocols, and began cloning his phone. It would need about three minutes to complete. I followed Calvin as he walked to his next class.

Two and a half minutes.

Because of Bluetooth's limited range, I would need to remain within ten meters of my tall quarry until the cloning completed. At his current pace, he'd be in Statistics by then. After a few more high-fives, Calvin walked up the steps to another generic brick structure. He went in the front door, and I followed him. His long strides devoured the stairs two at a time. We emerged on the second floor.

Seventy seconds remained.

Calvin paused for a drink from a water fountain, so I busied myself looking at my phone. A few seconds later, he was off again. We passed room 219 before he ducked into 221. I followed him because I had to. A few quizzical looks greeted me. Calvin walked to the left side and sat in the middle row of desks. I grabbed one nearby and opened my notebook.

We were under half a minute.

"Are you supposed to be here?"

I looked up. The professor, who'd been staring at her notes when we entered, now stared at me. "Me?" I said, even though it was obvious I was the target of her question.

"Of course, you. This is Statistics One. Are you in the wrong class?"

"Two-nineteen, right?"

She shook her head. "Two-twenty-one."

I offered my best sheepish grin. "Sorry. I guess I'll need another cup of coffee after class." A tight smile served as the only response. I flipped my notebook shut and stood. My pen clattered on the floor. I crouched and picked it up, offering an additional sheepish grin for this latest intrusion on the placidity of Statistics I. My phone buzzed in my pocket. I walked around my desk and out of the classroom.

Once I was back in the corridor, I checked my phone.

The clone completed.

* * *

HAVING GOTTEN the boot from Statistics, I plotted my next move. My Bluetooth program cloned Calvin's phone and SIM card, and I'd brought a spare so I could use a separate device to see what he did. I pondered going home. No pressing need jumped out at me. On my way back to my car, however, I saw a sign directing me to the athletic department offices.

It was too good to pass up.

I walked into the building and found the basketball coaches' rooms. Lou Baker, the head coach, sat behind his desk. His glasses perched on his balding head, and he frowned at a set of papers. A TV of about forty inches was mounted on the wall behind him, and a still image from paused game footage lingered on the screen. I knocked on the door.

He looked up. "Who the hell are you?"

"My name is C.T. Ferguson, and I'm a private investigator." I showed him my badge and ID, which he scrutinized through squinted eyes.

"Don't know what you're doing here."

Despite not being offered a seat, I plopped down in a chair before Baker's desk. He pursed his lips but didn't say anything. "Have you seen any shady characters around your players?"

"Do you count?" he said.

"Much shadier than I am. Think wiseguys and gamblers."

He shook his head, and his jowls wobbled faster than the rest of his face. "None of that shit around here." The coach glanced back to his papers. "We done? I got a game tomorrow to plan for."

"I have reason to believe at least one of your players is in league with someone who's . . . interested in the outcomes of games."

"Lot of people are interested in how the games turn out."

"Financially."

Baker paused. "You mean shaving points?"

"It's exactly what I mean."

"Doesn't happen anymore." He shook his head. "I been in this game a long time. I got started as an assistant coach in the 'eighties. The big programs always had some mob guy sniffing around. It's an artifact of the times, though. You don't see it anymore."

"I think you still could. Local bookies and online casinos make it easier than it was back then."

A quiet stare was the only answer I got. Baker looked between his papers and me. "What makes you think one of my players is involved?"

"I can't tell you exactly, but a concerned and reliable person hired me."

Baker waved his hand. "You got suckered." He stood, and his desk groaned in protest as he leaned on it. "Lots of people don't like it when others are successful. I run a good program. Have a couple great players. Some folks out there don't like it, and they'll come to people like you to try and tear it down."

This should be good. "People like me?"

"You're probably not so different." He studied me for a moment while I remained silent. "You look like you're in shape. Probably helps in your line of work. No one who's successful does what you do, though. So you attract other failures, and sometimes, your clients point you at someone like me. Someone who's built a nationally-recognized program."

I took a deep breath and avoided the bait. For now. "Then there's no harm in giving me some copies of your game films. If everything is on the up-and-up, there won't be anything for me to find."

Baker crossed his arms. "No way," he said. "I'm not legitimizing this witch hunt."

"Have it your way," I said. "But if I find something, I'll come back, and you probably won't like the conversation."

"I didn't much like this one." He sat again, his office chair creaking under the load. "I don't expect I'll be seeing you again."

This wouldn't go any further. Baker dug in his heels and wasn't going to give me an inch. I got up and turned toward the door. "Oh, Coach?"

"What?"

"Two thousand twelve, Loyola College, national lacrosse champions. Look me up."

Baker stared at me with a slack jaw. A few seconds later, he said, "I didn't . . . most people—"

"Go fuck yourself," I broke in.

I left the office.

* * *

AT HOME, I loaded the cloned image of Calvin Murray's phone and SIM card onto a spare Android model. This would allow me to review his texts and calls, plus see his communications in real time. If he shaved points, I would know about it, and the hope was this would also snag whoever masterminded the scheme.

Gloria walked into my home office—sparser now with the real one up and running—and sat in a guest chair. "New phone? It looks kind of old."

"It's new to me, you could say. I cloned it." I gave her a brief technical rundown on duplicating someone's device. To her credit, Gloria nodded at the important parts, but I knew she didn't understand most of it.

"Is that legal?" she asked.

"Doubt it." I shrugged. "I've built my career, such as it is, on being a scofflaw. Why start doing things the right way now?"

"What if this Calvin finds out?"

"He won't."

"You think this'll catch anyone?"

"It's my hope," I said. "Once it does, I'll destroy the clone." Gloria watched me as I scrolled through the phone. I got the feeling she wanted to tell me something. "What's going on?"

"Nothing," she said.

I didn't buy it, but I also didn't press it. "Just like watching me work?"

Gloria smiled, and her chestnut hair slid across her shoulder as she stared at me. "Sometimes more than others."

It was almost enough to make me leap across the desk between us. JHC had a game coming up, however, and both Calvin Murray's infant daughter and sick mother could be in the crosshairs if things went badly. "Give me a couple minutes," I said.

"Don't keep me waiting," Gloria said. She sashayed out of the room, and I watched her walk all the way to the stairs. It took me a minute to breathe normally and get back to work. I flipped through Calvin's emails. Nothing jumped out. His texts were similarly mundane.

Most people didn't communicate in these ways anymore, however, especially if they wanted discretion. Much of this was now the purview of messaging apps, and Calvin's phone featured the top choices in the category. He even kept them in their own folder and sorted alphabetically. I hoped nothing bad happened to this kid. Anyone who alphabetized smartphone apps was a winner in my book.

I needed to make it to WhatsApp to see something of interest. A contact identified only as Eddie sent a message to Calvin earlier today. *The line for the game is now 9.5. You've already been taken care of. I know you know what to do.*

Already been taken care of? I wondered if this meant someone footing the bill for Denise Murray's cancer treatment and recovery. Those things weren't cheap, and if Calvin's means of payback meant shaving points in games, some serious money needed to be on the line.

Calvin answered a few minutes later. *We got you.*

Who else was involved? Another rabbit hole opened the more I looked around this case. I needed to talk to Calvin and maybe a few of his teammates. The coach wasn't going to cooperate, though. I'd have to pursue something unofficial.

The parties whose necks were potentially in the noose now consisted of Calvin, Denise, Calvin's baby, and at least one teammate. I wondered how much worse this case could get before it took a turn for the better.

CHAPTER 6

THE NEXT MORNING, I STARTED MY DAY BY RUNNING laps around Federal Hill Park. It always afforded a great view of the city, and I loved looking out over the harbor as I pounded the pavement. I wore a light Under Armour jacket this morning. A couple about my age walked their small, yappy dog, but I didn't see anyone else out exercising. Many mornings, attractive women in exercise attire also ran laps. Today, I was alone.

I sprinted back home, showered, threw on jeans and a sweater, and explored my breakfast options. The status of my refrigerator and pantry is often lamentable, but I'd been to the grocery store recently. I settled on some ingredients and whipped up a scramble of potatoes, diced peppers, and eggs. The smells of this and a brewing pot of coffee summoned Gloria downstairs. She was predictable in this way. "What trouble are you getting into today?" she said as we ate a few minutes later.

"I think I'll go back to campus," I said. "Hanson's game is tonight. I want to see if anyone disreputable is skulking about."

"Skulking?" Gloria said with a grin.

"It's a favorite pastime of the disreputable."

"You would know."

I raised my coffee mug in a mock toast. "I can skulk with the best of them."

After breakfast, Gloria kissed me goodbye and advised me to stay out of trouble. I told her I would do my best, which was true but would likely come up short, which was also true. I drove to JHC and parked in a remote visitors' lot. Many more cars dotted the campus today, and the first two areas I tried were full.

I walked from my car, crossing a small grassy field with a path worn in its center. The athletic buildings were on the other side, across another stretch of asphalt. From there, three large men approached me. I got the feeling they were not just out for a stroll as each stared at me with every step. Coach Baker must have talked about our little chat. Maybe I shouldn't have told him to fuck himself. A simple go-to-hell might have earned me a smaller welcoming committee.

When they were about five paces away, I stopped. "Morning, guys," I said. They offered no response. Up close, each possessed the height and girth of linemen on the football team. "I figured spring practice would consist of more than leisurely strolls."

"We'll definitely get some exercise," the tallest one, a short-haired blond, said. The other two were about my height, maybe an inch taller, with dark hair—one sported a mullet—and full goatees. As someone who struggled to grow more than patchy facial hair, I felt a pang of envy.

"Let me guess," I said. "Someone told you to discourage me from coming onto campus." One of the dark-haired ones nodded. "You should have stood out by the road, then. I already drove on and parked my car."

"Get back in it," the blond one said, "and we won't beat your ass."

"You the only one who can talk? Maybe Tweedledee and Tweedledum here took a few too many shots to the head."

"Fuck you," the one on the left said. He started forward, but the fellow with the 'eighties hair restrained him with a hand to the chest.

"My comment stands."

"Last warning," the fair-haired spokesman said.

"Guys, you should know something. I've been beating up football players since I was sixteen. I'm sure you're all really good with the tackling dummy, but this isn't going to end well for you. How about *you* turn around and walk away?"

"There are three of us," Mullet said.

"I'm impressed. Maybe you go to math class after all."

Mullet must have reached his breaking point because he charged. As I expected, he tried to wrap me up in a tackle. This probably worked very well for him on the football field. Today, however, I grabbed his right arm and flipped him onto his back. The grass cushioned his fall some, but his head still bounced off the ground. As he looked up at me with a dumbfounded expression he probably wore often, I kicked him hard in the face. The light went out.

I turned and looked at the other two. Blondie gaped while the other dark-haired idiot worked on his best menacing glower. The threat in it dissipated significantly before it spanned the fifteen feet between us. "Want to walk away now?" I asked them.

Dark Hair's bull rush served as his response. I expected him to try and tackle me like his compatriot, so I readied myself to grab his arm and flip him. Instead, he drew his arms in, lowered his shoulder, and plowed straight into me. I tried to sidestep the hit when I realized what he had in mind, but the impact still drove me from my feet and sent me sprawling to the ground. He stalked toward me as Blondie advanced.

I let him grab my sweater and pull me to my feet, riding the momentum and kicking the blond one hard in the gut. While he doubled over, I blocked a punch from Dark Hair and elbowed him in the face. He rocked back a step. I gave him a hard shot in the gut, which drove him to one knee. Before I could follow up, though, someone grabbed me from behind. "Come on," Blondie's voice called out from my rear.

This guy already knocked me down once, and I didn't care to let him try again by punching me. As the dark-locked one stood, I snapped my head back. I'm six-two and Blondie probably had four inches on me. The crown of my head probably took him in the nose. I felt his grip weaken. Dark Hair drew his fist back. His eyes brimmed with hatred.

I bashed my head into Blondie's face again. A soft crack preceded his grunt. His grip slackened, and I ducked as fast as I could. The onrushing fist took him squarely in the jaw. The resultant crack was much louder this time. Blondie's hands fell away completely as he collapsed to the grass. The other stared ahead with wide eyes.

Before he could recover, I punched him hard in the balls. He groaned and staggered back a couple steps. I regained my feet and snapped off a quick kick to my attacker's midsection. He bent in half, and I drove a knee up into his face, snapping his head rearward and dropping him to the ground.

I looked around. We hadn't drawn a crowd. This part of the campus didn't see a lot of traffic, foot or otherwise. At some point, though, three large men lying on the grass would draw attention. I reversed course and headed back to my car before this happened.

* * *

I DIDN'T LINGER on campus after dealing with the three football players. Once word spread, the only people who would want to talk to me would be the campus police. Instead, I drove to my office. JHC's first tournament game was tonight. I'd already scheduled a recording of it. To figure out if Calvin Murray and others actively engaged in point shaving, however, I needed game film. There was no way Coach Baker would provide it.

People like me always counted on other means of gathering information. I spent a few minutes researching JHC and their network, devising the best course of attack. After reviewing everything, I settled on good old phishing. There were many more advanced attacks to try, but all carried either a higher risk of detection or a lower chance of success. Phishing was a popular attack across the world for a reason.

It took a few minutes to craft the payload my message would carry. It was a PDF purporting to be a listing of restaurants in the tournament areas, complete with menus. In reality, it was a few pages of Towson-area sub shop menus, along with a rather insidious piece of malware. Most email programs now warned users not to open attachments from people they didn't know. A lot of folks ignored this advice.

I boosted my odds of success with a spoofed email. It identified me as working for NCAA catering, which is not a thing but looks official enough to pass muster. I wrote a quick message saying I was emailing this information to all coaching staffs in the conference, sent it only to Coach Baker and his assistants, and waited.

With a game tonight, they were no doubt deep in preparation. By now, the players were likely reviewing film and prepping for a final run-through. I figured I would need to wait a few hours for someone to open the email and attachment.

Forty minutes later, I'd found a victim.

Assistant Coach Joe Coffey opened the PDF. I imagined him reading the email, grousing about the choices, and firing off an angry reply. The address I used would accept replies for the veneer of authenticity, but I wasn't checking it. By now the payload in the attachment would've installed a remote-access trojan onto Coffey's computer. I checked with the command and control software, and it reported a live endpoint.

Now I needed to wait for Coach Coffey to leave his office for the game.

THE PRESIDENTS TIPPED off at seven-thirty. I knew the coaches would be offline well before then, but I've also always thought patience was a great virtue for hackers to have. In the meantime, I'd gone home and ordered delivery for dinner while Gloria showered upstairs. She'd wanted to go out somewhere and seemed a little disappointed when I told her I'd planned a riveting evening of basketball.

About ten minutes before the opening whistle, I fired up my remote access trojan. Coach Coffey dutifully left his computer on. Most enterprises prefer this so they can update systems after working hours. The program began by harvesting his login credentials and passing them to the system. I was soon logged in under Coffey's profile. The coach and his Rottweiler—who was the better-looking of the pair—stared back at me, the image serving as the desktop wallpaper.

Video files tend to be large. College basketball games consist of two twenty-minute halves. On TV, this can take well over two hours with halftime, and the final few minutes of a close contest can consume what feels like seventeen days. I'd never seen official game film, but I figured it would be the forty minutes of action plus some additional time spent focusing on timeouts. A forty-five minute high-definition video would eat up a lot of space. A season's worth could take up a typical computer's hard drive.

My hunch was JHC stored footage on network drives or in the cloud. The former would be easier for me. I was logged in as Coach Coffey, and today's networks offered single sign-on to common resources. I poked around in Windows Explorer, eventually finding a video archive kept on the X: drive. A quick search showed games indexed by year.

I only cared about this year's contests, so I went after those. Transferring files out of a network boundary is something systems log and administrators will eventually notice. Some networks even throw alerts about data exfiltration in real time. I perused the suite of security software and concluded JHC didn't have this capability. I connected to an anonymized server I use for secure file transfer and moved the videos this way. Even over a fast connection, it would take a while.

Gloria came downstairs. Our food arrived a few minutes later. We enjoyed some excellent Chinese while watching the game and making sure my session as Coffey stayed alive. I tried to keep an eye out for anything suspicious on the court, but I really didn't know what I was looking for. I enjoyed basketball enough but didn't consider myself more than a casual fan. The Presidents moved the ball well, though they made a few bad passes and missed a handful of open shots. Maybe those were examples of players trying to keep the score close. A buzzer-beating three by Drexel just before half-time left Hanson up by only two.

During the second half, my file transfer finished. I used

the remote access trojan to erase the system logs, then disconnected to watch the remainder of the game. Gloria occasionally asked questions about what transpired on the court. I was about fifty-fifty in being able to answer them. I knew lacrosse from playing it, and baseball and football from being a lifelong fan. Gloria understood tennis. By the end of tonight's event, though, she knew what a pick-and-roll was. This counted as progress.

The final score was Hanson over Drexel 79-72. The Presidents, favored by nine and a half, won by seven. Anyone taking Drexel and the points would win the bet. I wondered how much money changed hands on this game and what quantity was handled by some random offshore casino. Maybe Margaret Madison turned a tidy profit on the night's action.

After the final whistle, I was no closer to knowing if any points had been shaved than I was at tipoff. This needed to change.

CHAPTER 7

I WAS THE PROUD OWNER OF A FEW TERABYTES OF JHC
game film stored on an external hard drive. Overnight, I
backed it up to cloud storage. In the morning, I came downstairs, made coffee, and looked at my list of questionable
contests. I queued the first game of interest. It was a
December tilt against Drexel. The Dragons went in as nine-
point underdogs and only lost by three.

The game played much like last night's playoff against
the same opponent, only with a closer final margin. Hanson's
offense favored guards and motion, and they kept Drexel
defenders off-balance much of the night. Bad passes led to
turnovers, however, and the Dragons made the most of their
opportunities. Calvin Murray, a good shooter, finished the
night nine-for-twenty-four from the field.

This alone didn't indicate much. Players could follow up
a great game with a dud or vice versa. In my lacrosse days,
there were times I felt every shot would go in and others
where I couldn't find the goal if someone held my hand and
steered me to it. No one sniffed around our Loyola teams for
goal shaving. Then again, maybe there wasn't enough action
on college lacrosse games to make such a thing a reality.

Before I could immerse myself in the second half, Gloria appeared in the doorway. She wore a long T-shirt as a nightgown and sipped coffee from a mug. "Right back at it?" she said.

I spent a moment regarding her legs before I answered. Gloria played tennis and practiced a lot, and the results showed in her tone. "I wanted to start early in case I need to go back to campus."

"You're so dedicated you forgot about breakfast."

"Maybe I was hoping you'd cook."

Gloria grinned at me. She knew I didn't feel this way. I barely trusted her to make toast without summoning the fire department. Anything more complicated butted against her low level of kitchen competence. "Your homeowners insurance is current, right?"

"I think I can spare a few minutes to cook," I said.

I whipped up a quick yogurt parfait and made a couple pieces of sourdough toast for Gloria. She ate in the kitchen while I took my bowl back down the hall. My basketball expertise remained low. Compared to Gloria in the kitchen, I was a hoops savant, but clearing this low bar didn't help me on the case.

My hypothesis confirmed itself as I watched the next game. This time, Calvin enjoyed a pretty good night shooting, finishing ten-for-eighteen and contributing 26 points. Hanson didn't cover the spread, however. I wondered about the subtleties of point shaving. Anyone looking into Calvin's performance would see he made all five of his free throws, half of his six three-point attempts, and put up solid numbers overall. He even dished out nine assists against five turnovers. Did the lack of clangers mean he tried? Was someone else on the take? Was this game merely closer than expected, and no one enriched themselves too much on the result?

I needed someone who knew more than I did. A name floated into my mind, and I made a phone call to arrange a lunch appointment, and I knew from experience it would be an expensive one.

* * *

As usual, Joey Trovato already enjoyed an appetizer by the time I sat across from him. I was only a few minutes late. Joey always managed to be early for these lunches, and whatever he ordered before I arrived came out in record time. We occupied a booth at Della Notte in Little Italy, his favorite spot of late. "Just because you're Italian doesn't mean we need to eat here all the time," I said.

Joey grinned. He was a black Sicilian of good humor and enormous appetite. "I like it here."

There really weren't any bad places to go in Little Italy. Sabatino's was the most popular with tourists. I preferred Chiaparelli's, though I doubted I would share my enthusiasm for it with Tony Rizzo. Apart from specials and a few health-conscious items, most of the restaurants served much of the same food, anyway.

Joey worked on a basket of fried calamari. Watching him dunk the squid in the marinara sauce reminded me I'd been watching too much basketball. I scanned the menu, and a pretty waitress appeared a moment later. She possessed a classic Italian complexion and dark hair. Her white button-down shirt strained to hold in her breasts, and I spied Joey eyeing her up as I ordered an iced tea and veal parmesan. Joey opted for mozzarella sticks and a seafood dish. As the waitress left, Joey watched her with interest. I didn't blame him. The view was equally good from this side, too.

"Need an extra napkin for your drool?" I said.

"I'll be all right." He paused and smiled. "She's beautiful."

"Is she why you've been on a Della Notte kick?"

"It's one of the best reasons to like a restaurant." I rolled my eyes. "Hey, we can't all talk to girls as easy as you."

"Talking to people isn't so simple," I said. "It's a matter of acknowledging the challenge and doing it anyway. If you think it's easy and then you can't do it, you only end up discouraging yourself."

"Jesus," Joey said. "If I knew you were gonna spout all this Tony Robbins shit, I woulda offered to buy lunch."

"You can come to my seminar for five thousand dollars."

He chuckled. "I'll pass." The waitress set down our drinks and Joey's second appetizer. She smiled at him, which only seemed to encourage him.

"I asked you here for your professional opinion," I said after waving a hand in front of Joey's face to snap him back to the here and now.

"Who are you trying to find this time?" It was a reasonable question. Like me, Joey skirted the law in a business setup to help people. While I investigated crimes, he provided new identities for those who needed them. They'd stand up to scrutiny, and Joey was able to charge well for his services, which proved to be a mix of art and science. I'd seen him work before and came away impressed.

"No one yet. You still follow basketball?"

"It's about the only sport I can stand to watch these days." He frowned. "Why, what's going on?"

"I need you to study some game film."

"How the hell did you get game film?" I spread my hands and tried to look hurt. "Right. Never mind. Who's the team?"

"John Hanson College."

"Good squad," Joey said. "They should win their conference tournament, which gets them a ticket to the dance. From there, it's all about the matchups."

"I'm not as concerned about their future as some of their previous games." I glanced around. Della Notte drew a decent crowd for lunch. A couple of middle-aged guys in starched shirts and expensive suits sat at a table nearby. I lowered my voice and explained my concern. Joey didn't say anything and provided no visible reaction. Our food arrived after I finished. When the server walked away, I said, "What do you think?"

"It's possible," Joey said. "Hasn't been done in a while, so the kind of people likely to do it might think it'll go unnoticed." He was careful not to use the term "point shaving" in public. I appreciated it. "It might be retro enough to fly under the radar."

"I think you're the first person I've mentioned it to who really agrees with me . . . no, the second. The other one works in gambling."

"We're just a pair of visionaries," Joey said, raising his soda glass.

"You think you can start watching the games?" I cut my veal as Joey stewed on his answer. The meat was tender enough to require almost no pressure from my knife.

"Sure." Joey worked on a mozzarella stick while he talked. Other than chatting with food in his mouth, the man possessed good table manners. If he didn't, my parents wouldn't have invited him to so many dinners over the years. He was on his best behavior around them, of course. I got the raw version of Joey. "I'll watch them. I know hoops better than you."

"You're not clearing a high bar there." The fact was Joey loved basketball. He served as the student manager of the team in high school. I didn't bring it up, though, because it was a sore spot for him. The coach thought he was too fat to play and wouldn't let him try out. Joey downplayed his disappointment and assumed a supporting role for a few years. The story went he got onto the court at the team's last practice his senior year, showed a few players up, flipped off the coach, and walked away. I didn't see it, and I'd never asked him about it, but I wanted to believe it.

"How many games you got?"

"The whole season. There are a few in particular to watch because I think the outcomes may have been . . . manipulated."

"I'll need to go through the others to get a baseline, though."

"I knew you'd understand."

"When are you looking for results?" Joey moved on from the last mozzarella stick and started in on his entree without a pause to breathe inbetween. I long ago stopped wondering how he did it.

"The sooner, the better," I said.

"Good thing I ain't too busy right now."

"And I know I'm not keeping you from your exercise routine."

"You're hilarious," Joey said.

* * *

LATER THE SAME EVENING, Joey called. "Twice in one day," I said as I answered. "To what do I owe such a singular honor?"

"I watched a couple of the games," he said. "One not on your list at first, then one of the ones you highlighted."

"And?"

"It's two games. Small sample size. I'm not sure I have enough to go on."

"Like you said, it's two games."

"I mean, I'm not sure I'm enough of an expert."

I closed my eyes and blew out a deep breath. Where would I find someone to analyze the games and keep everything confidential on short notice? "How are you not enough of an expert on basketball?"

"I haven't been involved since high school. Sure, I've watched a lot, but it ain't the same. The game's changed a ton since then, and the way people evaluate players and everything is different."

"You're saying I need someone still involved with the game?"

"Yeah, and I got someone in mind."

I heard the hair dryer fire up on the second floor. Thus began the ritual of Gloria getting her chestnut locks presentable enough to be seen in public. I thought she did at least three times the work she needed to—Gloria could be very pretty even with no effort—but I'd never gotten her to believe it. "Who were you thinking of?"

"Luther Bowser."

I frowned as I struggled to recall the name. Sometime years ago, I'd heard it, but I couldn't retrieve it. "Name's familiar, but I can't place it."

"He was the head coach at Loyola when we were freshmen."

"Didn't last long, did he?"

"They fired him at the end of the year. He's bounced around since. Right now, he's the coach at Howard Community College."

"So in eleven years or so, this guy went from being a Division One coach to heading up a community college program?" Joey didn't say anything. "What's wrong with him?"

"He's a stathead," Joey said. "He embraced all the numbers early and didn't really get along with his players."

"Or administrators, I imagine," I said.

"No doubt. But he's a hell of a basketball mind."

"And he's willing to help us out?" Upstairs, the dryer clicked off. This meant Gloria would be wearing a ponytail. I think it took her more than a year into our relationship to loosen up enough to pull her hair back. Gloria, like me, came from a wealthy family, but she didn't relate to people as well as I did. To her credit, however, she was improving.

"If you pay him for his time, yes."

"Fine. Tell him I will. Can you get the game files to him?"

"Sure. I'll put him in touch with you."

"Thanks, Joey."

We hung up. A couple minutes later, Gloria came downstairs. It must have been casual night. She wore a pair of designer jeans, a V-neck sweater with a very interesting neckline, two-inch heels, and her hair in a ponytail. "Where are you taking me, stud?" she said, swinging her leg over the chair and lowering herself onto my lap.

I looked at her sweater, then met her gaze. "Maybe back upstairs."

She gave me a lingering kiss. It didn't help. "Patience, grasshopper. Come on." She stood and slipped into a jacket. "You're not working tonight, right?"

"I'd scuttle any plans I had," I said.

"My hero," she told me as we walked to the car.

CHAPTER 8

THE NEXT MORNING, I DID TWO VERY IMPORTANT THINGS before making coffee. First, I read recaps of the Drexel-JHC game. With a day to process everything, I expected the takes to be hot. Even the most cynical of columnists didn't broach the specter of point shaving, however. A few commented on the Presidents coming out with an uncharacteristically sluggish offense. None pointed a finger at Calvin, who played a good game.

The next thing I did was look at the cloned phone. I scrolled through a few meaningless texts and other messages from Calvin's friends and well-wishers. Then, I saw the one from Eddie over the encrypted app. *Good job. Everything went very well on this end.* Using my amazing private investigator powers of deduction, I inferred Eddie made a nice bit of coin on the game. Calvin offered no reply, so Eddie kept the thread going. *Next game opened at 7. Will keep you posted.*

I checked the conference tournament schedule as I put the java on to brew. Hanson played another home game tomorrow evening, taking the court against the Dukes of James Madison University. The Vegas sportsbooks kept the line at seven points. The Presidents took both games against JMU in the regular season.

While I toasted a bagel, the cloned phone buzzed on the countertop. I saw another message from Eddie. *We should talk today.* I wondered what he had in mind. His earlier messages made it clear tomorrow's game would be of interest, too. Fixing two consecutive tournament contests seemed reckless to me.

Gloria remained upstairs while I ate my bagel and some turkey sausage. A few minutes later, another message flashed on the screen. *Get back to me. I'll send someone to talk to you if I need to.* Eddie grew impatient. Calvin would be in class now. Maybe he saw the missive and chose not to respond. If Eddie paid for Denise's cancer treatments and then held it over Calvin's head, I understood the player's resentment.

I also thought I could use it to my advantage, at least in the short-term. I wolfed down the rest of my breakfast, got dressed without waking Gloria, and headed to the car.

After parking on campus, I checked Calvin's schedule. He was in the middle of a biology class in McCormick Hall. I walked toward the building, keeping an eye out for angry basketball coaches and vengeful football players. Maybe those three idiots were back to spring practice by now.

I made it to McCormick without incident. Calvin's class was on the top floor. I wandered up and down the halls to get a lay of the land. Most of the classrooms weren't being used. Calvin looked bored in 307. I checked the doors leading down the hall to the exit. While 305 was locked, the knob at 303 turned. I padded into the room, kept the lights off, and sat at the teacher's desk. Might as well try to look official.

Keeping the door open allowed me to monitor Calvin's class easier.

Ten minutes later, chairs slid over nearby linoleum, and students milled about. I checked my copy of Calvin's phone. He texted someone named Belle. Other people filed past. I stood and moved toward the door, standing close beside it. All was quiet on the hallway front. I edged my head out. Calvin talked to another guy in the class. He headed in the opposite direction while Calvin walked toward me.

The hallway was empty.

When he passed 303, I took a step to the side, reached out, grabbed his arm, and yanked him into the room. Before he could swear at me, I kicked the door shut with my heel. Calvin glared. "What the fuck?" He raised his fist.

"Go ahead," I said, sticking my chin out. "Free shot." The brows above his hard eyes pulled down. "When you break your hand on my jaw, though, what will you do tomorrow night?"

"What do you mean?"

"What do you think I mean?"

Calvin lowered his fist but continued to eye me warily. "Who the hell are you? Who sent you?"

"What if I told you Eddie sent me?"

He pulled away a step. "I was gonna get back to him. Honest, I was." Another retreating stride made Calvin bump into a desk. He felt for it with his hand but didn't look behind him. Whoever Eddie was, Calvin was scared of him. He stood at least four inches taller than me and probably outweighed me by thirty or more pounds. I couldn't imagine many people made him afraid.

I thought about continuing the ruse, but I preferred having Calvin on my side to making him fear me. "Relax. Eddie didn't send me. I'm here on my own."

The rigidity of his posture eased. "Who the hell are you?"

"C.T. Ferguson. I'm a private investigator."

"I heard of you. Didn't you bust a bunch of pedos or some shit?"

"A few months ago, yes."

"Why you here now?" Calvin said.

"You have people who are concerned about you, Calvin."

He waved a hand. "Ain't nothin' to be concerned about. I got shit under control."

"So why did you look like you saw a ghost when I mentioned Eddie?"

He scowled at me. "Fuck you, man. I'm out." Calvin started toward the door, but I was still blocking it. I didn't step aside as he approached. "Move."

"You've got it all under control," I said. "Big man on campus. You don't need my help with Eddie. Why don't you move me?"

Calvin laughed. "You don't think I can?"

"No, I don't." He stared at me. "Three guys on the football team recently tried to discourage me from asking around. I'm not sure they're back to practice yet."

"Three of them?"

"Three of them. One's probably eating through a straw for the next six weeks. So what do you think your odds of getting past me and leaving this room are right now?"

The stare persisted a few more seconds before Calvin broke eye contact. He shuffled back a few paces. "Who sent you?" he said in a small voice.

"I told you people are concerned about you. Why don't you tell me what's going on?"

"Nothing I can't handle."

"Seems like Eddie has his hooks in you pretty deep."

Calvin didn't say anything. "How many games has he asked you to fix?"

"How do you—"

"In addition to being able to beat up three linemen, I'm really smart. Good-looking, too, but it hasn't helped me here so far."

A small smiled played on Calvin's lips. Finally, I got a reaction other than anger or fear. All it took was the truth. "A few." Calvin couldn't meet my eyes. "I don't know."

"Anyone else on the team involved?"

"Here and there. It's hard to take it all on myself."

"You're being awfully vague for someone who's in so deep," I said.

"I said I don't need help."

"You're wrong. I've dealt with guys like Eddie before. I can get you out."

Now he looked up at me. "Ain't no getting out for me yet." Calvin shook his head. "You don't get it."

Behind us, someone cleared his throat. I turned to see a bookish Indian man in a cheap suit standing outside the doorway. "I have a class in here soon," he said.

"We're done," Calvin said as he moved past me.

I didn't have many good options, so I let him go.

* * *

CALVIN MAY HAVE BEEN the BMOC at John Hanson, but on social media, he was merely one of billions. Being a college-aged Generation Z type—I tended to think of anyone younger than me as a Gen Z'er—he was all over various platforms. His bite-sized thoughts, written in grammar forcing me to question how much he paid attention in English class, dotted the Twitter landscape. They were rarely about basket-ball and made sense every bit as often.

On Instagram, Calvin posted a lot of pictures of himself in uniform, plus an occasional video at practice. I wondered who worked the phone camera for him. Many people his age posted pictures of everything they ate. I guessed Calvin avoided this because he was confined to eating on the JHC meal plan. College athletes aren't supposed to accept gifts from anyone, even a free meal, and uploading a plethora of food pics would've brought the NCAA Gestapo to his doorstep.

His Facebook profile was a different animal altogether. Calvin went to some effort to hide it or at least make it harder for people to find him. He used his middle name of Richard Murray, didn't identify himself as a basketball player, and rarely uploaded a shot of himself in uniform. It consisted of other pictures of Calvin, plus some of his family and friends. This would be where the treasure trove lay.

I found some photos of his mother both prior to and after her cancer diagnosis. She looked pretty and full of life and vigor before, but in more recent pictures, she appeared tired. This matched what I saw when she came to my office. Calvin posted a few shots of him and his mother together in the hospital, then of him in the kitchen cooking her first post-treatment meal. He seemed like a loving and devoted son, and this was something a person like Eddie would exploit. I saved a few pictures and kept looking.

Several albums were dedicated to Iris. She was a beautiful baby with bright eyes and an infectious smile. According to a video, she started walking at ten months. Calvin's post mentioned her as a future star athlete. Her mother, who was tagged in many of the photos, ran track in high school and competed in college until pregnancy forced her to back away from the team. Iris certainly possessed the genes for athletics.

Tagging the mother would also make her a target for Eddie. Her face alone would be enough. They'd have ways of figuring out who she was. Identifying her only made things easy. More people needed to understand the ramifications of sharing so many details of their lives and others'. I wondered if Calvin ever told Tamika Robinson about how he earned the money to pay for his mother's cancer treatments. I wondered if he ever mentioned the danger she and Iris would be in if a game didn't break the right way. Then, I shook my head. Of course he hadn't. Tamika looked too happy in recent snapshots to have been burdened with this sort of news.

As before, I saved a few choice photos. Once I felt I'd collected a strong sample, I put a few in a text message to Calvin. I attached a picture of his mother smiling and giving a thumbs up during her recovery, one of Iris looking delighted at the fact she crawled across carpet, and a final one of Tamika holding their baby.

You have a lot to lose, Calvin. You're risking way too much. Let me help you.

I waited a few minutes. My phone buzzed as he replied. Rather than accept my gracious offer of help, he opted to be confrontational. *How'd u get this number? I told u I didn't need no help.*

I sent a reply. *If it were just your funeral, I'd be happy to let you plan it. But it's not. If you don't want my help, fine. Don't do it for yourself. Do it for everyone else Eddie might hurt.*

A few minutes passed, and no reply came.

* * *

MY STOMACH RUMBLED, and I pondered what to make for lunch when Rich called. "Just want to be sure you're staying out of trouble," he said.

"Never. I am incorrigible."

"You doing anything for lunch?" I told him I wasn't. "Mind if I come by?" I told him I didn't. We hung up. I looked outside my living room window. Gray dominated the sky, and fresh raindrops danced in puddles on the sidewalk. This took grilling off the table. I inventoried my fridge to see if I would need to make a mad dash to Harris Teeter before Rich arrived. I figured it couldn't hurt.

When I got back, two grocery bags in tow, Rich and Gloria chatted at the kitchen table. My girlfriend smiled at me as I walked in. My cousin seemed more interested in the contents of the brown paper bags. "What's for lunch?" he said.

"You invite yourself, and I have to shop and cook?"

"Yep." He and Gloria exchanged grins.

"This seems to be a one-way arrangement." I unpacked the bags, putting items into the fridge or pantry as appropriate.

"You never answered my question," Rich said.

"I bought three steaks," I said, "plus some potatoes and green beans." I busied myself with turning the oven on, getting out my cast-iron skillet, and plugging in the vegetable steamer. When the oven beeped its readiness, I put the lightly-oiled and foil-wrapped potatoes in. Next, I removed the steaks from the fridge and let them grow closer to room temperature before I seasoned them. I put them in the hot skillet to build a sear on all sides. The green beans went in the vegetable steamer as I turned the cooktop down to let the New York Strips cook throughout.

At the end of the process, I plated a steak, a baked potato, and a serving of green beans times three. Rich went to the Herculean effort of opening three beers while I cooked. At least he didn't insult me by pretending to wipe his brow. I joined him and Gloria at the kitchen table, which was exactly the right size for the three of us. A fourth diner would have been as unlucky as someone crammed into the backseat of Rich's Camaro. My cousin cut into his steak and examined the piece. "Medium," he said, nodding in approval.

"Of course," I said. "I'm not a barbarian."

"Jeanne eats hers rare," Rich said. He didn't often mention his girlfriend, who served as a uniformed officer in the BPD. The infrequency led me to believe they'd split up on more than one occasion.

"I suspect anyone who eats rare meat of being a were-wolf," I said.

"Your father takes his steaks rare," Rich pointed out.

"Why do you think I avoid him when there's a full moon?"

Gloria laughed around a mouthful of beer, covering her lips with a napkin. We settled into eating our lunches. It was a bit decadent for a midday meal, but I didn't have a lot of advance notice. Besides, a slight lapse into degeneracy now and again could only be a good thing. This had been one of my beliefs for most of my thirty years, and it never did me wrong.

"You working on anything?" Rich asked when all our plates were mostly empty.

"Just took a case." I filled him in on the details in brief, along with my suspicion.

"Point shaving?" he said. "Seems a little . . . old-fashioned."

"Doing it the original way would be. Everything's moved online. Courts and governments are slowly warming up to casual gambling. You don't need smoke-filled rooms and wiseguys anymore. Between local books and the offshore casinos, I think it could work."

"Someone still stands to profit, though."

"Of course. In this case, it's someone named Eddie."

"Eddie who?" Gloria asked.

"I don't know. None of the info I've gleaned from Calvin gives me anything besides his first name. Whoever he is, he's pretty careful."

"I haven't heard of an Eddie doing anything like this," Rich said. "You think he's operating in the city?"

"Doubt it." I cut the last chunk of my steak into three manageable bites. "I talked to Tony. He's in the dark. If this guy's doing it in Baltimore, he's doing a hell of a job of making sure no one knows about it."

Rich frowned. "Of course you talked to Tony."

"If he's such a criminal, Rich, you guys should arrest him. Oh, wait. You can't because the system doesn't actually work."

We'd engaged in similar arguments before. This time, Rich didn't take the bait. "Hanson's in the county. Maybe he's out there."

"I'm working with Gonzalez," I said. "So far . . . nothing."

"Don't the athletes normally get a cut of the proceeds in these schemes?" Rich said.

"Usually. Calvin's mother has cancer, though. She thinks he arranged to have her treatment paid for."

"Nice kid. Too bad he'll be in hock to this Eddie for the rest of his life."

"I'm trying to get him out, but he's not terribly cooperative."

"Doesn't he have a baby?" Gloria said. She set her fork

down, leaving only a bit of potato skin and a couple pieces of steak fat on her plate.

"He does. I think it should make him concerned. He's not married to the mother, but they seem to be together. If you add his own mother, it's three places he's vulnerable."

"I don't think Eddie will want to let him go," Rich said. "He's probably making good money, and he doesn't have to share any of it with the kid." He paused. "He going pro?"

"He certainly could," I said. "Everything I've read indicates he'll be among the first three picks if he comes out."

"Maybe Eddie has a say in whether he comes back for another year." I frowned. "Think about it," Rich continued. "The NBA is huge. National. Media all the time. Hanson's a medium-sized school in a small state and a fairly minor conference. A lot less attention."

"And a lot less scrutiny," Gloria said.

"I really need to figure out who Eddie is," I said.

"Yeah," Rich said, "you do."

CHAPTER 9

AFTER RICH LEFT, MY PHONE BUZZED ON THE KITCHEN counter. It was a number I didn't recognize, a frequent hazard in my line of work. I use an app to filter out as many spam calls as I can. A few inevitably slip through. I do my best to answer the rest, and this one was no exception. "Hello?"

"You Joey's friend?" said a voice as unrecognizable as his number. Whoever it was spoke quickly and, in the three-word sample I heard, sounded serious.

"I'd like to think I'm not so easily categorized," I said.

"He asked me to look at some basketball film." Pause. "I don't want to say much more over the phone."

Great. When I met the coach Joey contacted, I wondered if he'd be wearing a tinfoil hat and saving jars of his own urine. "Yes. Did he tell you specifically what I was interested in?"

"He did."

I expected him to elaborate there. Maybe we could only continue this conversation where the government and the aliens couldn't eavesdrop. If I met this guy in anything other than an underground bunker, I'd be disappointed. "And?"

"And if you want to know more, we gotta meet in person . . . plus you gotta pay me for my time."

"No problem. When do you think you might be done?"

"Could probably have something for you tomorrow."

"Wow." He worked faster than I expected, especially considering the community college he coached should be playing its own games. Maybe Coach Bowser didn't sleep much. "Sounds good. Call me tomorrow, and we'll figure it out."

"Will do." He hung up right away. I'd gotten used to such abrupt discourtesies talking to cops like Rich or Gonzalez. Add socially inept basketball coaches to the list.

"Who was that?" Gloria said, correctly reading my puzzled frown.

"A very strange man. He's a basketball coach, and I think he can help me shed some light on my case."

"You work with some interesting characters," she said.

"Don't I know it," I said.

I hoped Coach Bowser would come through.

MY POPULARITY CONTINUED to run high as my phone rang again a short while later. This time, it was a video call request. I saw the familiar pretty face and red wavy hair of Melinda Davenport. Ever since I rescued her from her life on the street as Ruby, we'd been close friends. I patted my hair to make sure it looked good before I answered. "Hey, Melinda."

"Hi, C.T." She smiled, and it was a good one. A girl Melinda saved from a life of prostitution, T.J., told me Melinda liked me in the way which compelled girls and boys to pass notes in high school. I'd never seen a sign of it, but we men tend to be pretty dense about these things. Besides, I was happy in my relationship with Gloria. "You up to anything tonight?"

"I just took a case. Haven't done much with it today, so I figured I'd get back to it."

"That's too bad." Her brows pulled down into a delicate frown, "I know it's short notice, but I have a pair of extra tickets to my father's big fundraiser tonight."

"Really?" The same fundraiser Gloria told me she couldn't get an invitation to attend. "How did you wrangle those?"

"I don't know. Someone backed out last minute, I think. Anyway, Dad gave them to me to see if I could unload them. No charge—whoever can't come already sent in his money."

"You know Gloria helped your father plan this soirée, right?"

Melinda's head bobbed, causing her hair to bounce in a wave. "I know he's worked with her a few times. He's very impressed with how she does things."

"So impressed she didn't even get an invitation to attend."

"I heard." She sighed. "I'm sorry. I don't know how it happened. Dad isn't the only one who allocates tickets. I guess this one got away from him."

"I guess so."

"Do you guys want to come?" she said after a pause.

"Gloria's pretty salty she didn't get an invitation before," I said. "However, I know how much work she put into this, and I'll bet she wants to be there."

"So you're in?"

"We're in."

She flashed a winning smile again. It would make some lucky man's knees turn to jelly someday. "Great. I'll leave the two tickets for you, then. See you tonight."

"Thanks, Melinda." We hung up. I walked down the hall.

Gloria sat on the couch reading something on her phone. "Guess where we're going tonight?"

She perked up at the mention of a social engagement. "Where?"

"Actually, you'll need to tell me because I don't know the venue. But I just scored us two tickets to the Davenport gala tonight."

Her eyes widened. "How'd you manage that?"

"Someone needed to cancel on short notice. Melinda asked me if we wanted to come, and I said yes. I know you're perturbed about Davenport not inviting you himself. Maybe you can spit in his champagne when we see him."

Gloria grinned. "I would never do something like that."

"Too bad," I said. "It'd be pretty hot."

She got off the couch and slinked to me. "How hot?" She wrapped her arms around my neck. I felt the heat of her body as she pressed it against me.

"Why don't I show you?" I suggested.

"Yeah." Gloria gave me a lingering kiss and led me toward the stairs. "Why don't you?"

* * *

GLORIA LOOKED stunning in a purple gown. The first time I saw her was at a fundraiser at the Walters Art Gallery in Baltimore. She wore a similar red number then, and she drew more eyes than the artist we were all there to see. I feared we'd encounter similar reactions tonight. Though if people focused on her instead of Vincent Davenport, I'd consider it a win.

I sported a Calvin Klein tuxedo—one of two I own—and I complemented Gloria's gown with a purple bowtie. In deference to my inability to tie one properly, it was a clip-on, though a convincing one. To celebrate being the best-looking couple out on the town tonight, we took Gloria's Mercedes coupe. It only had two seats, and was the color and approximate shape of a rocket. It also drove like one on the highway and sounded like its engine came from NASA under open throttle.

The fundraiser was at Martin's Valley Mansion in Hunt Valley. The town sat north of Baltimore. I navigated the coupe out of the city, enjoyed putting my foot down on the highway, and we took I-83 North most of the way there. The venue was constructed almost entirely of brick, white columns, and tall windows. We parked amid a sea of Lexuses and walked hand-in-hand into the Empire of Brick and Glass.

Inside, we collected our tickets from a tuxedoed man standing behind a podium and entered the ballroom. The walls were covered in white and gold, and a similar pattern continued on the ceiling. Even the tables were done in the same color scheme. The floor, at least, featured black instead of white. I wondered if this were the default configuration or something Davenport recommended. He struck me as the type of man to not know which colors to pair together.

Along the far wall, a podium sat in the center, flanked by two long tables covered in chalk-colored cloths. At least the napkins possessed the good sense to be dyed black and inject some color into the room. We walked in close to the witching hour, so plenty of people sat or milled about. The din of conversations was loud.

Gloria and I snagged two open seats near the center of the room. Four couples, all older than us, occupied the other eight chairs. The men all wore tuxes, and none of the women looked as good as Gloria. We exchanged pleasantries, accepted a drink from the waitress, and waited for the festivities to commence.

We didn't need to wait long. A couple opening acts took the podium and told us what we could've read in our programs. After the preamble, Vincent Davenport strode up to a standing ovation. To avoid being the only one who remained sitting, I dutifully got to my feet and clapped as little as I could. Davenport was about my parents' age, making him around sixty. He still looked pretty fit, though I guessed the dark hair came from a bottle. His glasses lent him a professorial look. "Good evening," he said to the crowd. "Thanks for coming tonight."

More applause arose, but this time everyone stayed seated. Thank goodness. I didn't want to expend the energy of standing for forced politeness more than once. Davenport continued. "I know this wasn't a cheap ticket. I promise you my speech isn't worth the price of admission."

This drew some laughter, and I had to admit it was better self-deprecating humor than I figured Davenport capable of. "We're here tonight for two reasons. The first is to recognize my daughter Melinda. Go on, stand up." Melinda did so reluctantly, giving a polite wave as the audience cheered. She wore a medium blue gown and looked terrific.

"Many of you know Melinda heads The Nightlight Foundation. Rescuing girls from lives on the hard streets of this city is near and dear to both our hearts. She's only been doing this a few months, but last week, the foundation saved its twentieth young woman." Everyone clapped, and I joined in with sincerity. Melinda worked a hard job and did it well.

"The other reason we're here tonight also ties in to the future of our city. I want to talk about the recent past for a moment, however. Baltimore has seen two mayors get forced out of office over corruption scandals. The leadership at the police department has been in flux, and this started even before Freddie Gray died. Baltimore is routinely cited as the most dangerous city in America. I want to change this."

Short of hiring his own paramilitary force to supplement the police, I didn't see how Davenport would accomplish his goal. A packed ballroom paid a lot of money to find out, so I bit down on my skepticism and listened. "Starting tonight," Davenport went on, "I'm forming a political action committee. Making a Difference for Baltimore—yes, you could call it 'Mad for Baltimore' if you wanted—is going to identify and recruit new leaders. The ones we've had for years have let us down. It's time for new ideas and new voices. I want Baltimore to be a cleaner city, a safer city, a less corrupt city, and a city which earns back the nation's trust."

Davenport paused for applause. I noticed Melinda's tepid reaction at one of the long tables. The idea sounded good, but I trusted Vincent Davenport about as far as I could drop-kick him. I hoped to test the distance one day.

While the man of the hour blathered on, my phone buzzed. Denise Murray. I ignored the call. A minute later, she tried again. I did the same thing but texted her this time. *Can't talk at the moment. What's up?*

I'm worried about Calvin.

I already knew this. It was why she came to me in the first place, of course. Something must've happened to ramp up her concern. *What's going on with him?*

He's talking about staying in school. Calvin's been wanting to turn pro for a while.

Another year in college meant more games for Eddie to profit on. I texted back. *You seen anyone strange around Calvin lately?*

No.

What about the name Eddie?

I heard it once. Don't think I was meant to. I'm worried. Who's Eddie?

I didn't have a good answer for her, so I went with the truth as I knew it. *He's the guy your son is in debt to. He must want another year of profit.*

A minute later, her reply flashed on my screen. *Can you get him out?*

I really didn't have a good answer. I didn't even know who Eddie was. He'd done well to mask his identity so far, and I'd been focused on the basketball aspect rather than the man counting the money after the game. This would need to change.

Yes.

I hoped she believed it.

I hoped I did, too.

CHAPTER 10

GLORIA LET ME DRIVE THE MERCEDES HOME, TOO. I relished every chance I got behind the wheel. Tonight, however, more weighed on my mind than the performance of the AMG-made engine. Davenport's new political action committee worried me. He'd been a power broker in the city for a long time. Being the most prominent business owner brought a high level of cachet, and I felt sure Davenport used his influence over the years. What did a PAC get him he didn't already enjoy?

I was all for new ideas and new leadership. The city needed both. I was not all for Vincent Davenport being the driving force—and funding source—behind these efforts. He denied it any time it came up, but I knew he was aware of Melinda's life as a prostitute. He reconciled with her when I'd removed all the obstacles between them, and then he managed to turn it into a positive for himself.

Maybe he was a decent man and a good father. I could never shake the feeling he was an asshole. "Huh?" I said, vaguely aware of Gloria saying something and interrupting my stream of thoughts.

"You seem preoccupied."

"Oh. Yeah. Your buddy Davenport brings it out in me."

I felt Gloria bristle in the seat beside me. She knew how I felt about Davenport, but she enjoyed a good relationship with him. He liked working with her for fundraisers, even giving her a first big break when she started doing it. Whenever I referred to him as her buddy, she didn't care for it. "He means well," she said.

"I hope so."

We drove the rest of the way down I-83 and into the city in silence. I swung the red rocket onto my parking pad, and we walked into the house. "More than Davenport is upsetting you," Gloria said. She rubbed my shoulders. "I know you don't like him, but this feels like more."

I nodded in time with her massage. "I'm concerned about Calvin. His mother thinks the pressure's getting ramped up on him. She's not convinced Eddie's going to let him go pro next season."

Gloria's fingers stopped working their magic. "He could do that?"

"I guess so. If he paid for Denise's cancer treatment . . . I'm sure it wasn't cheap. She said it was some kind of trial. Medical bills like these bankrupt people. Let's say it cost him half a million dollars. He's going to make Calvin shave points to pay it off. They can't do it every game, though, or people will catch on. Maybe they get ten or twelve games a year. He'd have to be making about fifty grand a game to break even, and I doubt he's getting such a rate."

"I'm sure he'd want to keep Calvin around to make a profit, not just earn his money back."

"Right. Let's say Eddie makes twenty grand a game. He'll need to fix twenty-five games, and they all need to go his way. Calvin alone, good as he is, can't always guarantee the outcome. But let's say he hits on all his games. He'll need twenty-five to break even. Over twelve a year. He has to pick and choose the games carefully. Even after next season, Eddie might think Calvin's still in debt to him."

Gloria's hands gripped my shoulders and went back to work. "I know you'll be able to get him out."

"I need to find him first."

"You will," Gloria said.

I hoped so.

* * *

MY PHONE VIBRATED on the nightstand. Morning sunlight framed the edges of my curtains. I reached for the phone, almost dropped it, swore under my breath, and looked at the time. Seven-thirty. Coach Bowser was an early riser. I didn't want him to blow me off, however, so I slid out of bed and answered the call.

"I wake you?" he said. Considering how sleepy I sounded in my greeting, he must've known the answer.

"Of course you did. We lazy millennials sleep past sunrise."

"You and most of my players. Can you meet me at my office?"

"On campus?"

"Yeah. We don't have a game for a few days, so there shouldn't be anyone else here." He gave me the building and room information, and we hung up. I rubbed sleep from my eyes, threw water on my face in the bathroom, then freshened up and got dressed. Downstairs, I made coffee, drinking one cup with my quick breakfast of yogurt and fruit and taking another with me. I left the remainder of the pot for Gloria when she woke up and set off for Howard Community College.

The school is in Columbia, which sits between Baltimore and DC just off I-95. The city loves to boast of itself being a "planned community," which always makes me wonder how many unplanned ones there have been and what they look like. Columbia is in the affluent Howard County, and despite some of its patently absurd street names, it's a nice suburban town.

I pulled onto the campus shortly before nine. Finding the athletic buildings proved easy enough. Maybe good signage was the lynchpin of a planned community. I parked in a nearby visitors' lot and went inside, traversing the labyrinthine corridors until I came to Coach Bowser's office. His door was cracked. I rapped on it.

"What?" he bellowed.

I poked my head in. "I'm here for my film study."

"You Ferguson?"

"You expecting any other handsome visitors?"

He smirked. "Come in, come in. Shut the door."

I did. As I looked around, I realized doing so would also block the view of this hideously messy office. I pegged it for ten feet a side at most, making it smaller than a lot of extra bedrooms. The ritzier areas of the county featured larger sleeping quarters for servants. Bowser put his desk near the center of the room, which was probably the worst place for it, and it forced all the other furniture into bad places. Navigating the room on foot required a map. I picked my way past a table and over piles of paper to a shopworn guest chair.

Whiteboards hung on the walls with basketball plays diagrammed on them. Bowser seemed to grasp Xs and Os but not feng shui. A few other small tables existed mostly to support more stacks of paper. A TV sat atop a rolling cart with a DVD player and a freaking VCR connected. Why it hadn't been consigned to the incinerator or a museum was not the mystery I'd been tasked to solve. More documents and an impressive collection of Red Bull cans littered the oaken desk. "Want one?" Bowser said, offering me a can of his favorite beverage.

"No, thanks. I prefer my caffeine the old-fashioned way." I held up my travel mug and sipped the delicious coffee within. Maybe it didn't give me wings, but it also wouldn't kill me before I turned forty.

"You got money?"

"Maybe. You got more for me than shitty beverages?"

"You bet." He got up and carried his laptop to the TV. Bowser was a tall man, which seemed to be a desirable attribute in a hoops coach. I pegged him for six-five. He probably tipped the scales at close to three hundred pounds. His shaved black head combined with a perpetual frown to lend him a serious and even unfriendly appearance, something his demeanor also supported. Somehow, Bowser found a folding chair amid the chaos, set it up, and plopped down onto it. It groaned but held. I turned in my seat.

The coach connected his computer. "I've watched a bunch of the games." Considering the quantity of Red Bull cans strewn about the room, I wondered if he did anything else.

"Any conclusions?"

"They're playing Nellie ball." I felt I should nod as if I understood. "You know what it is?" I turned up my hands. "Don Nelson ring a bell?"

"Nope."

Bowser sighed. "Longtime NBA coach. He basically popularized an offense with three guards, sometimes no true center, and lots of passes. The Warriors play a version of it now."

"I've seen their games."

"So you get the idea," he said.

"More or less."

"Great. Let's look at some things." He called up the file for a game early in the season, a non-conference tilt against Towson. I recalled the Presidents being decent favorites but only putting the game away on a late three-pointer from—of all people—Calvin Murray. Bowser consulted one of the many documents near him, but he found the moment he wanted to show me. "Watch this play."

He advanced the film. Another JHC player pulled down a rebound and immediately passed the ball to Calvin. He dribbled it up the court, looking around at the defense and taking his time. Then he drove to the basket and fired off a quick pass. It missed the mark and sailed into the stands for a turnover. "He threw it away on purpose," Bowser said, sounding as confident as if he walked outside and confirmed the grass was in fact still green.

"How do you know?"

"Let me be clear. I don't know any of this for certain. I can only tell you what I think is extremely likely. You understand?"

I nodded. "I took a lot of math. I get probability."

"All right. Good." The coach rewound the film and paused it about a second before the errant pass. "Calvin moves the ball well," he said. "Kinda have to if you're a point guard. He's got good vision, and he can put the ball where it needs to go. I've seen him fit them in really small windows. This one, though . . ." He shook his head. "Watch."

I leaned forward as if getting a few inches closer to the screen would guarantee an epiphany. The game resumed. Calvin took a couple steps and heaved the ball into the crowd. "What am I supposed to see?" I asked when Bowser paused the video and offered nothing.

"Look at his head and feet." We watched the clip a third time. Bowser slowed the footage down and narrated the action. "His four is on the other side of the paint. Not a hard pass. The closest defender doesn't have a good angle." Pause. "We can't see his eyes, but his head ain't in line with the four. And look at his lead foot." I did, and it pointed about twenty degrees to the left of where the ball would need to go.

"What's a four?"

"Power forward. Now follow the ball." Bowser resumed the clip, and the would-be assist followed Calvin's foot, zipping past every other player to land in the hands of a very surprised fan in the first row of seats. "One bad pass, right?"

"It's possible."

"It's not. Calvin's too good. His footwork is too clean. He doesn't make this mistake."

"Unless he's on the take," I said.

"Now we're on the same page," Bowser said. He exited this game and scrolled to a video he must have made himself. "I did some shooting charts. Looked at the games you didn't suspect as a control group and compared them to the fishy ones." He fired up the footage. It showed plays from an assortment of games. "He misses all these shots. Every single one. They're all open looks at the top of the key."

"Does he normally make them?"

"For the season, he's a fifty-six percent shooter overall. Pretty good. In the control games, he's seventy-seven percent from the spot I showed you."

"Seems high," I said.

"Above average," Bowser confirmed. "Hell, I wish I had a player who came within five points." On the TV, Calvin tossed up another brick. "In the other games, he made the same shot about forty percent of the time."

"Wow. Quite a drop."

"Sure is. Now, it's probably consistent with probability and random chance for him to be a good shooter from this area some games and a bad one in others. I get it. But when you add in the possibility of point shaving, you see the pattern."

"Impressive," I said. "This is great work. Thanks, Coach."

"I have some notes I'm gonna type up and send you in case you need them. Meantime, you can grab those two papers closest to you."

I snagged the sheets before they got lost in another mountain. "I appreciate it."

Bowser asked me for five hundred dollars. Considering the time he must've put in, I scored a bargain. I paid him six hundred, saying the final C-note was for the extra information he would prepare and send. This seemed to make him happy, and I got the impression few things outside of basketball achieved this.

I drove away from campus more certain than ever Calvin Murray was shaving points. What did this get me, though? I was pretty confident before. I still needed to figure out who Eddie was, and I needed to devise a way to get Calvin out from under his thumb.

Knowledge was nice, but I still had work to do.

* * *

WHEN I GOT HOME, I tried Calvin again. Before, I approached him like I harbored a suspicion. Now, I felt certain he was on the take. I sent him a text. *Calvin, I know what's going on, and I know you're in trouble. This is bigger than you. Let me help.*

I waited a few minutes, but no reply came. Calvin would be in class now, but this rarely stopped someone his age from answering a message or doing something else with their phone. Count this among the reasons I was glad not to be a college professor. I checked on my clone of his phone. My message sat unread.

Eddie piped up again over WhatsApp last night, though, after Calvin didn't answer him last time. *You know what to do.*

Calvin replied this time. *Yeah, I know. Quit hounding me. We're good.*

It seemed Eddie didn't care for being told what to do by Calvin. *I'll hound you as much as I need, you little shit. Don't forget what I did. You're not even to the halfway point yet.*

This must have been the genesis of what Denise told me. Eddie was laying it out here—he expected Calvin to remain at JHC next season. Calvin's feeling about this were neatly summed up in his next message. *I'm out after this year.*

No you're not was Eddie's retort.

The conversation ended there. Calvin didn't have any idea how much trouble he was in. I didn't either, as Eddie remained an unknown, but I got a glimmer of a much better idea. While I pondered how short-sighted and selfish he was behaving, Calvin answered me. *Fuck off.*

He was in over his head. Whether he wanted it or not, I meant to throw him a life preserver. I only hoped he didn't drag me to the bottom with him.

CHAPTER 11

THE REST OF THE DAY PASSED UNEVENTFULLY. GLORIA and I tried tandem cooking. My kitchen barely allowed us both space to move—hers would have been a much better choice—and I did a good eighty percent of the work. Still, she tried and seemed to enjoy the effort. I chalked it up as a small win, though I still didn't want to leave her unsupervised near the oven, microwave, or anything else which could catch food on fire.

The next morning, I got up and went out for a run. I took my usual laps around Federal Hill Park. The chill in the air no longer bothered me by the middle of my first circuit, and I felt the first drops of sweat as I began the second. I'd skipped yesterday to meet Coach Bowser, and while it was productive, I did an extra lap to make up for it.

At home, I showered, got dressed, and made a quick breakfast of oatmeal and yogurt. Gloria joined me once the coffee finished brewing. We chatted a bit over breakfast—she told me she'd be going home and invited me to stay the night with her—and then she left. After I kissed her goodbye and closed the door, I pondered where I stood with my current case. As usual, I didn't know nearly enough. I normally have a suspect after a few days. Eddie made for a convenient villain, but I didn't even know who he was, let alone if anyone pulled his strings.

I got in the S4 and drove to the office. After parking in the lot, I walked into THB Bagels and Deli for another cup of coffee. Maybe the third would help me crank out a powerful insight. If nothing else, at least it tasted good. When I left the shop, I glanced to the right and saw two men standing near my car. I paused and watched them. They continued to loiter in open defiance of laws forbidding it. I crossed the street and approached. One elbowed the other as I drew near.

When I was a few steps away, I took a sip of coffee. It was almost too hot to drink. I also caught the lid in my teeth and pried it up just enough to make it loose. "You guys know loitering is illegal, right?" I said as I sized them up. They had the height and builds of the football players I'd tangled with a few days ago, but these two fellows were older, more my age. I presumed this made them more formidable, too. One wore his blond hair in ridiculous spikes while the other failed to hide a receding hairline by reversing his Orioles cap so its adjustable strap and gap were in front..

"You gonna take us in?" the fair-haired one said.

"I think I have to. First, it's loitering, and then what's next? This is how societal decay begins."

"Ain't you a fucking philosopher?" the hat-wearing one said.

"Let me guess," I said. "You two assholes are here to get me to back off." They both nodded. "We could do the whole song and dance where I pretend not to know what you're talking about, but I think we can skip it today. We're all professionals here, right?" Their heads bobbed again. "Great. So let's fast-forward to the point where I tell you to go piss off."

"Thought you might want to do it the hard way," Orioles Cap said. He took a step forward, and I threw my hot coffee in his face. He screamed, and his hands went up as he dropped to the asphalt.

His partner barely spared a glance at him. "He made me waste good coffee, dammit," I said. "You walk away now, I'll take five bucks from your friend here to replace my drink, and we'll call it a wash. What do you think?"

He threw a punch. "A simple 'no' would've sufficed," I said as I blocked another couple haymakers. To my right, the other man moaned still flat on the parking lot. The goon with the ridiculous hair advanced. He fired off a pretty good side kick, which I turned away. He launched another. I stepped to the side and put my foot in the back of his knee. It buckled, but he staggered forward and regained his balance without toppling over.

I barely avoided a wild swing as he recovered faster than I expected. Out of the corner of my eye, I spied a couple people across the street near the entrance to my building. I'd hoped we weren't attracting attention, but I didn't park very deep in the lot. A few more rows back, and we might've gone unnoticed. I blunted another couple punches and countered with a hard right jab in the gut. My foe backed off a step, and I walloped him again. This bent him in half. I grabbed the collar of his shirt and rammed his head into the door of a nearby SUV. He bounced off it, hit the asphalt, and didn't get up.

By now, the other guy stopped moaning. He took his hands away from his face, which was red and swollen already. His eyes, already narrowed from the puffy tissue around them, glared at me. As he tried to get up, a kick to the head sent his baseball cap flying and put him down again.

I heard the first siren. Great. Whoever saw us across the

street called the cops. In the grand scheme of things, I supposed it was preferable to getting sweet footage for Instagram. Our scuffle drew a few more onlookers, some of whom now pointed at me. I turned away to spoil their videos. Leaving the scene wasn't an option at this point. The SUV blocked the first guy I knocked out from view. I crouched beside him and took out his wallet. I pocketed a five-dollar bill for my coffee and snapped a photo of his driver's license.

Then I saw his mobile peeking out of his right front jeans pocket. How could I not look at it? It was an iPhone and it asked me for Touch ID or the passcode. I put the unconscious goon's thumb on the sensor and unlocked the device.

Another siren joined the first one. Both drew closer. I looked in the contacts and was disappointed to find Eddie listed by only his first name. I quickly memorized the number in his entry, locked the device, and put it back where I found it.

Then, I waited for the cops.

I'D NEVER BEFORE SEEN the two officers who questioned me. A man and a woman, both black and around my age, frowned at me as I truthfully recounted the events of a few minutes prior. They took my PI license, checked it in their car, and returned it to me with a warning not to take on two large men in parking lots. I didn't bother telling them I hadn't sought the encounter.

When they were finished with me, I replaced the coffee I'd used as a weapon and went to my office. The number I got from the goon's phone didn't help. It matched the one I had from Calvin's. In the futile hope something changed, I conducted another reverse lookup. No results. Eddie continued to be a local man of mystery. I added the first names Edward, Eddie, Ed, and Eduardo to the search. *Nada*.

Next, I scoured social media for the name of the assailant whose license I'd photographed. Christopher Horace Robbin, whose parents must have loathed him from the moment of conception to saddle him with such a dreadful name, maintained a fairly small online footprint, especially for a millennial. He had no LinkedIn or Instagram, a barely-used Twitter, and a Facebook profile he mostly used to share lame memes and send creepy DMs to uninterested women. He showed one friend whose name was a variation of Eddie. Ed Fells looked to be about sixty years old in his profile picture, quite a bit overweight, and listed his city of residence as St. Paul, Minnesota.

It made him an unlikely local bookie, or whatever Eddie was supposed to be.

I still had little to go on. What did I know about Eddie? He was some kind of bookie or big gambler who made money on point shaving. He employed at least two supposed toughs. Rumors swirled he worked in the county. What else? He exerted a lot of control over Calvin Murray.

An obvious fact finally hit me—he paid for Denise Murray's cancer treatment. She told me she'd been to Hopkins for her program. The Johns Hopkins Hospital was a national and world leader in many areas. It attracted people from all across the globe who came to Baltimore for advanced treatments from renowned specialists. However Denise's payments were resolved, the hospital would keep a record of it.

My fingers hovered over the keyboard. Did I really want to try and hack Hopkins? It wasn't a question of skill. I never doubted my abilities. When I lived in Hong Kong, my hacker friends and I broke into the biggest bank in China. The police only found us because of a rat in our ranks.

The issue was really one of time. I'd need to be very careful going after a major institution. The hospital could afford top-tier security and countermeasures. It wouldn't be easy. I missed having a small team working alongside me at times like these. If it took hours and hours to get in, find what I needed, and get out without detection, was this the best use of so much time? Eddie and Calvin seemed to be at logger-heads about the latter's basketball future, and my money would be on Eddie to win. By playing dirty if he needed to.

I needed a shortcut.

* * *

I PONDERED who I might know at Hopkins. The dreadful shrink my parents forced me to see after my sister's death might still be there, but I'd rather heave him out a window than ask him for help. I didn't know any doctors well enough to ask them, and I didn't know if they'd be able to access the records anyway. If Hopkins set things up well, they'd only be accessible to the oncology staff and the billing department.

An idea sprang into my head. My first client, Alice Fisher, worked as a patient coordinator--I still didn't know what this actually meant--for Upper Chesapeake Health. Maybe she knew a colleague at Hopkins who could help. I sent her a text to find out. A few minutes later, she replied.

C.T.! It's great to hear from you. I'm doing really well. I left UCHS just after you wrapped everything up for me. Needed a new start. Funny you should ask, but I'm actually with Hopkins now.

Bingo. I would take any lucky break I could get.

I sent her a response, telling her I needed a favor and

didn't want to discuss it over the phone. A half-hour later, we met at a tiny place called JC Romero's Neighborhood Cafe. I'd never heard of it, nor the road it sat on--Cornwall Street, which lay just off Eastern Avenue. It would be a short walk from the Hopkins Bayview campus.

Like most people who meet with me, Alice was already there when I arrived. The café was a brick end-unit rowhouse. This made the inside pretty small, but the place possessed a definite charm. People sat at every table. Before I could order from the counter, Alice stood and hugged me. "It's great to see you," she said.

"You, too." She looked good. The time away from her husband's death and the loan shark hounding her made a difference. Her color had improved, her hair held more shine, and her smile looked sincere. Alice was a pretty woman then and remained so today.

I ordered a latte and joined her at the small table. She nibbled on a wrap of some sort and paired it with a fruit smoothie. I sipped my drink and let her eat. She probably ventured out to see me over her lunch break, and I didn't intend to monopolize her time with chatter. For her part, Alice seemed content to eat.

A few minutes later, with the first of half her wrap gone and a nice dent made in the second, she said, "What did you need help with?"

I cast my eyes around the room. The older man behind us left, but an Asian couple replaced him. The place was still packed. I lowered my voice and hoped Alice would follow suit. "I need some information. I could probably get it, but it would be . . . time-consuming."

"What kind of information?" The cozy nature of JC Romero's created a constant din, making it hard to converse in *sotto voce*. Note to self: don't meet a potential hitman here. "You have anything to write on?"

"Uh . . . sure, I think so." Alice fished a small piece of paper from her purse. "You need a pen?"

I shook my head and pulled one from my jacket pocket. She handed me the paper. I wrote Denise's name, a few other identifying details, and what I wanted, which was the name and other info of who paid for the treatment. I folded the paper in half and slid it back across to her. She frowned before picking it up.

Alice's eyes widened as she read it. "I'm not sure I can do this." She shook her head. "I don't think I should."

"I wouldn't ask if it weren't important," I said. Her frown remained. "Alice, I can get the information on my own. I'm . . . let's just say I'm good with computers. But it would take time to do it right, and I'm not sure how much of it I have." Institutional pride was a factor, too—I didn't want to do anything to damage Hopkins' reputation. Even a small data breach could harm their name. Alice didn't say anything. "The woman on there . . . her son plays college basketball. He's getting squeezed by someone who reminds me of Vinnie."

She scowled as I mentioned the name. "I hate him." Vinnie Serrano, a former classmate of mine, put the screws to Alice a little over two years ago.

"Then help me stop someone who's a lot like him. The player has a young daughter. I'm worried about all of them but her the most. I don't know what kind of enemy we're dealing with yet. This is where I need you." I paused while she stared at the paper in her hand. She held it as it if might burst into flame at any second. "Can you help me?"

Her eyes flicked from the folded note to me. "Yes. I don't want to see anyone like Vinnie ruin someone else's life."

I smiled. Alice didn't reciprocate, but her expression softened. "Thanks. Let me know when you have something."

"What's your timeline?"

"Sooner the better."

Alice nodded. "All right." She stood, leaving the rest of
her wrap uneaten along with a quarter of her smoothie. "I
need to get back to work. I'll contact you later."

"Great. Thanks again." Alice hustled from the restaurant.
I knew she didn't want to do this, and I hated putting her in
this spot. Alice was a good person doing a questionable thing.
What tipped the scales was the mention of Vinnie. I didn't
want to drop his name, but I did it to maximize my odds of
saving Calvin and his family from Eddie.

Now I needed Alice to come through.

* * *

A FEW HOURS LATER, Alice called back. "I think I have
something for you," she said, sounding hesitant.

"You're doing the right thing," I told her, doing my best to
be reassuring.

"I hope so." I heard papers shuffling in the background. "I
don't know the best way to get this to you."

"I suppose giving me the physical file is out."

"Of course it is," she said, her voice hushed but firm. "I
can't have something like this go missing for long."

"All right . . . I have an idea. What kind of phone do you
have?"

"An iPhone Eight."

"Good," I said. I recommended a scanner program which
would allow her to take pictures of each page of the file and
send the whole thing to me as a PDF. "I'm going to setup an
email address specifically for this so it looks as official as

possible on your end. Text me when you're ready to send."
She said she would, and we hung up.

I setup a temporary email account which sounded like it
dealt with HIPAA compliance. The American health records
law required much overhead and effort from doctors and
hospitals to remain compliant. A patient coordinator—or
whatever title Alice currently held—emailing a file to such an
address wouldn't raise suspicion.

Fifteen minutes later, Alice said she had everything
ready. I sent her the email address, and she followed with the
file a minute later. Once I confirmed I'd received the PDF
and I saved it, I sent her a text. *You've been a big help.
Thanks.*

She wrote back quickly. *I hope so, but please don't don't
tell anyone what I did. At the very least, I'd never work in this
field again.*

I couldn't blame her fear, and in fact, I felt a bit like a jerk
for involving her in the first place. She shouldn't have the
impression my helping her two years ago came with strings
attached, because it didn't. I assuaged my guilt with a freshly-
brewed coffee, deleted my temporary address, and opened
the PDF.

Alice sent everything, including specific details of
Denise's cancer and treatment. I didn't need to know any of it
—and probably didn't understand much to begin with—so I
flipped past those pages. Billing information resided near the
end of the file. The entire sum, which was a little cheaper
than my initial guess but still in the ballpark, got billed to a
man named Edward Ferrugia.

"I got you, Eddie," I said to my empty office.

CHAPTER 12

EDWARD FERRUGIA RAN A DATA MINING BUSINESS, according to my initial searches. It didn't look like a shell company, either. Both Google and Yelp posted client reviews, and the business received high marks from a few current and former employees on Glassdoor. If this were a con, it would rank among the best I'd seen.

The company listed an address in Towson. The man himself tried to make his residence harder to find. It took a minute or two, but I uncovered it. After days of working this case, I finally knew the identity of the mysterious Eddie. I wished I knew what to do with the information. Storming the man's home or office didn't seem like a good plan. I figured I'd encounter more resistance than one could reasonably expect from a data company.

So I kept digging. Like most young entrepreneurs, Eddie Ferrugia maintained a LinkedIn profile. He had few connections, however, and none of them jumped out as me as someone to exploit to get closer to Eddie. I looked at his personal information. Ferrugia earned a bachelor's in data analytics and an MBA. He listed his home town as St. Paul, Minnesota. His pictures showed a black-maned fellow who wore his hair slicked back and looked like he just stepped off the set of a *Jersey Shore* reunion.

I frowned as a recent memory of seeing the city flashed into my head. I saw a profile for a man named Ed Fells who hailed from St. Paul. A minute later, I learned he ran Fells and Son, a gaming company still based in his home city. A quick online search found no such business. I stared at the screen. Something was here . . . something I wasn't seeing.

Fells and Son. Gaming. Minnesota.

"Son of a bitch," I said to the empty room. If this case continued for a while, I'd be having full-blown conversations with myself. In the meantime, I figured out what was bothering me. Eddie Felson, AKA Fast Eddie, was the main character in the movie *The Hustler*. His antagonist at the billiards table was the fictitious Minnesota Fats.

Did Eddie Ferrugia maintain an identity as Ed Fells? I dug into both and found a few similarities. Both allegedly attended the same college, though about thirty years apart. Fells' Facebook page listed an email address of realeddiefelson@yahoo.com. I brought up Yahoo and tried to sign into the account. It failed as I expected.

I clicked the link to reset the password. If Fells, or whoever set the account up, required two-factor authentication, this wouldn't work. I caught a break: only a security question. *What was the name of your high school mascot?* I scanned Fells' profile. He didn't list a high school. I took a shot in the dark and went with the most popular.

Eagles.

No dice. I tried again. *Tigers.*

The site asked me to set a new password. I went with a strong and obnoxious one Ferrugia wouldn't guess and couldn't reasonably assemble the resources to crack in time. Once I finished, Yahoo presented me the account homepage.

Eddie Ferrugia's LinkedIn picture stared back at me.

* * *

I CALLED Gonzalez and asked to meet him. He offered a Dunkin' Donuts near the police station, and I agreed. When I arrived, he sipped some ridiculous chilled beverage through a straw. I ordered a dark roast coffee, added some creamer, and slid onto the seat opposite his. "What's the sugary mess?"

He shrugged. "Chocolate something or other. Sounded interesting."

"How's it taste?"

"You called it—a sugary mess." He frowned at the drink and set it aside. "What'd you want to talk about?"

I kept my voice low. The place was about half full, and without a ton of real estate, all the tables sat close together. "You heard of Eddie Ferrugia?"

"Should I have?"

"Depends," I said. "What's your opinion on point shavers who threaten college kids and their families?"

"Name's not familiar." Gonzalez picked up his drink again, narrowed his eyes at it, and set it back down. "You think we should look into him?"

"On the surface, he runs a data mining business. Seems like it's legit, too, not just a front for the shady parts of the operation."

"Probably why he hasn't been on our radar." Gonzalez snatched his drink off the table. "Hang on. I gotta replace this shit with something edible." He spiked the offending beverage into the closest trash can, ordered a coffee, and returned to the table with it black. After taking a sip, Gonzalez said, "Much better. What were we talking about?"

"You were expressing the department's gratitude at me putting you onto a numbers racket."

"Doesn't sound like something I'd do." He paused for some more java. I was several drinks ahead at this point. "This guy has his hooks in the Hanson player, right?"

I nodded. "And potentially his sick mother and infant daughter. If Calvin doesn't cooperate, I'm worried about all of them."

"Is Calvin worried?"

"I can't get through to him. Maybe you guys could. Roll up with the lights flashing, and maybe he'll start taking this seriously."

"This Eddie can't hurt him," Gonzalez said. "Not directly, at least. Calvin's the meal ticket, and he knows it."

"It's cause for concern."

"I hear you. Twenty-year-old athletes ain't exactly the smartest people on campus."

The two people behind us cleared out. A young professional woman in a very tight gray skirt entered the café and got in line. Black hair spilled down her back, and she stood close to six feet tall in heels. Gonzalez and I fell silent for a moment. "I didn't know who Eddie was until now," I said. "Maybe it'll be different the next time I talk to Calvin. Eddie's already told him he can't turn pro after the season."

"How do you know this?"

"I have my methods." I drank some coffee as Gonzalez glared at me. "I know . . . you do things the right way in the county."

"We do."

"I'm sure you'll turn down the commendation when this case is over, then. Wouldn't want to strain your principles."

"Don't get ahead of yourself," Gonzalez said. "We gotta get Calvin away from this asshole first. Then, pinning something on Eddie would be nice. What's he done besides allegedly fix some basketball games and make vague threats?"

"Sounds like something the BCPD would be great at finding out," I suggested.

"We gotta have some place to start. Some of us actually do things like talk to judges and get warrants."

"Here we go. The system lets down more people."

"Look, I'll do what I can. But if what you said earlier is true, and a lot of this stuff happens online and offshore, I don't know how much we'll be able to pin on this guy."

"As long as you try. I'll let you know what else I uncover."

"Make sure you do." Gonzalez picked up his coffee, took a swig, and stood. "I gotta get back to work." He walked toward the door without waiting for me to bid him adieu. I finished my drink and drove back to my office.

Once there, I checked on the BPD's network for Eddie Ferrugia or Fells. Neither returned a hit. Eddie kept his nose clean. It made sense; if he'd stepped over the line, Gonzalez would've recognized the name. Of course, I'd neglected to mention Eddie Fells to him. I added this info to a text and received a curt thanks in return.

I couldn't count on Gonzalez and the BCPD to be much help. As usual, I was on my own here.

* * *

A FEW HOURS remained before tipoff in JHC's quarterfinal game. I checked the Vegas lines and saw they were favored by seven and a half. If Eddie wanted to keep Calvin in college through next season, he'd probably want to fix this game, too. I wondered at the wisdom of it with more eyes on the game than normal, but this was still a small conference tournament. If Hanson made the big dance, the temptation and the difficulty would get ratcheted up again.

I sent Calvin a message. If he were deep in practice and preparation at this point, he wouldn't answer, but I still wanted him to know. It might make him more amenable to working with me and getting out from under the man who pulled his strings. *I know who Eddie is, and I can help you with him. I've dealt with bigger and tougher before, but you need to work with me. There's more at stake than just where you're playing next year.*

Calvin seemed like a decent kid, so he probably realized his mother, Iris, and Tamika were all at risk if the point-shaving scheme turned sour. A reminder couldn't hurt, however. I'd played in a major college sports tournament more than once. You get tunnel vision. Everything becomes about the next practice, the next game, the next pass. Winning makes it all worthwhile, but it's a pretty tough road to navigate, especially when you're young and without a lot of your support network.

I'd moved on to figuring out how to use my time before the game when Calvin got back to me. *How'd you find out who he is?*

I responded. *I'm really good and really smart. Let me help you, Calvin . . . you and your family.*

His reply came quickly. *I'm willing to listen. Can't talk now, though. Maybe in a day or two.*

It was a start.

CHAPTER 13

With a couple hours remaining before tipoff, I drove into Little Italy. Cars lined the streets as early arrivals for dinner filed into the various restaurants. I valeted the S4 and walked into *Il Buon Cibo*. I usually got a knowing nod from the maitre d', who'd seen me come in and out a bunch of times. Today, his expression was inscrutable.

I didn't understand why until I started toward the back. Tony wasn't at his table. Since I'd returned from Hong Kong and well before I left, Tony always parked himself in the table by the fireplace. Some restaurants would use it as a signature seat for their best customers. Not Tony. He claimed it for himself. "Plenty of other fucking tables," he told me once when I asked why he reserved such a prime one for himself.

Today, Bruno sat there, accompanied by a nameless goon. Bruno was Tony's *consigliere*, though he lacked most of his boss' personality and charm. He looked to be in his late forties, wavy black hair graying above the ears, and olive skin showing the classic initial wrinkles of middle age. Bruno's dark eyes never looked at me fondly, and today was no exception. The other fellow at the table followed his supervisor's lead.

"Where's Tony?" I said, stopping behind the chair opposite Bruno.

"Vacation," he said. "Everybody needs one from time to time. Tony ain't took one in years."

He didn't look to be in good enough health for a vacation the last time I saw him, but I let it pass. Maybe he recovered quickly. "Mind if I sit?"

"If I say yes, will you leave?"

"No."

He narrowed his eyes and sighed. "Fine," he said, waving a hand in the general direction of the chair I stood behind.

"Thanks." I pulled the chair out and sat.

"Let's get one thing clear," Bruno said, thrusting his finger at me. He did a good job of not raising his voice beyond a conversational volume. Tony taught him well. "Tony's way too good to you. You're practically a cop. You come in here and ask for information, and he gives it to you. I tell him he shouldn't, but he's the boss." Bruno withdrew his finger, putting both his hands on the table. "I'm the boss right now, and I ain't telling you shit."

The goon beside him smiled as if he provided input. I pressed on. "I'm not here for information. Not directly, at least. Maybe we can help each other."

Bruno stared at me until it became obvious I wouldn't blink first. "Fine. Whadda you want?"

"I've become acquainted with a guy running a numbers racket," I said. "Point shaving, to be specific."

"Jesus Christ, someone still does that?" The other man frowned at Bruno, probably for his blasphemy.

"The more you talk to me, the more you realize I'm right a lot." This truism didn't impress either of my table companions. A waiter approached but retreated at Bruno's quick head shake. "I know he's making money. I'm not sure how much yet, and I still need to figure out exactly how he does it, but—"

"So what?" Bruno broke in. "Lots of people make money. Capitalism."

"What if he's making it in the city?"

"Is he?"

I shrugged. "I'm still working on it. As far as I can tell, he's based in the county, but it doesn't mean he stays there."

Bruno steepled his fingers under his chin and studied me. He brought the other fellow in close for a quick whispered confab. They came to a hasty consensus. "Who's this guy you're talking about?"

"Name's Eddie Ferrugia," I said. "He sometimes uses the surname of Fells. Like to imagine himself as an Eddie Felson type."

This made Bruno chuckle. I couldn't recall seeing him display a sense of humor before. "For Christ's sake. He probably calls himself Fast Eddie and tries to hustle people at pool."

"He might." I wouldn't put it past him, based on what I'd uncovered online so far. I wondered if a billiards table sat in the lobby of Ferrugia's data company headquarters. "He's making money at a lot more than pool, though."

"And you think we might have an interest in this."

"If he's crossing into the city, I think you should."

"Yeah? You think so?"

"The player he's putting the squeeze on has a young daughter." Bruno's scowl softened a little. "You can dislike me all you want, but I know you're a father, and I don't think you'd want to see anything happen to a little kid." I turned my eyes to our silent tablemate. "I don't know anything about you." His neutral expression and slight shrug told me he was fine with continuing this arrangement.

"Anything else you think we should do?" Bruno said. I didn't know if appealing to his sense of fatherly justice made a difference or not.

"You could try smiling more," I offered.

Bruno crossed his arms under his chest and glared at me. "Tony indulges your sense of humor too much."

"Maybe he just understands how funny I am."

After rolling his eyes, Bruno said, "Anyone else you want us to look into to make your life easier?"

"Hey, if you don't want to know about people trying to get around the system, it's all good. Not what Tony would expect, but like you said . . . you're the boss right now."

"You're right," he said. "I am. And I don't need you to tell me what Tony would expect. We're done here."

I didn't get up. The goon at the table stood. This was my cue to leave. "All right. Thanks for your time." Bruno grunted. The enforcer remained standing as I turned away and returned to the front of the restaurant. "The atmosphere's a little lacking," I said to the maitre d' as I passed his station.

He didn't reply.

* * *

Tipoff loomed. I couldn't recall the last time I stayed home to watch a college basketball game, especially a local one. With the interest in Calvin and JHC spiking, a local TV station carried the contest. Gloria and I sat on the couch munching on tortilla chips and salsa. I didn't expect her to watch the game with me, but I was glad for her company.

The first several minutes were a taut affair. The Presidents came out quickly, opening up an early eight-point lead on the strength of their ball movement and general speed. William and Mary took a time-out and devised an answer on defense. They went smaller, removing their plodding center for a small forward who could slash to the basket and still get back on defense. The pace of the game remained high, but the Tribe—team nicknames which weren't expressly plural bothered me—chipped away at the deficit. With about ten minutes remaining, JHC held a three-point lead.

"Good game so far," Gloria said as a batch of commercials began. I tried to get tickets to see the game live, but they were sold out. TV timeouts in basketball games are more palatable with the energy of the crowd buzzing around you.

"It is." I checked an online box score. Calvin led JHC with nine points so far. No one else scored more than five. So far, he didn't look to be throwing the game. A margin of three over each of the remaining ten-minute blocks would lead to the Presidents comfortably covering the spread. I wondered if this was the desired outcome. Playing a bunch of squeakers against lesser teams would attract attention. Drubbing a team you were supposed to beat would not. Before the game, the Vegas lines closed to seven, and the vig on Hanson went down, indicating a lot of action on William and Mary. Maybe Eddie Ferrugia planned to turn a profit on this game by bucking the trend.

The rest of the opening half saw a lot of back-and-forth. Hanson led by six when Calvin went to the bench for a breather after incurring his second foul of the game. It seemed a bit of a conservative move by Coach Baker, a sentiment the announcers echoed a moment later. During their star player's absence, the Presidents struggled. It exposed how much they depended on Calvin. The team had other good players, but the offense moved differently with someone else at the helm. The game slowed down. Slashes and cuts got replaced by fadeaway jumpers. The Tribe capitalized, closing the deficit to two before Calvin came back in with a bit under four minutes until halftime.

Those four minutes went much more according to plan for the Presidents. In his first play back, Calvin came off a pick to drain a three from the top of the key. The crowd roared, chest-bumping ensued, and William and Mary regrouped with another timeout. The remainder of the second quarter went quickly, with both teams forsaking defense in the name of more shots. At the end of twenty minutes, JHC enjoyed a five-point lead.

"They're on pace to cover, right?" Gloria asked.

I grinned at her. "Look at you using gambling terms. Next, you're going to chide me for not putting a dime on the over."

A blank look passed over her face, which she compensated for by smiling. It worked. "I'll pretend I understood that."

The over-under sat at 154 before tipoff. At the half, Hanson led 51 to 46. Unless the second half saw the players in torpor, this game would cruise past 154 combined points. Now I wondered if Eddie bet on the total, too. Maybe he used his pernicious influence on Calvin—and whoever else on the team—to emphasize offense over defense. This is why organized sports needed to be free of the influence of gambling—everything came into question once legitimacy cracked.

The second half opened with more of the same. The Tribe kept their smaller lineup on the court, and the teams traded baskets and occasional free throws. Calvin absorbed a hard foul, made both his free throws, and went to the bench. William and Mary brought their center back out, and the pace of the game slowed. The Tribe moved the ball more deliberately, using the big man effectively and narrowing the lead.

Calvin remained on the bench until the twelve-minute whistle. He took the court with his team up by a single point. William and Mary countered with their smaller package. The center snatched a towel from someone on the sideline and sat angrily in a chair much too small for his seven-foot frame. I would've been salty in his spot, too. He was a good player, and it wasn't his fault the coaches couldn't devise an effective counter to Hanson's quickness with him on the hardwood.

With Calvin running the show, the Presidents' offense played like it did in the first half. By the eight-minute mark, their lead was back up to five. With the last regular TV timeout at three minutes and change, JHC had pushed the lead to eight. This exceeded the Vegas line by one. I leaned forward on the couch and felt Gloria do the same beside me. "Now, we'll see which way they're going on this one," I said.

"What if there's no action on the game? You said they can't rig them all."

"True. But if Hanson wins their conference and goes to the big dance, the stage is a lot bigger. National reporters will nose around and maybe pick up on trends. They won't be as deferential to the players and coaches as the local guys."

"You think they have something in the works for this one?" Gloria asked.

I nodded. "They only have one game after this one before the scrutiny ramps up. I think Eddie and whoever's in league with him will squeeze Calvin dry before then."

"Sounds like he could be in trouble."

"It's his family I'm worried about. They can't break Calvin's legs because he's the meal ticket, and he's smart enough to understand this. But his mother, daughter, and girlfriend could be collateral damage."

Gloria rubbed the center of my back. "You need to get him out of this . . . get them all out."

"I know. I'm working on it. Calvin might be more willing to cooperate now."

At the sixty-second mark, the Presidents led by nine. Then the slew of timeouts began. The end of a close basketball game is nearly interminable. Fifty seconds of game time plays out over a quarter-hour of fits and starts with frequent breaks to strategize and give the sponsors another word. Gloria fidgeted beside me. I sympathized.

With fifteen seconds to go, Calvin hit a three from the corner to put Hanson up by ten. Following yet another stoppage, the Tribe put on a furious rally. They hit a quick trey, then fouled Calvin as soon as he received the inbounds pass. This was the other factor slowing close games to a crawl. Score, pass, foul, shoot free throws. Sprinkle in a timeout here and there and repeat.

These free throws would be key. The Presidents' lead was back to seven, exactly the Vegas line on the game. Calvin hit these uncontested shots at an almost ninety-percent clip. The odds of him missing both were a shade more than one percent. If he sent both clanging off the rim, I knew the fix would be in.

The crowd hushed as Calvin lined up the shot. *Swish.* Hanson led by eight. A cheer spread through the arena. Eleven seconds remained. Every point JHC scored made a Tribe comeback so much more unlikely. Calvin got the ball and lined up his second attempt. The fans fell silent.

Swish.

The lead was nine. If the fix were in the usual way, the Presidents could play shoddy defense and concede the shots from William and Mary. They didn't. Calvin intercepted a pass, got fouled on his way to the basket, and made it eleven with six seconds to go.

"It's going to be more than seven," Gloria said.

"And well over a hundred fifty-four," I added.

The horn sounded. The final: John Hanson College 92, William and Mary 81.

In the postgame celebration, Calvin looked legitimately happy. I wondered if Eddie Ferrugia felt the same.

FOLLOWING THE GAME, I made the mistake of watching the sports highlight shows in a search for meaningful analysis. I am far from a basketball savant, and none of the talking heads told me anything I didn't see with my own amateur eyes watching the game. Shows like this compelled many people in my generation to cut the cord. Maybe I would join my brethren soon.

The only useful thing I learned was when Hanson would play their next game. They would tip off against an opponent to be determined in about a day and a half on Saturday afternoon. The betting lines wouldn't be released until someone won the next game. I wondered how happy local bookies were with tonight's result, so I called the one I knew best.

"What now?" Margaret Madison said.

"You salty because you took a bath on the Hanson game?"

"I just finished watching it." Her voice brightened.

"Do you set the same lines Vegas does?"

"Mostly. If I vary, it's not by much."

"You seem happy with the result."

"I am."

I played a hunch. "What about Eddie?"

She paused for a beat too long. "Who's Eddie?"

"You'll be pleased to know I've figured it out," I said. "Or maybe you won't."

Her answer was noncommittal. "I don't work for Eddie or anyone else. I learned my lesson from your buddy Vinnie."

"Tell me, Margaret . . . is Eddie ambitious?"

"Why?"

"It doesn't always end well in his line of work. I know you know how to play the game." Like most people working in the shadows in Baltimore, she tithed a chunk of her money to Tony Rizzo. It may have been the one good thing Vinnie taught her.

"You don't need to worry about me," Margaret said. Before I could tell her I didn't, she hung up.

Now, she'd never know.

* * *

I FOUND a channel carrying the second CAA semifinal game, so I watched it. As I did, I wondered if this fell more under dedication or masochism. Maybe some of both. After forty minutes of occasionally interesting action, the Northeastern Huskies earned the right to take on John Hanson College for the conference title. The opening whistle was confirmed for Saturday at two-thirty.

Checking the Vegas lines within moments of the game ending made me feel a bit like a degenerate gambler. JHC opened as five-point favorites. I figured point shaving became more difficult as the expected margin narrowed. Then again, sometimes the bookies bucked the trend and made money the old-fashioned way.

Even though it grew late, I sent Calvin a text. When I

was his age in college, I don't think I went to bed on the early side of midnight. *Good luck against Northeastern. I think we should talk before then.*

No answer came. I gave it a few minutes and tried again. *I heard everyone was happy tonight. You know this trend won't continue forever.*

As before, no reply came. I hoped Calvin would come to his senses and want to talk to me before the next game. The more contests he tilted a certain way, the deeper he got in with Eddie. And the deeper he got in with Eddie, the less chance I had to pull him out.

CHAPTER 14

THE NEXT MORNING, I WOKE UP EARLIER THAN USUAL thanks to my phone vibrating on the nightstand. I picked it up. Ten after eight. Denise Murray called. If this were a real emergency, it would have come in four hours ago. I sent it to voicemail while I got out of bed and readied myself to face the day.

Once I settled in downstairs with a cup of coffee in front of me, I returned her call. "How's your investigation going?" she said.

In my two years or so of doing this job, I've found things I like and others I don't. My least favorite aspect is the client update. I get why people ask for them, but what I can provide never seems to match their expectations. Cases often start out slowly and meander along before hitting a rapid *dénouement*. No one really wants the boring details. I've seen plenty of yawns and glazed-over eyes when I've provided these status reports in person. Denise's reactions over the phone would probably fall in line with my expectations. "I figured out who Eddie is," I told her.

"Oh." I heard disappointment in her tone. Why didn't I know before? What did this mean? I covered my phone and sighed. People weren't keen on incremental updates. "Who is he?"

"A guy who runs a data mining business. Most people who do what he does have some kind of legit operation going."

"What's data mining?"

I could've provided a long answer here but went with a shorter, simpler one instead. "It doesn't matter. I know who he is and where he's probably operating from."

"What does that get us?"

"It's a start," I said. "I think Eddie enjoyed being anonymous before."

"What are you going to do next?"

"This isn't an exact science. Some will depend on what he does. But I'm going to get Calvin away from him and keep you all safe."

"You don't need to worry about me," Denise said.

"Calvin does, and I'm sure Iris will want to know her grandma. Speaking of all this, how's your health?"

"I told you not to worry about me." Denise tried to give her voice a hard edge, but she didn't have the strength for it. It sounded depressing, and despite her protests, I would maintain my level of concern.

"Not much of an answer," I said.

She remained quiet for a minute. I waited her out. Most people don't do silence well, and they'll fill in the gaps once the conversation gets too awkward for them. Denise proved to be no exception. "I'm all right. Doing better than a few months ago when Calvin got involved in all this mess." She sighed, and it came through my phone as a weak hiss. "I'll need another round of the immunotherapy I'm in. It's a chemo alternative. I have an appointment at Hopkins soon."

This didn't sound good, and it also didn't sound cheap. "Does Calvin know?"

"No, and don't you tell him, neither."

"I won't," I said. "It's your place."

"I know." She paused. "Maybe I'll tell him. I probably need him to drive me there. I'm just worried he'll stay in college another year and keep dealing with Eddie."

I didn't think this likely. If Calvin were an early NBA draft choice, he'd have the money to afford the therapy without needing to deal with an asshole like Eddie Ferrugia. He'd need to wait a few months for the process to play out, though. If Denise required the money sooner, Calvin might go running to his banker. None of us wanted this outcome. "I'll get him out," I said. I still had no idea how I would make this happen.

"Good. You worry about Calvin, Iris, and Tamika. Don't lose sleep over me."

I would try to work things out for everyone, including Denise. Damn her objections—if I could solve her problems, too, I'd do it.

* * *

AFTER BREAKFAST at a much more reasonable hour, Calvin texted me. *Hey. I'm taking my mom to the doctor soon. Maybe we can talk after?*

"Finally," I said aloud. Gloria looked up from reading something on her phone and shot me a quizzical look. "I think Calvin is ready to talk to me."

"Wow, that's great." She smiled and squeezed my hand. "I knew you'd wear him down eventually."

"I think the situation got to him more than anything. I'll

take it, though." I replied to his message. *Sounds good. When and where?*

While I waited for him to respond, I brewed a second carafe of coffee. Once it finished, I poured myself a cup, stirred it, carried the elixir back to my small kitchen table, and sat. No reply. I fixed Gloria a second mug. Still nothing. For someone who seemed eager to talk to me, Calvin clammed up in a hurry. I went upstairs, put on actual clothes, and came back down. Silence. I frowned at my phone.

"You think he ghosted you?" Gloria said.

"I'm not sure. He seemed sincere . . . as far as I can tell from a short message at least. He certainly needs the help."

"I'm sure it'll work out."

I didn't share her optimism, so I sent Calvin another message. *Hey, you there?* While helping clients in my job has been something I've enjoyed more than I expected, some people made the process into an ordeal. I remembered what Denise said earlier: she had an appointment at Hopkins soon. Maybe even today.

Health information like this is surprisingly easy to get. Hacking Hopkins would be time-consuming, so I opted for good old-fashioned social engineering. I called the oncology department, said I was Calvin, and wanted to confirm my mother's appointment time. The helpful receptionist told me Denise was due in at twelve-thirty, about three hours from now. I thanked her and hung up. These tactics work because people want to be helpful. Far less scrupulous hackers than I have exploited similar situations to disastrous ends.

"I'll talk to him later whether he wants to or not," I said.

"Using your powers for good?" asked Gloria with a grin.

"Mostly." I checked for messages and found none.

A few minutes later, I left to run an errand. The Caprice sat on the parking pad, and Gloria's coupe took up the other spot. I walked out the front door toward my S4 a few houses down. I've lived on this street for almost two years. By now, I knew most of the neighbors' cars. A gray BMW SUV I didn't recognize stood out. Its engine fired up, and the driver steered it away from the curb.

I moved behind a pickup truck, standing behind the engine as I slid my 9MM out of its holster. The SUV crept toward me. I held the gun in front of my midsection, hidden by the truck's hood. The BMW's windows were already down. The driver and someone behind him both glowered at me. I recognized the fellow in the back as one of the men I tangled with at Hanson. I raised the gun to the point they could see it. The vehicle sped away.

I watched it drive up the street and make a right turn before I walked back inside.

* * *

I FELT like I'd been talking on the phone more than usual with this case. Like most millennials, I preferred to text. The world doesn't always cooperate, however. I needed to make another call after the goonmobile did its slow cruise up Riverside Avenue.

"Been a little while," Rollins said when he picked up. I first worked with him when I hired him as a bodyguard about a year ago. A particularly tough case saw a couple attempts on my life, and I needed someone to watch my back. A family friend and retired colonel recommended Rollins. We've worked together a few times since. He's retired Army, knocking on the door of forty, and very capable.

"Sometimes, I wear my big boy pants and solve cases on my own," I said.

"And other times, you come running to me?"

"I don't think I'm running . . . more of a stroll at this point." Rollins didn't say anything. I could picture him rolling his eyes. He didn't find me nearly as funny as I actually was. His loss. "I'm working something, and it's taken a serious turn recently."

"Fill me in," he said. I did. When I finished, he asked, "These guys know who you are now."

"A hazard of being in the phone book." I wondered who put the BMW crew on to me. I didn't tell everyone who I was. Word got around, however. Would Calvin dime me out? What about Coach Baker? If he gave me up, it meant he was also in league with Eddie Ferrugia on some level. This got worse the more I thought about it.

"You want me to hang around for a couple days?"

"I think it'd be prudent. I don't know a lot about the guy I'm ultimately going after yet. He's something of a wild card."

"What's your next move?"

"*Our* next move. Calvin is supposed to take his mother to the doctor later. He said he wanted to talk to me, but then he fell off the face of the earth."

"You want to crash the woman's cancer appointment?"

"Not crash," I said. "It'll be a polite interruption. If we can leave her out of it, I'd like to. Maybe Calvin doesn't go back with her. If he's in the waiting room, we can get to him."

"You don't think the mom will recognize you?" Rollins said.

"Let's worry about it when we're there. The appointment is at twelve-thirty. They'll be driving from Waverly. You know it?"

"A little."

"Same here. I think I know the route they'll take, so we can tail them after they leave."

We made arrangements for Rollins to pick me up in his

obnoxious pickup truck, which would go unrecognized by Denise, Calvin, and the goon squad. We would then tail mother and son to the former's appointment. If this worked, maybe I could make some ground in this case for once.

I couldn't summon the optimism.

* * *

"You sure they're going to come this way?" Rollins asked as we sat in his truck. I much preferred cars, but this monster featured a nice interior, tinted windows, and enough horse-power to turn heads on the street racing circuit.

"No," I admitted, "but it's the most direct route."

"You assume the kid's driving?"

I nodded. "Probably using a GPS, too. If he does, it should take him this way." We were parked in a lot off Harford Road, more or less around the corner from where Denise Murray lived. If they drove past us, they would continue past Lake Montebello and Clifton Park Golf Course, then head into downtown and the hospital via either Wolfe or Broadway. "Either way, we know where he's headed."

"Why are we following him, then?"

"I presume he'll go in with his mother. Considering he ghosted me after saying he wanted to talk, though, I'd like to have eyes on him in case he doesn't."

"All right." We lapsed into silence. I glanced at my watch. They should be passing us any moment now. About a minute later, we watched a silver Hyundai Elantra drive past. The driver looked crammed into the front seat.

"There they are," I said, even though Rollins had already put the truck into gear and pulled out. I told him the color, make, and model of the car when we began our vigil. He probably saw it a hundred yards before I did. We settled in behind Calvin and Denise, always keeping at least one vehicle as a buffer. They rode in the left lane all the way; Rollins changed lanes periodically, even getting ahead of them at one point before falling back. If Calvin were paranoid enough to think he might be tailed, he wouldn't suspect the pickup.

They turned down Broadway. After a few blocks, it became obvious they weren't veering off, stopping, or doubling back as a counter to being followed. Rollins zoomed around the Elantra, and we made good time on the way to the hospital. "I'll wait in the garage," he said as I got out. I walked in and scanned the lobby. Hopkins is a terrific hospital with many of the finest doctors in the world, and their facilities are above par, but the budget didn't extend to improving the lobby. I watched a video about the oncology department, which helpfully provided a list of the doctors working in it.

When it was my turn at the desk, I said, "I'm here to see Doctor Cheng" to the receptionist. She didn't ask any other questions and printed me a guest badge showing my destination as the cancer wing and Cheng as the doctor I would see. For a major hospital operating in a violent city, this struck me as lax security. Considering how easy it made what I needed to do, however, I saved my complaints for another day.

I rode the elevator to the fourth floor and veered left to the oncology area. Once I stepped off, the familiar smells of hospitals filled my nose. Antiseptic, cleaner, and general sickness made for an unpleasant mix. Once I walked into the cancer wing, I added malaise to the mix. Some of the people in here had already received the worst news of their lives. Some were about to hear it today. I wondered how many of them wouldn't survive to see their next visit. The whole place made me morose. I didn't have a lot of good memories of hospitals--I figured few people did--so I picked up a random copy of Sports Illustrated. I faced away from the entrance and made sure I could see it reflected when I held up my phone.

A few minutes later, Denise Murray opened the door, followed by her much taller son. I covered my features entirely, shifted in the chair, and eyed them from the side as they walked past. Denise exchanged pleasantries with the receptionist, who told her Dr. Cheng would be out to see her shortly. They sat behind me and to my left. "You need me to go back with you?" Calvin asked.

"I'll be fine," Denise said, though the words didn't match the lack of strength in her voice. I hoped she would.

I glanced over my shoulder to see Calvin watching basketball film on a tablet. At least he possessed good study habits. A short while later, Denise was summoned behind another door. After she left, I put the magazine down again, walked around to the next row of chairs, and plopped down beside Calvin. He spared me a brief glance. Plenty of open seats remained. I wondered if he would notice and look at me again.

He did.

I said, "Hi, Calvin."

His eyes widened, and he scooted back as much as the chair would allow him. "Who are you? Did Eddie send you?"

"No. We were talking about me helping you with your Eddie problem, and then you fell silent."

Calvin's posture eased as recognition dawned in his eyes. Our first meeting had been contentious. This one didn't shape up to be much better. "Yeah. I'm busy, man. Got a game to prep for."

"You've got a lot more to prep for. We need to have a chat."

"So chat."

I rolled my eyes. "Not here. Let's go downstairs. We can be back before your mother comes out."

Calvin sat in silence. He seemed like he remembered me, so he must have also recalled the part of our conversation covering the fate of three football players turned goons. He powered off his tablet. "Fine. I'll talk to you."

"It's the first good decision you've made in a while."

Calvin didn't respond. He probably knew he deserved it.

CHAPTER 15

WE SAT AT A TABLE IN THE VAST HOSPITAL CAFETERIA. The lunch crowd complicated matters, but I found us a secluded spot. I drank a mediocre coffee while Calvin chowed down on a turkey sandwich. I'd considered making a crack about buying him lunch affecting his college eligibility. The reality, of course, was news of his arrangement with Eddie would torpedo his college career anyway, not to mention damage his NBA prospects. This was another complication in the case. Guaranteeing the young man's present couldn't come at the expense of his future. I walked a tightrope, and the wind blew from many directions at once.

"What are we doing here?" Calvin said between bites.

"You're eating the most expensive shitty-looking sandwich I've ever bought," I said. "Take your time, but we need to get down to brass tacks. This is important. It's not just your neck in the noose."

"You think Eddie will go after people I know?"

I sipped my java. Cream and sugar did not improve it. Mediocrity can only be elevated so far. "He can't very well go after you, can he? You're not much good to him with a broken leg. Maybe he can get another guy or two on the team, but without you, the lines are going to be different . . . harder to manipulate."

"Wow," he said, "you've really thought about this."

"Good thing one of us is."

Calvin winced. "Ain't cool."

"What 'ain't cool' is your entire arrangement." He scowled, but I pressed on. "I get why you did it. But you had to know where this was going to end up. Someone like Eddie doesn't just let you go once he's got the hooks into you."

"I can't lose my mom, man." Calvin punctuated this point with an angry chomp of his sandwich. "Can't."

"We need to figure out how to get you away from Eddie."

"Good luck." Calvin sighed and set his lunch down. "I thought I'd be done by now. Eddie said he'd cover the treatment, and I owed him some games. He told me about ten or twelve if the action was good." This jibed with what I discovered going through the results of JHC's games. "Early on, I asked how things was going. He told me it's all good. Money's coming in. So I figured I'm out after ten games or so, like the man said." He shook his head. "Turns out Eddie likes the money. He don't want to let me go."

"And now your mother might need another round of this treatment."

His thin brows pulled down. "She told you?" I replied with a single nod. "Yeah. Some new immunotherapy. It's working well. She's still kinda weak, but she's a lot better than she was a few months ago." Calvin showed a small smile. "They told us it could take two rounds."

"You're going pro," I said. "A portion of your signing bonus would pay for the next round."

"It would . . . if we had time to wait. The draft ain't for a while. I'd be looking at months until I got paid."

"But Eddie could give you the money now."

"Yeah. I'd owe him another year."

"Then what?"

"What do you mean?"

"After another year, you'll graduate. Does he think his scheme is going to work in the pros?" Calvin could simply write Eddie a check out of his bonus if he went pro this summer. He probably understood this, but I didn't want to push him to defy the man funding his mother's climb toward good health.

"I don't know," he said. A few nurses walked by, and we paused our conversation as they passed. One of them eyed Calvin like she recognized him, but they didn't say anything as they sat a few tables away.

"There's a lot more visibility in the NBA," I said, keeping my voice lower and hoping Calvin would follow suit. "Local and national media, all the sports shows, talk shows, Twitter analysts . . . it's going to be a lot harder to pull this off at the next level. You're in a small conference now. Fewer eyes on you. Even in the tournament, fixing a game becomes a lot harder."

"I tried to tell Eddie this," Calvin said. "He's determined to try. He says he's got analysts who can get us past all the attention."

"You believe him?"

"He's been pretty smart so far."

"Maybe he's been pretty lucky, too. So have you. If word of this got out, you'd be cooked. You may not even get drafted."

"I know." Calvin couldn't take his eyes off the tabletop as his head bobbed. Maybe he'd already explored the depths of his situation and found them hopeless. "So how do we get Eddie out of the picture without exposing everything?"

"It's tough. I think I need to talk to him."

"Talking ain't gonna get it done."

"It works for diplomats." While I didn't think I possessed a great deal of diplomacy—especially when seated across from parasites like Eddie Ferrugia—I needed to try.

"I'm worried about my daughter, too," Calvin said. "It ain't just my mom."

"I know. There are a lot of moving parts here."

"Can you juggle them all?"

"I'm sure gonna try," I said. We fell silent while Calvin went back to his sandwich. I stared at my coffee as if compelling it to taste better. I took another sip. It didn't. Something about Coach Baker jumped into my mind. My offensive line welcoming committee only visited after I talked to him. "Does your coach know what's going on?"

Calvin looked at me for a few long seconds before answering. "Yeah," he said in a quiet voice.

"You tell him?" He shook his head. "We can presume Eddie did, then. You think he's on the take, too?"

"Maybe. It's another way to try and control the outcome. If I'm doing better than I should, he can take me out of the game." I remembered wondering about Calvin's time on the bench in the last game. This filled in the gap.

"I may need to chat with your coach, too."

"You think he sent the football players after you?"

"I don't see who else could've done it," I said. "I guess he needs to have some pull with the team or his counterpart."

"He's the assistant athletic director," Calvin said.

"Interesting." I should have checked this. The nameplate on Baker's office only listed him as the coach. Maybe he had a separate space carved out in the administrative offices. "Now I dislike him even more."

"Don't be too hard on him."

"He's an asshole, Calvin. I'll be as hard on him as I need to."

"I ain't trying to mess things up too much," he said.

At least the young man was aware of his situation. Still, my expected conversation with Coach Baker could turn into something more. "I'll do my best," I said.

* * *

AT HOME, I conducted some basic research into Lou Baker. He'd been the basketball coach at John Hanson College for six years. About a year ago, he added assistant athletic director to his duties. The primary AD at the time resigned, replaced by the current one, and then Baker ascended to the deputy role. Local reports suggested some kind of power struggle with the previous guy, which Baker obviously won. His additional title didn't garner a lot of publicity at the time.

As assistant AD, Baker held sway over the rest of the athletic programs, which would explain his influence over the football players dispatched to teach me a lesson. Reports of him in any capacity other than basketball coach were scarce. If Baker abused his power, either no one discovered it, or no one reported on it. Even the school's newspaper—which often sang a contrary tune about the college, like most similar publications—remained silent on the issue.

Personally, Baker lived in a recently-purchased house on Edgar Terrace, a side street between Echodale and Walther Avenues. The dwelling itself wasn't far from Rich. I frowned when I saw Walther Avenue, though. It meant Baker also lived pretty close to Calvin and Denise. Thanks to the availability of housing records, I found out a lot about his home and mortgage.

Considering my cousin lived nearby, I called him in the

interest of pursing justice together. "What did you have in mind?" he said in a guarded tone, like he expected me to suggest calling in an air strike.

"I'm going to have a talk with the coach," I said. "I'd like you to be there to make sure he doesn't summon any reinforcements."

"You think he might?"

"He's already sent three football players after me. Next time, he might call the entire offensive and defensive lines."

"How's this chat going to go?" Rich asked. The skepticism in his voice practically oozed out through my phone. "You going to knock on the front door and hoist a couple brews inside?"

"If I thought I could. I don't think he'll talk to me willingly."

"So you're going to break in."

"You sound so dramatic, dear cousin. Perhaps the coach left his back door open . . . or a window."

"You're still entering his home illegally."

"My tax dollars pay his salary," I pointed out.

"Great. Even if the state owned his house, you couldn't just walk in." Rich sighed. "Tell me why you're working this one again." I filled him in about Calvin, Iris, Denise, and the whole mess. When I'd finished, Rich remained silent a few seconds before saying, "It sounds like a good cause, at least."

"It is."

"Fine. I'll tag along. If it goes south in there, though, you're on your own. I'm not getting dragged down for your shady operation."

"I'll be sure to point out your self-righteousness to anyone who asks," I said.

"Likewise," Rich said. We made a plan for what time all this would go down, and he hung up.

* * *

I NEEDED a way to know when Baker would be headed home. Coach Coffey's computer was offline, so my previous foothold wouldn't work. With a game tomorrow, Baker would probably put in a late night at the office. The longer I lingered in his neighborhood—not to mention sat in his house—the greater the odds I'd get discovered. Rich might deter anyone coming to scare me away, but I didn't think he'd wave his badge and quell the suspicions of nosy neighbors. His help always went only so far.

Early in the case, I visited Baker in his office. It was small, cluttered, and messy, like the workspaces of many college coaches. He kept a Dell laptop sitting on the desk. It would have a webcam built-in. With some skilled searching and a little luck, I could find it. I went to a search engine called Shodan, which is like Google for Internet-connected devices.

From there, I hunted for Dell webcams, narrowing my focus to the JHC campus. Many results popped up in red. Classes were still in session. A lot of computers would be online. I would need to wait until later. After the professors went home, anything left would belong to an enterprising administrator—of which there were few, in my experience— or a coach looking for an edge. With the field narrowed, I could find Baker more easily then.

So I waited. Gloria left for some tennis event, so I had the house to myself. Feeling a little sluggish, I went out to pound the Federal Hill pavement for a few miles. This time, I kept a .38 holstered under my light jacket. The blued revolver went well with the navy running outfit I wore. If you're going to carry a gun while you exercise, you might as well be sure it pairs with your clothes. There's no excuse to be unfashionable in the face of danger.

I encountered no miscreants while exercising. After showering and putting on clean clothes, I whipped up a late lunch of a turkey sandwich and tortilla chips. Few men can dress well and be gourmets. It's a gift. Once I finished eating, I checked for webcams at JHC again. Still too much noise to find the signal. If the location could be isolated more precisely, I'd be able to make a better guess, but such were the limitations of the technology.

A couple hours later, with the afternoon rush hour in full swing, I checked again. Four remained active. Connecting to these devices over the internet proved easy. The laptops were assigned IP addresses by the college. Rather than using private ones, they made them public. Using the IP address and the camera identifier in a web browser brought me to a screen with a button saying *Login.* Clicking the button revealed whatever or whoever was on the other side of the camera.

The first was a secretary frowning at something. I disconnected right away. The next was a conference room. I watched for a minute in case someone like Baker walked in, but closed the tab when it became clear nothing would happen. Two remained. The third was a middle-aged man in a cheap suit whose face was buried in his phone. Clearly an administrator hard at work bettering the lives of students. I disconnected from this one, too. Now I needed Baker's laptop to be the last one.

Once I bypassed the login button, a messy office came into view. I recognized the chaos right away as well as the man sitting in profile to the camera. Baker studied what I presumed to be game film on another monitor and scrawled notes on a piece of paper. I watched this riveting scene play out for several minutes before I decided a hearty observation of paint drying might be preferable.

I whiled away the time as best I could. Baker seemed to be in no hurry to leave his office. This way, he could point to how late he stayed as a sign of his dedication. Finally at about seven-thirty, he packed it in. The light on the webcam would give away its activation. Disabling this required a different level of attack. If I'd known I would have hours to wait, I may have done it. Baker didn't pay the glow any mind. He packed a bag and closed the laptop lid.

I called Rich. "We're on."

* * *

I MET Rich at his house in Hamilton. He owned a large Victorian with a driveway fit to host a flag football game. We left the S4 there and took his Camaro. The jaunt to Baker's house was quick.

Edgar Terrace is an L-shaped street. Shortly after the 90-degree curve at the bottom, it dead-ends onto Crosswood Avenue. This road, taken right or left, would enable a hasty retreat should we need to make one. Baker lived immediately around the curve in the second house from the Crosswood intersection. Rich parked across the street, where the houses were more spaced out. Baker's was dark, and no cars sat in front of it or in the driveway. "You're sure this is how you want to do it?"

"What's the alternative?" I said. "You flash your badge and get us in?"

"He *does* live in the city."

"But he doesn't have to let you in. It's not like I have a lot on him. I'd rather surprise him."

"All right," Rich said, his voice tinged with disapproval. He frequently sounded like one of my high school teachers whenever we worked together. Apparently, my exemplary success rate did not factor into Rich's calculus.

I got out, scanned for nosy neighbors, and closed the Camaro door quietly. A large tree in Baker's front yard gave me excellent cover as I checked again for anyone taking an interest in me. The coast looked clear. I hugged the house as I padded down the driveway, across Baker's back yard, and onto the rear porch. The storm door wasn't even locked. The one behind it was, so I took out my special keyring and got to work.

In Hong Kong, a couple of my hacker friends also specialized in breaking and entering. I learned how to do it from them just for the knowledge. It's served me well since coming home and stumbling into this job. A minute later, I bypassed the lock and slipped inside.

The interior was dark, and the drawn blinds prevented any moonlight from creeping in. I took my phone out of my pocket, using only the luminescence from the screen to cast my surroundings in a dim blue. It was enough, and it wouldn't alert anyone who happened to be looking at the house. What I could see appeared as messy as Baker's office. His dining room was cluttered with boxes, and papers lay on the table in loose piles I couldn't bring myself to think of as stacks. The living room featured a couch, loveseat, and coffee table, plus a shabby recliner near the eating area. It was a lot of seats for a man who lived alone and was too much of an asshole to have many friends.

I sat in the recliner and waited. If Baker drove home after leaving campus, he should be pulling up soon. I waited. No Baker. While I passed the time, I got up and poked through the mail on the coffee table. I found junk mail, a couple bills, and the latest issue of Playboy. Would the college find it interesting their assistant AD ogled women who were the same ages as the athletes he served? From my experience with administrators, probably not.

A few minutes later, I sat in the recliner again. Rich texted, *Car pulling into the driveway.* I heard the engine an instant later, and the headlights struggled to seep through the blinds on the front windows. The engine cut off a few seconds later. Footsteps soon landed on the front porch. A key scraped the lock, and the door swung in.

Baker entered, his head down, clutching a bag of carry-out in one hand and his water bottle and keys in the other. For the first time since I met him, I sympathized. He carried everything to the coffee table, set it down, and pulled the ceiling fan cord to turn on the overhead light.

"Hi, Coach," I said, and Baker jumped high enough to pull down a rebound.

"What the hell?" He stared at me. "You're the detective . . . Ferguson?"

"Detective and NCAA champion lacrosse player."

"Now, I remember. You told me to go fuck myself. Maybe I'll tell you the same thing when the police arrest you."

"Go ahead and call them," I said, inclining my head at the cell phone now in his hand. "While you do, why don't you mention your association with a guy who's running a point shaving scheme?" Baker frowned. "Maybe you could also volunteer how you afforded to pay cash for this house."

"How did you--"

"Public records . . . plus a few other clever searches. I can do the math, Coach. You don't get paid enough. But help fix some games, and you can buy a house conveniently close to your star player."

Baker sighed, tossed his phone down, and sagged onto the couch. For a man who hoped to lead a championship basketball team, he surrendered easily. "What do you want?"

"To know how deep this point-shaving rabbit hole goes."

"You going to get me out of it?"

"No."

"No?" he said, his mouth hanging open.

"No. I don't care about you. You're a fully-formed adult. You took the money and made your choice. Calvin has better motivations."

"He's also about to turn twenty-one."

"Frontal lobe development continues until twenty-five," I said. He gaped at me again. "I took a couple semesters of psych. You should try dropping in on a class sometime."

"You expect me to work with you for no gain?"

"I'm trying to get Calvin out from under your friend Eddie." He frowned. "Yeah, I know who he is. Anyway, if Eddie goes down, you're in the clear, too. If you help me, you help yourself."

Baker stared at the ceiling. He didn't say anything, and I let him stew in silence. Considering I needed to explain cause and effect to an employee of a supposedly good college, I figured we'd be here a while if the coach tried to think his way out of this mess. Eventually, he said, "What do you want to know?"

"Is Eddie a bookie?"

He shook his head. "I don't think so."

This surprised me. Not doing the books himself added another player, but it also reduced his personal risk. "You know who is?"

"He's never told me. I've never asked."

"Fair enough," I said. "You guys have a big game tomorrow. How's it going to play out?"

"I'm confident we'll win."

I'd checked the line earlier in the day. Vegas favored Hanson by six. "A squeaker or a blowout?"

"These conference title games are usually hard-fought."

So the big man wanted it to be close. "Where does Eddie watch the games?"

"He's got a buddy owns some little shithole sports bar in Middle River. Final Score or something close to it. He's usually there."

"I think I'll take in the game there." Something nagged at me. "You knew about this whole thing early."

"Yeah . . . so?"

"Doesn't seem like something a player would tell his coach."

"Well, Calvin told me."

I couldn't come up with a good reason for him to let Baker in on the scheme. There were way too many excuses which were way too easy to offer for things like missed shots and bad passes. Hanson still won the games, so Baker would be unlikely to care so long as the results remained good.

"Any other players involved?"

"Maybe."

I figured there would have to be. Even someone like Calvin can only affect a game so much. There would need to be contingencies if he got hurt. Multiple players and the coach being in the know and on the take pointed to a big operation. Something of this scale could find its genesis some-where besides shaving points. "Anything going on here besides basketball?"

Baker shook his head a little too quickly. People rarely deny things the instant they're mentioned. "Nope."

I didn't believe him, but pressing him didn't seem likely to work out. What else could be happening? I stood. "We should probably keep this chat between us."

"Yeah, yeah." Baker waved a dismissive hand.

"I mean it." He nodded. I let myself out.

CHAPTER 16

BAKER GAVE ME THE RIGHT NAME. THE FINAL SCORE Sports Bar sat on Eastern Boulevard in Middle River, not far from the eponymous body of water. I wondered what kind of welcome would be awaiting me. Baker was a toady; if he were on Eddie Ferrugia's payroll, he'd call the boss and give him a heads-up. This meant I couldn't go alone.

I'd recently asked Rich for a favor and didn't want to impose. The place was in the county, but I couldn't ask Gonzalez. His by-the-bookness rivaled Rich's, and I didn't know him well enough to ask him to go in off the clock. Lacking a better option for backup, I called Rollins. "You need me again so soon?" he said. As usual, he answered the phone before the second ring no matter the time.

"I can't think of anyone better to go with me to a sports bar."

He chuckled. "I actually like basketball. We watching the game?"

"More or less," I said. "I'm going to talk to the man behind the scheme. He may be aware I'm coming, so I don't know what it's going to look like in there."

"So I'm playing bodyguard again."

"For a couple hours. You can eat and drink on my tab."

"You're lucky I like you," Rollins said, and he was right. "Where are we going?" I told him the where and when. "See you at thirteen hundred tomorrow." He hung up.

When I put my phone down, I realized how hungry I was. I cooked a chicken breast on the stove, pairing it with broccoli and a pouch of microwaved rice. In line with its status as *haute cuisine*, I ate it on the couch while watching Netflix. After I finished eating, my phone buzzed. Gloria texted from her tennis tournament. *Who knew West Virginia could be so nice?*

I replied. *Probably in for the night. I can talk.*

She called a moment later. After we exchanged pleasantries, she said, "Slow night on the case?"

"It's been a busy day," I said, filling her in on what I'd done and what lay ahead tomorrow. "It finally feels like I'm making some progress."

"That's great."

"How's your tournament?"

"Today was just practice. Matches start tomorrow morning."

"You'll do great. I wish I could come and see you play."

"My coach is going to take video."

"I'll watch it with you. Let me know how you do tomorrow."

We chatted a few minutes more before Gloria said she needed to get a good night's rest. After a round of I-love-yous, we hung up. I put on a basketball show talking about the CAA tournament final tomorrow. All three analysts expected Hanson to win, citing Calvin as the best player on the court. They all expected the game to be something of a runaway.

If only they knew.

* * *

MIDDLE RIVER never managed to impress me, and the Final Score tavern fit right into this perception. The decor was shabby and basic. Shopworn wooden booths ringed the exterior of the dining area. Four-seat tables filled the rest of the space. TVs hung above the bar and on the walls. The air inside smelled of cheap beer and mediocre fried food.

Rollins walked in behind me and made a beeline left toward the bar. He sidled onto a stool on the far side, affording him a view of the entire dining room. The TVs showed a mix of events, though most displayed either the pregame show for the Hanson contest or an Orioles' spring training game.

I recognized Eddie Ferrugia from one of the rare photos of him I saw online. His classic Italian complexion went well with the dark gray pinstriped suit he wore—white shirt, no tie. Gotta look casual on the weekend. A pair of short-haired goons flanked him at the table. The trio left one seat open. I've never been one to pass up so obvious an invitation.

The enforcers both glared at me but waited for their boss before making a move. "Who the hell are you?" Eddie Ferrugia said, "and why shouldn't I let these two toss you out of here?"

I was ready to say they probably couldn't but held my tongue. This wasn't the time or place. "I'm Calvin Murray's new agent," I said.

"Kid never had one before."

"So he clearly needed a new one."

One of the goons pointed at me. Eddie shook his head. "I like this guy . . . for a while, at least. Now, friend, I know you're not a fucking sports agent. What are you doing here?"

"Can't a man just be here to watch the Hanson game?"

"Plenty of empty tables or seats at the bar."

"Fine," I said. "Calvin's made you a lot of money already. He should be free to turn pro next season." Over Eddie's head, a TV showed tipoff was imminent. On the other side of another commercial break, of course.

"You seem to know a lot about Calvin and me," Eddie said, narrowing his eyes and studying me. "What's the deal? Who told you?"

"You know I couldn't tell you."

Before Eddie could reply, a waiter walked to the table. I ordered the one draft beer which sounded interesting. No one else requested anything despite having nothing in front of them. Coach Baker mentioned Eddie knew the owner. I guess it meant he could sit here and not run a tab.

The commercial ended, and the players lined up for the opening tip. "You staying to watch the game?" Eddie said.

"You expect it to be a close one?"

He smiled like a wolf looking at a field of chickens. "I think it will be, yeah."

JHC possessed the ball first. Calvin brought it up the court. Judging by the size of the players, Hanson again rolled out the three-guard configuration. Calvin passed the ball, moved up the right side of the court, and came off a pick. He took the return pass, put up a twelve-foot jumper, and watched it clang off the rim. I watched Eddie for a reaction. A small smile crossed his features.

After a few minutes of action left the Presidents with a small lead, I said, "What's your interest in Calvin?"

"It's not just Calvin," Eddie said. "I'm a data guy. You seem pretty smart, so I'll presume you know what my business does." I bobbed my head in confirmation. "I'm getting lots of good information out of this. It'll end up allowing the company to make better decisions down the road."

"The short-term financial gain doesn't seem bad."

"It's not. A little hard to setup at first."

"You're not doing the book yourself?" I asked.

Eddie shook his head. "Not trying to get so involved. I want to be able to make the money. I'm fine to outsource the rest. No one's heard of . . . what we're doing in a while." He was careful not to call it point shaving, even though he seemed to know I was wise to the whole scheme. "But I found a few people." He paused. "You know I had a significant outlay of cash before this season began, right?"

This presented me a conundrum. If I admitted I knew of the expenditure and what it was, I could be outing Denise as the person who told me about Calvin and, thus, the client. I couldn't take the chance. The two toughs with Eddie didn't look like they'd have any qualms beating a woman. "If you have a business, laying out cash is part of it from time to time."

"It wasn't a company expense." Eddie waved his hand. "Forget it. Suffice it to say Calvin is in my debt, and he's paying it off a game at a time." He leaned forward. The two guys with him both glowered at me. For the first time since I sat down, I felt the menace at the table. "Now tell me why I'd give it all up."

"It's the right thing to do," I said. "I can see you're into employing socially conscious gentlemen."

One of the goons chuckled. The other one knitted brows at his partner. Eddie maintained a neutral expression throughout. "I know you got a better reason."

"If he goes pro, it's a bigger pie. You can cut a nice-sized slice of it."

"Lot more of a challenge there, too. There's a ton more eyes on the NBA."

"You're a data guy," I said. "You're smart. Figure it out." I sipped my beer while Eddie ruminated on this.

"Maybe I could," he said after a moment. He'd probably thought about it already, and the result was he wanted Calvin to stay in school. "You know why I got involved in the first place? The kid needed help, but I ain't so altruistic. I did it because I graduated from Hanson."

"Really?"

"Yeah. Trying to help my alma mater."

I remembered asking Baker if this went beyond basketball, and he denied it right away. Now I could try and pry it from Eddie. "So this is bigger than just a kid on the basketball team."

Eddie shrugged. "Right now, I'm enjoying what Calvin does. After this . . . who knows?"

Not much of an answer. I checked the TV, which we'd been watching on and off during our conversation. Hanson led by two midway through the first half. A chyron crawled across the bottom of the screen, informing the viewers Calvin scored ten points on four-of-eleven shooting. "Come on," I said, goading him. "You told me I'm smart. You seem smart, too. I'm sure a guy like you has some ambition, especially considering your . . . employees."

Both goons now glared at me. Eddie looked both amused and curious at the same time. "What do you mean?"

"I mean, I don't think you hired these guys for their math skills." I leaned a little closer to the one on my left, whose expression was especially sour. "No offense. I'm sure you don't need to take your shoes off to count past ten." His expression softened for a second before a deep frown replaced it.

"It's a fair observation," Eddie said, and his two legbreakers stopped shooting daggers at me. "I guess you could say my guys match my ambition. I have people specifically for data and analysis, and I have employees with . . . other useful skills."

"There's a power vacuum in this county," I said. It was true. A few people maintained small criminal groups, but no one stepped up to control the county like Tony had done for years in the city.

"So I've heard." Eddie's smile widened. "The same could be true in Baltimore."

I didn't want to betray my association to Tony, so I played this one close to the vest, also. "I heard there's a guy there. Been in charge for a while."

Eddie shrugged. "People get old. Things change. Nature abhors a vacuum."

A couple years ago, I encountered an enterprising gangster who thought he could usurp Tony and run organized crime in the city in a much more modern fashion. His plans came to an end when a bullet burst his skull as he stood next to me. I'd never been able to get the windbreaker I wore on the fateful night clean again. While I felt no attachment to Eddie Ferrugia, I also didn't want to see him shot by someone in Tony's influence, especially if I would be close by. "You've watched *The Wire*, I presume? Omar's wisdom seems to apply."

"If I go after the king, I won't miss. Big if, though."

"It would be," I said.

We lapsed into silence as the first half pressed onward. Some good back-and-forth action in the final minutes saw Hanson take a one-point lead into the locker room. "Good game," Eddie said.

"So far."

"I think it'll stay this way." He excused himself to take a phone call, walking outside the tavern.

The goons stared at me in silence until it grew uncomfortable sitting at the table. They looked brawny and capable, but I'd seen larger men working for Tony. "It's been real, fellas," I said, getting up and walking to the bar. I grabbed an empty stool near Rollins to his right, keeping two vacant between us.

The second half started as I nursed my second beer. It was colder than the first but didn't taste much better. Adequate, as brews went. I caught Rollins' eye and shrugged my left shoulder. He didn't acknowledge it, but I didn't think he would. He was one of those people who didn't miss anything but didn't give any indication he saw anything, either.

Hanson opened the final twenty minutes with some quick passes and good offense, taking a five-point lead three minutes in. The Huskies pushed the ball up the court on their next possession. Calvin picked off a pass, however, sprinted down the court, and threw down a powerful dunk. He pounded his chest as the crowd roared, and the Northeastern coach called a timeout to corral his beleaguered players.

It didn't help much. I noticed Eddie watching the game with interest, but his jovial expression of the first half vanished as the Presidents maintained their lead. When the whistle for the TV timeout sounded with inside of eight minutes left, JHC enjoyed a nine-point lead. The last I checked the line, it held at six. They still had opportunities to let Northeastern whittle away at it, but Eddie didn't seem pleased with the current progress of the contest. The announcers told us Calvin scored eight points this half but also dished out six assists.

As the rest of the game unfolded, it became obvious Hanson was playing to win. Eddie looked more and more unhappy, which prompted a couple conferences with his intimidating tablemates. The buzzer sounded a few minutes later. JHC won the conference as expected, vanquishing Northeastern by a final of 85 to 74. They won and covered, and Eddie's red-faced glower told me all I needed to know about his thoughts on the matter.

Now, I was worried for Calvin and by extension, Iris and Denise. If Hanson was supposed to win and not cover the spread, Eddie and a few others probably took a bath on the outcome. Why would Calvin risk so much to defy someone I could help him get away from? I fired off a quick text even though I knew he wouldn't see it until later. *Eddie looks pissed. I hope you know what you're doing. Let me know if anyone is in trouble.*

Rollins' eyes flicked toward the door. He got up and left, and I followed about a minute later after I paid my tab. As I walked out, I saw Eddie look at me and chat with his goons.

I got into the S4 and drove away. I'd gone about a block before I saw a car pull out of the lot and follow me.

* * *

ROLLINS WHEELED from the lot before I did. I called him as I drove down Eastern Boulevard. "I seem to have grown a tail," I said when he picked up.

"You sure?"

"Eddie was talking to his enforcers when I left. Thirty seconds after I hit the street, a car pulls out behind me."

"Lot of people could be leaving after the game," he said.

"True. I think this is someone tailing me, though. They're hanging back and trying to make it look like they're not following me."

"Where are you now?" I heard tires squeal over the connection.

"On a leisurely drive down Eastern," I said. "I'm not even speeding. Plenty of cars have passed me, but the one behind me just stays there."

The line was silent for a moment. Then Rollins said, "I see you. The car dogging you is a dark gray sedan, right?"

"Looks like it."

"I'm on him."

I stayed on the boulevard even though it wasn't the fastest route back into the city. It was direct, however, and it afforded me plenty of spots to turn off should I need one. "I'm not keeping you from a hot date, am I?" I asked as I traversed the bridge over Back River.

"He'll wait," Rollins said.

We passed the treatment plant Back River is infamous for. It took a couple blocks for the smell to dissipate. Soon, we crossed the border into the city, and Eastern lost its Boulevard status, becoming a mere Avenue. "There's a police station not far from here," I said. "I'm going to pull in there and presume whoever's following me won't do the same."

"I'll stay on him," Rollins said.

"Thanks. You'll tell me where he ends up?"

"Unless he loses me."

"I don't see it happening."

"Me, either," Rollins said, and he broke the connection.

A few blocks later, I turned into the small police precinct. Sure enough, the sedan behind me kept going. I watched Rollins' truck go by in the group of cars which happened to be behind them. I turned around, pulled out of the lot, and drove home. Gloria was still out of town, so I found a sports highlight show and watched it. Before long, the talking heads raved about Hanson and how they stepped it up in the second half. I didn't share their enthusiasm.

I tuned out the show when they started discussing where JHC would be seeded in the big tournament. As the winner of a rather small conference, they received an automatic bid but were unlikely to get a favorable matchup. They'd probably be the underdog. I wondered how Eddie would handle this. It was easy to shave points when you were expected to win.

A little while later, Rollins called. "Where'd they end up?" I said.

"You'll never guess."

"I definitely won't if you tell me."

"John Hanson College."

My mouth fell open. A few seconds later, I said, "Did you break it off there?"

"Yes," Rollins said. "Too hard to follow them without being seen on campus."

Eddie was an alumnus of JHC. I got the feeling from Coach Baker this mess went beyond basketball. Now the goons who sat with Eddie and spent much of their time glaring at me wound up on campus.

Something was rotten in the state of Maryland.

CHAPTER 17

GLORIA AND I WERE SKYPING WHEN MY PHONE BUZZED. Calvin. I told her I'd call her back and flipped my laptop shut. Calvin sent a text in response to mine from earlier. *I know what I'm doing. Fuck Eddie. I want to be done with him.* I shook my head and blew out a deep, exasperated breath. Calvin was still young, but how could he be so stupid? The last time we talked, I got the impression he would ride this out. Now, I wondered what happened to change his mind.

You're not the one he'll go after. How do you know your mom and Iris are safe?

I waited for a response, drumming my fingers on the desktop. It came in a moment later. *My mom is staying with a friend. Iris is with my cousin. He's got a nine.*

I presumed he meant a nine-millimeter. *Eddie has big guys on his payroll. They have guns, too. Your cousin might be in trouble. Where's Tamika?*

How you know about Tamika?

For Christ's sake, Calvin, I'm a detective. Is she safe?

She's with my cousin, too.

Great. A single point of failure. Eddie Ferrugia's goons would find the hiding place, storm in, shoot Calvin's cousin, and walk out with his girlfriend and infant daughter. Or they'd shoot Tamika, too, and simply take Iris. Eddie struck me as more ambitious than ruthless, but I didn't think the strong-arm squad on his payroll would have much compunction at the thought of murdering a woman.

You put them all in danger, Calvin. I hope you're happy.

A few minutes later, he sent a reply. *I am.*

I sighed in disgust and slammed my phone down. The idiot would get someone killed, and all because he wanted to spit in Eddie's eye. I could've gotten him out from under before, but at this point, who knew what would happen? All I knew was Eddie looked pissed at the end of the game, and I didn't expect him to take it lightly. Calvin could have held down the final score and didn't. In another situation, I may have applauded him for finding his spine.

Now, I lamented the likely collateral damage. I picked up my phone and sent Calvin another text. *Where's your cousin? I want to make sure they're safe. I can move them if I need to.* If he told me where they were, I could turn to a couple people to find temporary housing for them. It would be some place with no association to Calvin, his family, or me. Eddie and his legbreakers wouldn't be able to find them. It was more than Calvin deserved, but I wouldn't be doing it for him.

Don't worry about them. They're safe.

Dammit, Calvin, this is serious. Let me help them. You're putting them in danger.

I waited. He didn't reply.

* * *

THE NEXT MORNING, I drove to my office after breakfast. I logged onto the BPD's network and searched for Eddie

Ferrugia. They held no data on him. Not even a parking ticket. His business was incorporated in the county, so as far as the city of Baltimore went, Eddie Ferrugia didn't exist.

I recalled last evening at the Final Score. The guys with Eddie were total unknowns. Rollins followed them to the John Hanson campus. Then it hit me: someone as observant as Rollins would have gotten the tag number. I should have asked him for it last night. To rectify this, I sent him a text requesting it. He responded with it within a minute, adding to my suspicion he never slept.

While still in the BPD systems, I punched in the license number. It spat out a result almost right away: Ronald Garver, age thirty-four, and the member of the duo who actually showed a neck. I scrolled past his measurements and other useless information, and his job jumped off the screen at me.

Officer, John Hanson College Campus Police.

"Shit," I said to the empty office. As usual, it didn't reply. I wondered if the guy with him also served on the college police force. Eddie said he was an alumnus of the school. He must have also been a large donor, or he may have held dirt on a couple of the guys who wore badges on campus. And he counted the basketball coach and at least one player on the team among his stable.

I called Gonzalez, who answered with his usual bright and sunny tone. "The hell do you want?"

"You're always so happy to hear from me," I said.

"I love talking to people who create work for me and complicate my life."

"Today, I just have a simple question."

"Thank Christ," he said. "What is it?"

"Does the BCPD have any influence over the John Hanson Campus Police?"

His response came in the form of a deep breath blown into the phone. "What the hell do you need to know for?"

"I think it's important."

"Still on the basketball player?"

"Yeah."

"They're a qualified force according to the state, and they'll be the first to tell you. The thing is they're only allowed to handle certain things. We have oversight of the whole operation, and we step in for emergencies or things like major crimes."

"Like murder," I said.

"Sure . . . or rape and sexual assault, too. We get involved for the really bad stuff. The rest of the time, they're on their own for the most part. Once a year, we have someone who audits their work."

"Any problems?"

"I wouldn't know offhand, but I don't remember hearing anyone mention it. Why?"

"I may have seen one of their officers moonlighting. Let's just say his commander would probably be disappointed in his choice of employment." I hoped so, for the sakes of many. Eddie tossed around money on expensive cancer treatments. He could've kept a bunch of college cops on the payroll.

"Got a name?"

"Ronald Garver."

"Doesn't ring a bell, but I'll see if I can find something out." He paused. "See? You're creating work for me again."

"Think of it as laying the foundation for your next award."

"Right," Gonzalez said, and he hung up.

I put my phone down and sighed. I knew more than when I arrived at the office, yet the case grew murkier. Now, at least one member of the Hanson cops was involved somehow. The oversight by the county only came online in the forms of an annual compliance check and a takeover for serious crimes. Garver could fly under the radar for a while with those criteria in place.

Calvin had been quiet since last night. I sent him another text. No response came.

I didn't have a good feeling about this, and I didn't know what to do about it.

* * *

A COUPLE HOURS LATER, the elevator on my floor dinged. Footsteps rushed down the hall. I opened my right-hand drawer, grabbed the .45, and held it on the desktop. Calvin burst through the outer door. His eyes were wide. Despite the cool day, sweat beaded on his forehead. Before I could ask what was wrong, he launched into a tirade. "You were right. Dammit, I shoulda listened to you. I shoulda listened. Now, it's too late. Now—"

"Calvin," I said, breaking in. "Stop." I left the gun on the desk, stood, and put my hands on his shoulders. Despite him being bigger and stronger, I steered him into a seat with minimal resistance. "Take a breath." I took a bottle of water from the fridge and set it before him. "Drink this. You look like you need it. When you're ready, tell me what's going on."

He unscrewed the lid and guzzled the contents in a single drink. Calvin looked all around the office, his eyes still as big as dollar coins. He stared at me as if seeing me for the first time. "I shoulda listened to you," he said again.

"While I'm always glad to hear I was right, you're going to have to tell me more." A dark feeling as to where this conversation would go twisted my stomach.

"My cousin," he said after a few seconds. "My cousin Ben . . . he's dead."

I remembered what he told me last night after he defied Eddie Ferrugia and led Hanson to a decisive win over Northeastern. Tonight, they would learn their region and seeding in the big tournament. I didn't expect the news to be a happy occasion for Calvin. "Would this be the cousin who was watching Iris and Tamika?"

His head wobbled up and down as if the connection to his neck were loose. "Yeah. I tried him this morning and got nothing, so I went over there." He paused to collect himself. "Tamika was beat up and knocked out. Ben was dead, and Iris was gone." He gazed up at me, his eyes wet. "She's gone, man."

"All right, Calvin. Take some breaths." I fetched him a second water, which he picked up but didn't open. "Let's work this from the top. How long were Tamika and Iris staying with your cousin?"

"Two days."

"Did anyone else know they were going to be there?"

"No way, man. Even my mom didn't know."

I leaned back in my chair and pondered how this could've gone so wrong. Calvin shouldn't have stuck his thumb in Eddie Ferrugia's eye, but Eddie also shouldn't know where some random cousin lives. Either someone talked, or the Ferrugia regime was good at gathering information. It didn't take a big stretch to go from data analysis to hacking.

"Would Ben or Tamika have told anyone? Called anybody while they were there?"

Calvin wanted to say no right away, but he stopped. "I don't know. I hope not." He took an iPhone out of his pocket. A moment later, he said, "Nothing on their Facebook about it." Another pause. "Not Instagram, neither."

So social media was out, but this still left myriad ways for one person to contact another. Ben or Tamika could've let something slip to a friend. How Eddie and his crew found out remained a problem to solve. For now, however, the matter of a missing infant took priority. "Did you come straight here from your cousin's house?" I said. It took Calvin a moment, but he indicated he did. "How's Tamika?" I continued, trying to focus Calvin on the task at hand.

"She's busted up," he said. "They beat on her pretty good. Paramedics were looking at her . . . they say she should be OK in a few days."

"Great. Now tell me about Iris."

For the first time since he showed up, Calvin's expression brightened. "She's the best. I love my little girl, man. I'll do anything to get her back."

"Does she need anything above and beyond what's normal for a baby?" Calvin shot me a blank look. "Like special formula, medicine . . . those kinds of things." He shook his head. "Good. We still need to get her returned to you, but now there's no ticking clock hanging over our heads. Where does . . . did Ben live?"

"Park Heights."

In the city. Calvin told me he came here directly, so cops would still be processing everything. This meant I could lean on Rich. "All right," I said. "I want to see the crime scene and—"

"We gotta get Iris back," Calvin said.

"We will. There could be something there to point me in the right direction." He was about to say something else, but I cut him off. "Let me do my job. You said you should've listened to me before. Do it now."

Before the conversation could continue, Calvin's phone

rang. He stared at the number on the screen, unable to do anything.

"Is it Eddie?" I asked. He gave a single nod. "Pick it up." It rang another time before Calvin answered the call. He was aware enough to put it on speaker without me prompting him.

"Calvin," Eddie Ferrugia said, his voice filling the office. "How you doing?"

"You motherfucker, I want her back!"

I couldn't fault Calvin for his emotional response—I probably would have said the same in his place—but it didn't help. "Who are you talking about, Calvin?"

"My daughter, you son of a bitch."

"I have a way you can see her again." Eddie paused. Calvin stewed. I waited them both out. "Wanna know what it is?"

"I think I can guess."

"I'm sure you can, Calvin. You're a smart kid. It surprised me a lot when you went against what we had planned. It hurt. I know you're smarter than you showed."

"You didn't have to kill my cousin!" Calvin pounded my desk. He stood in a rush and stalked around the office. I held up a hand and moved it up and down in time with my breathing. He may not have been capable of calming himself, but I needed to try. Him being amped up didn't help anyone, especially Iris.

"You didn't have to defy me," Eddie said. "You cost me a lot of money and a little bit of reputation. I needed to do something about it. You keep blaming me, Calvin. This is on you."

Calvin paced around some more. After a moment, he stopped, leaned over the desk, and spoke through clenched teeth. "What do you want?"

"I want you to do what I tell you in the next game. We'll know tonight what it'll be. Once the line settles, we'll have a play, and I'll be in touch. You do exactly what I say, and you'll get Iris home unharmed."

"Fine," Calvin said right away. "Whatever you want."

"And no cops, Calvin. No cops and no private investigators. Did you know one of them came to see me yesterday?" I'd never introduced myself, but with a few high-visibility cases under my belt, someone puzzling out my identity wasn't a big lift.

"I ain't gonna talk to him," Calvin said.

"Good. Very good, Calvin. You wait for my next call. Do what I say, and it'll all turn out fine."

Calvin hung up and crammed the phone back in his pocket. "Can you find him?"

I shrugged. "Sure. Just because he's somewhere doesn't mean Iris is there, though."

"What are you going to do, then?"

"My job, Calvin, and it starts by going to your cousin's crime scene."

He pursed his lips and stared at me. "Can you get her for me?"

"Yes."

"Whatever you gotta do, then. Just get Iris back alive."

I said I would. Calvin left. I leaned forward in my chair, put my face in my hands, and wondered how this case careened so far off the rails.

CHAPTER 18

THE PARK HEIGHTS AREA OF BALTIMORE IS PROBABLY best known for containing Pimlico Race Course, the site of the annual Preakness Stakes. It extends north to Northern Parkway and south to the border of Druid Hill Park. For the most part, it's residential. The neighborhood has some nice homes, but on other streets, blocks of row houses sit boarded up. Crime in the heights, however, started trending downward in 2010 as urban renewal efforts began.

I called Rich as I drove toward this area. "I'm calling about a murder," I said when he picked up.

"Did someone kill his annoying cousin?"

"Actually . . . kind of."

"Oh." Rich paused, and when he came back on, his tone sounded more professional like it usually did. "What happened?"

"Calvin Murray's cousin Ben was killed over in Park Heights."

"Let me guess," Rich said. "You want to see the crime scene."

"I think it would help my case, yes."

"What else happened?" Wariness dominated his voice

now. Rich worked with me enough to know when I was
playing an angle.

"Whoever killed Ben also beat up a woman and abducted
an infant girl."

"Jesus. You headed over there now?"

"Sure am."

"I can't meet you," Rich said. "I'm tied up with something
else. Probably will be for a while. I'll call over there, though.
Someone will let you in."

"Thanks," I said, and I enjoyed the rare moment where I
got to hang up before Rich. Realizing where I was going and
what I would see upon arriving sobered my good mood. I got
on I-83 North, lead-footed my way to Cold Spring Lane, and
snaked through the neighborhood to Finney Avenue. The left
side of the road gave way to a park. Well-maintained
rowhouses lined the right, each with a brick front, ample
porch, and two flights of concrete steps leading up from street
level.

I parked behind the scad of emergency vehicles. A
uniformed officer eyed me skeptically as I approached and
showed him my credentials. "He's good," a familiar voice
said. Paul King walked from behind an SUV and gave the
thumbs-up.

"I'm actually very good," I said as the uniform let me
under the police tape. "He's selling me short."

My argument did not meet a sympathetic audience. King
waited for me. As usual, he looked more like a mediocre rock
singer than a cop with his mop of wild dirty blonde hair,
scraggly goatee, and casual clothes. I wondered if he'd ever
owned a suit in his life. Despite his appearance, King was a
damned good detective who'd toiled away in several different
departments over the years. "Rich told me you were
coming by."

"You're on homicide detail now?"

King shrugged. "A man can only deal with vice for so long."

"I'll take your word for it." As we approached the house, I noticed an ambulance parked very close. A woman sat in the back, her face cut and bruised and her arm in a sling. "You talk to her yet?"

"Figured we could after I gave you the tour," King said.

We walked up the red-painted stairs and into the house. King led me to the second level, where a black man lay supine on a bed. His shirt and the sheets under him were all stained crimson. I placed him in his mid-twenties, and the unfortunate reality was he'd never get any older. A pistol lay near him on the mattress. Four holes marred his chest. He never had a chance.

"He probably got killed first," King said. "We have some recent shoe prints going upstairs, so my guess is whoever shot this guy went upstairs, beat up the woman, and took the kid."

"One guy?"

"Two."

I nosed around the bedroom. The door jamb was pristine, so the door was either open already or the killers gained access without forcing it. "Bullets still in him?" I asked.

"Far as we know."

I didn't see any holes around the room, nor signs the police discovered any and marked them off. Apart from the grisly scene on the bed, the room itself looked neat and well-kept. No one ransacked the drawers after shooting Ben. They came in, pumped four bullets into him, and went upstairs. By then, Tamika and Iris were trapped. They couldn't jump out the window without a serious risk of injury, and they couldn't fight off or get past two men with guns.

We walked upstairs to a disheveled room. A tiny dresser

fell to the floor, its drawers and contents scattered. A fist-sized hole pockmarked one wall. The sheets and blankets on the bed lay in disarray. Drops of blood dotted the floor, all identified by the officers and crime scene technicians who'd already visited this room. "Looks like she struggled," I said.

"Yeah. I would, too, if I had a young child with me."

"They just beat her up, though? No signs of anything worse?"

"You mean other than taking the kid? No."

I looked around some more, but nothing jumped out at me. It didn't appear the police missed anything. King and I walked back down and emerged from the front of the house. Tamika still sat in the rear of the ambulance, tended to by a paramedic. We approached, and she glared at us. "You the detectives?"

"I am," King said, showing his badge. "He's a private investigator."

"It means I'll be the one who really figures this out," I said, ignoring King's eye roll.

"I don't care who does it. I want my daughter back."

"Miss . . . Robinson, is it?" Tamika nodded. "Can you tell us what happened?"

"Same thing I told the other cops. Me and Iris was upstairs. Ben was on the second floor. You know Calvin asked him to look after us?" I bobbed my head. "Poor Ben." Her eyes, already puffy and red, welled. A tear slid down her cheek, passing over a bruise to rest in a cut near her lips. "Anyway, they must have been all quiet. First thing I heard was Ben asking who the hell was there. Then, I heard some footsteps and a few gunshots." Tamika dabbed at her eyes with a tissue. We waited.

"Take your time," King said.

"I figured Ben was dead at that point," she said. "We

didn't have no good options. Can't jump from the third floor. Don't wanna get shot. It was two of them. They came in. I held Iris. The big one punched me in the face. I went down on the bed. Iris musta slipped out of my arms. The other one grabbed her up. I tried to stop them, but the first guy kept beating on me." She cried in earnest now, and we took a couple steps back.

"Anyone get a look at these guys?" I whispered.

King shook his head. "Nothing on the vehicle, either."

"Nobody heard four gunshots and a crying baby?"

"How long have you lived in Baltimore?" He made a valid point. "Even if someone did hear what happened, you think they're going to peek out the window? Uniforms are talking to the neighbors, but we don't expect to learn anything."

"Sounds like a professional job," I said.

"Yeah . . . worries me."

Tamika composed herself but didn't have much more to say. The men wore masks, so she didn't get a good look at either, but she thought both were white. Fairly tall and wide. She could've described the two goons who sat with Eddie Ferrugia last night.

"Body's on its way to the ME," King said. "You want to tag along?"

"I can't think of anything else to do," I said.

* * *

WE LEFT Park Heights a few minutes later. From there, we stopped at the precinct so King could file some paperwork. I sat in a guest chair and struggled to seem interested. "No point in rushing," he said at one point. "ME needs time, and the fucking body isn't going anywhere." He had a point, but

I would've preferred knowing about this detour before we left.

We eschewed the precinct's swill and stopped for proper coffee before walking to the medical examiner's office. The coroner on duty was Doctor Gary Hunt, whom I'd worked with a few times before. He directed King and me to an office while he finished with a body on the table. Only one cadaver lay out in the open. The ventilation system did a great job of pumping out the putrescence and replacing it with a neutral aroma.

A few minutes later, Hunt joined us, slipping his slender frame into the chair behind the desk. Brown hair framed his face, and his glasses showed a prominent smudge which would've driven me insane. "You're here about the shooting victim?" he asked. "Ben Murray?"

"We are," King said.

"Pretty simple. Four gunshots to the torso. Two in the upper chest, one in the diaphragm, and the fourth in the liver."

"The same gun fire all four?"

"Can't tell yet," Hunt said. "I collected all the bullets for testing. They look to be the same caliber to my eyes, but it doesn't mean all four came from the same pistol."

"A quartet of shots center mass," I said. "We're not dealing with an amateur here."

"Most likely not," Hunt said, "but I'll leave the investigation to you."

"You'd say our shooter was trained, though?"

"Probably. The odds of a novice clustering shots in such a manner, even from twelve feet, are quite long. You gentlemen would probably know better than I would."

"You got anything else?" King said to me. I shook my head. "Thanks, Doc. We'll be in touch." We left the office and hit the street a moment later. King looked at me as the exterior door swung shut. "I know you have something on your mind."

"One of the pitfalls of being a genius," I said.

"I hear you. What are you thinking?"

"How much did Rich tell you about this case?"

"Not a lot," King said. "Told me you had a bug up your ass about it."

I filled him in on the details, including my chat with Eddie and his enforcers yesterday. "After they left, they drove to the JHC Campus. The plate is registered to a member of the campus police."

"You think two college cops shot this guy?"

"I think they'd be trained in how to fire a gun like any other law enforcement officer."

"They would." King chewed on his bottom lip. "I hope it's not them, but it sounds like there's a chance. You working with anyone in the county on it?"

"Gonzalez," I said. "He told me BCPD has oversight of the JHC cops in certain circumstances."

King's phone buzzed. "I probably have to go," he said. "You good for now?"

"Yeah, thanks." He returned to the precinct. I walked back to my car, climbed in, and sighed. Calvin's cousin was dead, the hoops star's girlfriend took a beating, and someone kidnapped their daughter because Calvin defied a guy who was fixing the games. I wondered about Denise. If her son planned any more acts of rebellion, she would be the next one in the crosshairs. I didn't want to Calvin to lose his mom, and keeping a client from getting killed is a point of personal pride.

I needed to stash her somewhere safe.

* * *

CALVIN CALLED me a little later demanding an update. When I told him I was working on it, he launched into a screed, and I needed to shut him down. "I just saw your cousin's body," I said when he paused for a breath.

He didn't have part six of his rant ready to go anymore. Calvin stammered a couple of times. I took over. "Let me lay it out for you. I'm willing to help you get out from under Eddie Ferrugia, but I don't work for you, and I'm not putting up with your bullshit. I work for your mother, whom I'm still concerned about. Let's get back to reality, Calvin. Have you heard from her recently?"

"Uh . . . yeah. Yesterday, I think."

"You think?"

"It was yesterday," he said.

"So you haven't told her your cousin is dead?"

"No," he said slowly.

"While you're ranting at me for an update, you might want to consider her safety." I waited, but he didn't say anything. Apparently, I needed to do everything. "I'll talk to her. She should probably stay somewhere Eddie can't find her easily. Taking Iris probably puts enough pressure on you, but never put it past these assholes to double down."

"Where you gonna stash her?"

"I'm not sure yet," I said.

"You gonna tell me?"

"Why? So Eddie can have some grunt beat it out of you? No. You'll be in the dark. You worry about basketball for now. Let me handle the rest. And stop calling me for status reports." I hung up on him before he could respond.

I didn't care for having all these phone conversations, but

I needed to make another call. I dialed Joey Trovato. "Need more of my basketball expertise?" he said.

"No, but I do need a favor."

"The same case?"

"Yes," I said. I told him about the game going awry, Ben getting killed, and Eddie's men taking Iris. "I'm concerned about the mother."

"This guy already has the daughter, though," Joey said.

"I know. But what if Hanson wins their first-round game? He may want to keep the run going."

Joey blew a deep breath into the phone. "I got someone in the Columbia safehouse already." Pity. I'd used it before on an earlier case and hoped to again. "I do keep a couple hotel rooms on standby for emergencies, though." When I didn't say anything, he clarified by adding, "The managers know me."

"Thanks. I'll take wherever I can get at this point."

"Sounds like recent events have you spooked."

"I guess they do," I said. "I didn't expect anyone to die when I started working this case, but I left the morgue a little while ago. It's all gone to hell over the course of a day."

"Let me get back to you in a little while. I should have somewhere you can use."

We hung up. At this point, I would gladly take the small sliver of optimism my conversation with Joey afforded.

* * *

About a half-hour later, Joey called me with some information. I got hold of Denise and said I needed to see her. She hemmed and hawed but eventually told me where she was staying. She was at a friend's house in Odenton, not far from Fort Meade and Columbia. I pulled into the townhouse community and marveled at the sameness of everything.

Inside, Denise's friend Jasmine cleared out, leaving us alone in the living room. I resisted scoffing at the dreamcatchers, crystals, and other new-age trinkets on display. "Should I sit a certain way to maximize the feng shui?" I said. Chairs and loveseats faced a variety of directions. The area was a mish-mash of styles, to say nothing of the more interesting accoutrements cluttering it up.

Denise smiled. "I don't think it matters."

She was right. "Did you know Calvin's cousin Ben?"

"Yes," she said. "He's Calvin's uncle's son on his father's side. Nice kid." She frowned as if realizing for the first time why I might be asking the question. "Why?"

"He's dead." Denise, already a little pale, blanched. "Someone went to his house and shot him four times."

"My God." She shut her eyes tightly and bowed her head. "What about Tamika and Iris?"

"They're alive," I said. "Tamika took a beating, but she should be OK."

Denise looked up at me, her eyes threatening to spill tears. "And Iris?"

"Eddie has her."

She cried and hid her face in her hands. Jasmine appeared in the doorway, but I waved her off. Healing salts and woo-woo wouldn't be any help to us. "Are you looking for her?" she said after taking a couple minutes to compose herself.

"The police are, too. At the moment, I'm concerned about you." Before she could try to allay my worries, I kept talking. "Eddie might want more leverage over Calvin, and if Hanson wins their first game, he might think he needs it. You need to go somewhere safe, and I've worked it out."

"But no one knows I'm here."

"I don't think anyone was supposed to know where Tamika and Iris were, either," I said. When I saw Eddie next, I would ask him how he came by the information.

"Where are we going?"

"A hotel. My friend uses it. He . . . helps people, too." She remained in the chair. "You already have a bag packed, I presume. You'll be safer there. I'm not going to tell Calvin where you are, and Eddie won't get the info from me."

It took a minute, but Denise nodded. She thanked Jasmine for lending a hand, grabbed her bag, and we left.

At least I kept one person safe.

CHAPTER 19

AFTER TALKING TO GLORIA FOR A BIT—SHE'D BE COMING back tomorrow—I drove to my office. The lot was pretty empty at this hour. Most of the offices were medical in nature, and many workers cleared out at the stroke of four. I was one of the few remaining tenants who didn't fit in with the CareFirst system, because they honored my lease when they took the building over from First Mariner Bank. I wondered how long they'd let me remain.

I eschewed the elevator and climbed the stairs. It was a lot of flights, and my legs burned after setting a good pace for the first ten. I slowed to a more reasonable rate for the next two when my phone started blowing up. The alarm I'd installed in my office threw a bunch of alerts. I quickened my pace again, and I was breathing hard by the time I popped out into the hallway next to the elevators.

Sure enough, a light was on in my workplace. The exterior door remained opened a crack, spilling a triangle of illumination onto the carpet. I hugged the wall, drew my 9MM, and walked slowly toward the burglary in progress. As I stalked closer, I heard muffled voices coming from within. A lock popped open, and my phone responded with a fresh series of notifications. Whoever was in there breached my inner sanctum.

I flattened onto the wall next to the door. Its hinges returned my stare. I needed to be on the other side to see anything. A quick peek told me the coast was probably clear, so I ducked and scampered across. Now I could see two guys inside. Both wore something covering their heads. Conveniently enough, they stood with their backs to me. I inched the door open and took a cautious step inside.

They didn't react. One looked at my desk while the other worked on jimmying the file cabinet I barely used. For the most part, it held a couple pictures of Gloria and me along with a Keurig on the top. I advanced, crossing the threshold of the interior space. The one at the desk was closer. I brought the gun up and whacked him behind the ear with the butt. His head hit the desk, and then he sagged to the side and slid onto the floor. The one who'd broken into my filing cabinet turned.

I held the business end of the 9MM about four feet from his head. He looked at me with wide eyes, glanced over to his fallen comrade, then returned his uneasy gaze to me. This guy was smaller than the two who lunched with Eddie at the Final Score tavern. Hell, he was barely even my size, though he looked young enough to still get carded at R-rated movies. "Let's chat," I said. His hand moved toward his back. "Don't."

To emphasize the point, I edged closer to him. The muzzle was maybe two feet from the tip of his nose. If he took a deep breath, he could smell the oil I used to clean it. His hand returned to where it had been. "Turn around," I said, and he did. I plucked a pistol from his waistband, stuck it in my holster, and gave him a quick one-handed pat-down. He was clean. "Have a seat. Feel free to move your friend's legs out of the way if they're blocking the guest chair."

I waited for him to get situated before I walked around the desk and sat. I tossed his gun into my top drawer and put mine on the desktop pointed in his direction. He eyed it. It lay in easy reach if I needed it, and he knew it. "Eddie send you?"

"Who?"

"Oh, piss off," I said. "I've had way too long a day for this. You and I both know who Eddie is and what he does, so can we dispense with the bullshit and have a conversation." Swallowing hard served as his answer. "Now . . . did Eddie send you?"

"Yeah," he said in a small voice. After I chastised him, he refused to look at me, spending his time glancing between his lap and the still-unconscious man lying on the floor to his right.

"See? Wasn't so hard, was it? Now, tell me why he sent you."

"Wanted to know what you know, I guess. He told us to bring back files and computers."

If he wanted computers, I presumed he thought he possessed a way to break into them. Let him try. My computer was tethered to the desk with a cable bolt cutters would have a tough time getting through. Even if someone lifted the unit—or only its hard drive—I used full disk encryption with a strong algorithm and a password no rainbow table would uncover. "Tell Eddie if he wants to talk to me, he can make an appointment. Let him ask his questions then." The guy didn't say anything. "You work for Eddie long?"

He shrugged. "Couple months."

"You in college?" His head bobbed. "Let me guess—John Hanson." Another bob. "You know where he's keeping the girl?"

"What girl?"

I glared at him. "I thought we talked about this. A young girl—not even two years old. Kidnapped from her mother, who caught a beating in the process." I left out the detail of Ben Murray getting killed. Kidnapping a baby and beating up a woman should be enough to raise most people's hackles.

He frowned so deeply it added ten years to his age. "I don't know anything about it."

"You're sure?"

"Yeah!" he said. "Eddie doesn't seem the type to do it. It must be . . ."

"Must be what?" I asked when he trailed off.

"Nothing. Forget it."

"A what or a whom?"

"Nothing. I'm just . . . surprised Eddie would do something like this."

"These are surprising times," I said.

The fellow on the floor stirred. He groaned, and his head poked above the top of the desk as he raised himself to a crouch. I picked up the gun and showed it to him. He frowned and rubbed his head where I'd clobbered him. "Jesus, we were just looking around," he muttered.

"What can I say? I like my privacy. You have a gun?" He shook his head. I glanced at the other guy. "He telling the truth?"

"Yeah. I had the pistol. He's the burglar."

"You might as well sit in the chair you're pulling yourself up with," I said to the groggy one. I pushed the speaker button on my little-used desk phone and dialed 9-1-1. When the cops arrived a short while later, I told them what happened, gave them the gun I confiscated, and watched them lead the two burglars out in handcuffs.

I'd originally come here to do work. No time like the present. I brewed a cup of coffee in the Keurig and set about conducting a little research into Eddie Ferrugia and where he might be.

* * *

THE NEXT MORNING, I woke up feeling antsy. Gloria was due back today, and thinking about it made me realize how much I missed her. I hoped her final match went well. She won a tournament about eighteen months ago and found herself on a dry spell since. Tennis was a sport where professionals debuted on the women's tour while still teenagers. Gloria was about to turn twenty-eight. She was far from washed up, but a younger wave of competitors managed to win all the titles since her lone victory.

Before making breakfast or coffee, I went out for a run. I wore a .38 snugged in an elastic holster under my warm-up jacket in case any more of Eddie Ferrugia's men decided to pay me a visit. The man himself continued to be mysterious. It impressed me in this modern age when someone kept a minimal online footprint. Eddie was one of the few. He'd avoided spilling a lot of personal information out into the world. Every time I visited social media, I wished more people took this minimalist approach. It would make my job harder but society better.

All this magnanimity must have been a side effect of being thirty.

I finished my morning constitutional and spied no goons, miscreants, or ne'er-do-wells. At home, I took a shower, got dressed, and made breakfast. It was more like brunch at the current hour of ten-forty. Maybe I should go back in the kitchen and whip up a mimosa and some avocado toast.

After eating, I checked in with Joey. He'd heard nothing about Denise, and he told me no news was good news.

Calvin still champed at the bit, and he only calmed down when I told him I had something potentially big in the works for today. And I did, as much as I disliked the idea of it. It all came from my inability to find a place Eddie Ferrugia would be stashing Iris. He wouldn't do it at his home or business. I knew who he was, and the police would find those places easily. Damn him and his tiny online presence.

I drove into Little Italy, parked the S4, and walked into *Il Buon Cibo* shortly after their eleven-thirty opening. A quick scan of the mostly-empty dining room showed me Tony wasn't back yet. Bruno sat at his table, accompanied by a couple tough guys who stared me down as I approached. "The hell do you want?" Bruno said.

It was a risk, but I sat uninvited. All three men glared at me. "I think I have some information you might find useful."

"Yeah?" Bruno kept staring at me. After a moment, he said, "You ain't getting a free meal."

"I just ate."

"Good. If I don't like whatever it is you're telling me, or if I don't think I can do anything with it, these two are going to show you out."

"I can leave on my own," I said.

"You *can*. You won't. They'll make sure you're back on the pavement real quick." He paused long enough to show me a predator's grin. "You still wanna talk?"

"I didn't come here for the company."

After I said it, I wondered if the line might have been pushing it. Bruno already didn't like me and wasn't inclined to listen. I didn't need to provide him much incentive to have the no-neck twins toss me out on my ear. Instead of ordering my eviction, he took a deep breath and said, "Speak."

"Remember the name Eddie Ferrugia?" He shook his

head. "I told you about him recently. He's out in the county. Data guy . . . running a point-shaving scheme."

"I think it's ringing a bell now. So what? What does this Eddie have to do with me?"

"I'm sure you know the county has something of a power vacuum. There's no Tony out there to run everything."

"Been the case for a while," Bruno said. "Why should I start caring about it now?"

"I know more about Eddie now. He's ambitious." A cute waitress neared us, then turned heel and strode away at Bruno's curt headshake. "I don't know how interested he is in the county, and I'm not sure I much care beyond how it affects my client's family. He specifically mentioned Tony, though. Eddie might have an eye on Baltimore."

Bruno waved his hand. "Tony's fended off a lot worse than some numbers geek."

"Sure. Look, I like Tony. I've known him most of my life. None of us are getting any younger, though, and he's had a pretty rough go of it recently."

"Meaning what?" Bruno regarded me though narrowed eyes.

"Meaning Eddie might see him as ripe for the picking."

"This is why Tony keeps us around." Bruno gestured to the two guys sharing our table as if I'd forgotten they were there. "I'm sure we can handle one guy." He inclined his head toward the goon on my right, and the man stood.

"There's more," I said. "The player he's using for his scheme has a young daughter. Eddie's men kidnapped her."

The enforcer didn't sit, and Bruno's expression didn't change. My pulse climbed. If I couldn't appeal to his loyalty to Tony, I hoped to win him over as a father. If both failed, I'd be out on the concrete. "Why do you think I care about some kid?" Bruno said.

"Because you're a father. If some asshole took your little girl, I'm sure you'd want her back." The goon advanced, moving behind me. He was ready to grab me at Bruno's command. "You don't like me. Fine. Don't do it for me. Do it for a girl who's not even two years old yet and is wondering where the hell her parents are."

Bruno frowned and stared at the tabletop for a few seconds. When he looked up, he said, "Tell me prick's name again."

"Eddie Ferrugia."

"Spell it." I did. "All right." He jerked his thumb, and the man behind me took his seat again. "We'll look into it. You can go."

I left while the leaving was good.

* * *

AFTER LEAVING *IL BUON CIBO*, I drove back to Federal Hill. From the parking pad behind my house, I walked around the corner to the closest bar, which was The Outpost American Tavern. Normally, I would have appreciated the dark wood design and pleasing interior. Right now, however, I simply wanted a drink. I ordered a double whiskey on the rocks and sipped it at the bar.

My failure to find anything usable on Eddie Ferrugia led me to making a bargain with Bruno. It felt a lot like negotiating with Tony, only with less charm and more hostility. I didn't feel good about farming the problem out to someone else, especially a person like Bruno. However, time was of the essence. Iris shouldn't be away from her parents longer than necessary. Appealing to Bruno's paternal sensibilities would reunite Iris with Tamika and Calvin and solve the Eddie problem.

All it cost me was any sense of accomplishment. And seven dollars for the drink.

I downed the remaining whiskey in a single swig, hoping the burning sensation cascading down my throat would improve my mood or clear my head. The results were inconclusive. I walked back home. A minute after closing the door behind me, a familiar German engine rumbled down the alley to the rear of the house. I opened the back door as Gloria sidled her Mercedes coupe next to the S4. When she got out of the car, I tried my best rakish lean against the frame.

She smiled, so it must have worked. My own smile faded when I saw Gloria limp from her car unable to put her full weight on her left ankle. Good thing her Mercedes only came with two pedals. I met her in what passed for my backyard. Before I could help her up the stairs, she wrapped her arms around me and kissed me like she meant it—several times. "Bourbon?" she said after we pulled apart.

"It's been one of those days already. Don't worry about me, though. Let me get your bag." She handed it to me, and I slung it over my shoulder. It looked like the one for her tennis equipment. At least one suitcase of clothes remained in the trunk.

As if reading my mind, Gloria said, "There are two more in the trunk."

"Of course there are."

I helped her inside, where she limped into the living room before plopping down on the couch. "I made the finals." A grin started to form on her lips before abruptly stopping. "Had to resign in the first set, though." Gloria swung her left leg onto the couch. "I twisted it running down a drop shot." She shook her head. "I should've let it go. I tried to play the next game, but it just wasn't happening."

"You did your best," I said, squeezing her hand. "You can't really compete when you're injured."

"People play hurt all the time."

"Big difference between hurt and injured."

"I guess." Gloria's eyes flittered between the couch and her swollen ankle. Her shoulders slumped. I knew she hadn't won a tournament in a while, but she took this loss hard. Getting all the way to the finals and then being unable to finish must've been heartbreaking.

"I sat out my sophomore year of college," I said.

She looked up at me. "Really?"

"Yeah. Medical redshirt. Didn't cost me the year of eligibility, but I couldn't play. High ankle sprain . . . took a long time to get better."

"What did you do?"

"Stayed around the team. Tried to keep myself in game shape. It was rough. We made the playoffs, and I watched them from the sidelines."

Gloria put a hand on my shoulder and squeezed. "Thanks."

"Any time." I kissed her. "How old was your opponent?"

"Twenty-one."

"They keep rolling out the young ones, don't they?" Gloria offered a somber nod. "Here you are not quite twenty-eight, and you're already washed up." She grinned. "Past your prime."

"I am not." She leaned in, and we locked lips again.

I eased her down on the sofa, and her eyes sparked up at me. "Prove it," I said.

* * *

LATER, I sought updates on Eddie Ferrugia and Iris. Rich didn't have anything to report. I tried Gonzalez next but got his voicemail. My next call was to Captain Casey Norton of the Maryland State Police, whom I'd crossed paths with on a few prior cases. I began the conversation by asking him about Eddie.

"Who?" was his reply.

I explained what I'd been working on the past several days, including the abduction of Iris, the assault of Tamika, and the murder of Ben. "Sounds like the city cops are all over it," Norton said, assigning work to *all over it* the phrase was ill-suited to perform. "What do you need me for?"

"The case crosses city and county lines. I was hoping the state had something on Eddie."

"Hasn't been on our radar," Norton said.

"What about cops from John Hanson College being on a criminal's payroll?"

"Sounds like the county has jurisdiction there, but as a captain in the state police, I'd certainly be interested."

"I'll keep it in mind," I said, and I hung up.

Gonzalez got back to me a few minutes later. "Got nothing for you," he said after we exchanged pleasantries.

"What's Eddie up to?"

"Running a legitimate business as far as I can tell. We got a few guys watching him in shifts. He goes home, he goes to work, he goes to the gym. For a criminal mastermind, he leads a pretty boring life."

He goes to work. An idea took shape in the back of my mind. "OK," I said. "I'll let you know if I figure something out."

"Likewise." Gonzalez broke the connection. Eddie Ferrugia, like me, was a millennial. A lot gets hurled at us by the older generations. Much of it doesn't make sense, but there's some signal to be found in the noise. One of the frequent accusations against us relates to frequent job-hopping. No one has a career anymore according to people who were bored out of their professional skulls for forty years. Eddie owned a business, but people our age can be serial entrepreneurs. It may not have been his first.

Before his current sports-based company in Towson, Eddie owned and operated Fast Eddie's Data Warehousing. It would tie nicely into analytics and business intelligence. From what I could discern, Eddie shuttered the operation over a year ago. The property management company maintained no web presence, so I called them. They confirmed Fast Eddie's was defunct, but the lease had been paid for another two years, which left ten months.

Before I could hang up, the helpful lady on the other end also informed me utilities were included in the lease. It was a place not many people would find, and the power was on.

Seemed like the perfect spot to hide a kidnapped child.

CHAPTER 20

EDDIE'S ERSTWHILE COMPANY MAINTAINED ITS OFFICE in a building on Crain Highway in Glen Burnie. It was close enough to BWI for the management company to boast of its proximity to the airport. The real downside, of course, was the Glen Burnie location. I pulled the Caprice off the main road. The lot held a pair of identical brown commercial structures and a white one which didn't fit in at all. The address placed the former Fast Eddie's Data Warehousing in the rust-colored one farther from the road.

I didn't know the layout of the building. The office could be closer to the front or the rear. I drove around the exterior. In addition to the main entrance, a smaller keycard-restricted one bisected the back wall. With few other cars in the vicinity, I parked near this door and found it locked. The card reader flashed its red light at me as I tried to gain access.

I walked around to the main entrance and went inside. Like many lobbies, a directory on the wall indicated where I could find the various tenants. A few suites on the first floor were abuzz with activity as people moved around behind frosted glass walls. Eddie's business, despite being closed, still appeared on the tenant list.

To avoid tipping him off via the elevator, I took the stairs to the third floor. A carpeted hallway led in both directions. I followed it past the elevators to the left. Across from Eddie's, an attorney's office sat dark. The data warehousing unit appeared dark as well, and the door was locked when I tried to open it.

I scanned for security cameras. A place like this was bound to have them—it would allow them to charge more for monitoring in the rent. I saw only one, mounted into the ceiling directly in front of the elevators. It swept left and right at regular intervals. I couldn't simply pick the lock. If someone watched the camera's output, they'd notice me.

What I could do was pretend to knock on the door when the camera was on me and work the tumblers when it wasn't. When its electronic eye pivoted away, I took out my tools and started. Twenty seconds later, I paused, pantomimed knocking and waiting, and watched the camera. Its circuit began again. Three cycles later, I lined everything up and opened the lock. I waited until the lens pointed away before I stepped inside.

The lights were off in the main entryway. A data warehousing company would need room for computers, probably a bunch of servers. It would also need to keep them secure. Even if Eddie didn't have racks of equipment mounted anymore, he still rented a pretty large space. If he brought a goon with him, an ambush could come from anywhere.

I didn't want to use a flashlight and give myself away, so I let my eyes adjust. The foyer opened into another hallway where more doors waited on either side. The corridor angled to the right. A server room would be large. The right side would be against the building's exterior, so I focused on the left side. The last door was about halfway down. Paydirt.

Before I could get there, one of Eddie's enforcers

emerged from an office to my right. If I hadn't heard his shoes, he would've gotten the drop on me. With a little advance warning, I ducked under his wild punch and backed up so he couldn't follow it with a better one. This guy was about my size, though a bit younger and much stockier. Maybe he was another football player on loan from the assistant AD.

Whomever he was, he pressed the attack and kept me on my heels. The walls and the door behind me meant little space to maneuver unless I could slip past him. Considering his speed and tenacity, I didn't like my chances. Rather than waste time and breath on a volley of punches, my foe threw them with purpose. He didn't wear himself out. Eddie must've asked for a higher caliber of goon since the last time.

Still, while this guy was better than any of the first three, he wasn't a trained fighter. He was smart enough to keep his wits about him, but I noticed his guard drop every time he threw a left. My forearms stung from blocking his blows. Time to turn the tables. When he fired off a left, I blunted it and countered with a sharp right to the jaw. My knuckles stung, but it staggered my opponent.

I tried to keep him at a disadvantage. His hands guarded his face, so I kicked him hard in the stomach. When he leaned forward, I grabbed his hair, elbowed him twice behind the ear, then drove my knee into his face. His head snapped back, and his body followed it. He lay on the carpet and didn't move. I checked the room he ambushed me from. A small empty office.

Might as well test my theory. I bypassed every other entrance and went right to what I presumed to be the server room. Eddie could be waiting on the other side with a gun. I drew my .45, stood to the side, and pushed the door open. No bullets greeted me. I dropped to a crouch and padded inside. Sure enough, this had been the data center. Four empty equipment racks lined the room. I saw Eddie hiding behind one. At the rear, a small monitor showed the security camera footage. He knew I was coming.

"Eddie, I'm here for Iris," I said. He stood with his back to me, so I couldn't tell if he held a gun. Never one to take too many foolish risks, I slid over and positioned myself behind the metal of a rack on the other side of the open space. "If she's not here, let me know where she is. This doesn't have to end badly."

"Go away," he said. "She's not here."

"Where is she?"

"Why should I tell you?"

"Calvin will play ball," I said. "You don't need to keep his daughter."

"Yes, I do," he said. He spun toward me. I saw the pistol as he raised his hand, so I ducked farther behind the steel frame. The sound of two gunshots thundered in the server room, but the thick metal soaked up both rounds. I peeked around. Eddie retreated to where he stood initially.

"Eddie, I don't want to shoot you. I just want the girl." My elevated pulse whooshed in my ears. I controlled my breathing in case I needed to return fire.

"I'll have no leverage."

"You have bigger things to worry about."

"Yeah?" he said. "Like what?"

"I heard you're on Tony Rizzo's radar."

He didn't say anything at first. "Tony don't scare me." The tremble in his voice told me otherwise.

"You might think Tony's an old codger, but he's got some smart people working for him. It's a matter of time before they find you, Eddie. What do you think they'll do when they get here?" He remained silent again. "Come out. No gun. We'll talk about it."

"Fine." He walked out, made a show of stuffing his gun in the back waistband of his pants, and crossed his arms. I moved from behind the rack.

"Smart decision," I said.

"You going to put your gun away?" he said.

"No."

"Why not?"

"Because you're a criminal. How do I know you don't have more guys waiting for me?"

"I guess you don't."

"I guess I don't."

We walked to the back of the room. The monitor with the security feed sat atop an otherwise empty desk. A window pointing to the rear corner of the building was behind it. Its tint prevented a lot of light from coming in. "All right," Eddie said, "let's talk."

I was about to say something when I looked out the window. Two large black SUVs pulled into parking spots. Five men got out. One of them was Bruno. "Shit," I said.

"What?" Eddie moved beside me. "Who are they?"

"Remember when I said Tony had some smart people working for him? Here they are."

"Did you lead them here?" Eddie reached for his gun again.

I grabbed his arm. "No," I said, even though I put Bruno onto Eddie in the first place. "I'd like to get us both out of this building alive. Can you work with me on this?"

"Why do you want to keep me alive?"

"Iris. Now, let's try to get out of here."

We headed toward the main entryway of the office. "There's another stairwell to the left," Eddie said. I held up my hand as we approached, nudged the door open, and scanned the corridor.

"All clear. Let's go."

We scampered ten feet to the stairwell, threw open the door, and headed down.

CHAPTER 21

WE DESCENDED THE STEPS QUICKLY WHILE STILL remaining vigilant. I went before him so any members of Team Tony wouldn't see Eddie first. We made it to the ground floor without incident. The stairs ended in a short, narrow corridor taking us directly to the back door. It offered no place to hide and no cover. Thankfully, it was empty.

Did Bruno take everyone in the front? Maybe he left a few guys here in case Eddie made a break for it. The rear exit door was metal but held a small window in its top half. Eddie and I crouched on opposite sides. I rose and peeked out. No one stood in the way, but off to the side, two goons leaned against one of the SUVs.

"See anyone?" Eddie asked in a quiet voice.

"Two guys. We won't make it without being seen."

"You think they have people at the entrance, too?"

"Sure." I almost identified Bruno by name but caught myself. I didn't want to betray how well I knew Tony and his organization to Eddie. "These guys look like they aren't stupid. Two cars, so they probably brought six or eight men. The pair out back leaves at least four. Could be two waiting out front while the others raid your office."

"Any ideas?"

The Caprice was parked right in line with the door. Eddie and I looked different enough to prevent these two mistaking me for him. I could get the Caprice, back up, and have him make a run for it. I didn't see an alternative, so I suggested the plan to Eddie. He concurred with a nod.

I holstered my pistol, pulled the collar up on my jacket, and walked outside. From the side of my eye, I watched the enforcers at the SUV as best I could. One tapped the other on the arm to get his attention. Both looked at me. The tappee shook his head. I unlocked the door of the Caprice and slid in behind the wheel.

Phase one: complete.

The V8 fired up with a satisfying rumble. I loved the smooth supercharged V6 in my S4, but it couldn't match this engine for sound. I put the car in reverse and backed out of the spot, swinging wider than necessary to end up closer to the curb. I heard my heart in my ear over the V8's growl.

Eddie threw the door open and ran. It was maybe a hundred feet to the car. I watched the goons in the mirror. They noticed him right away and stood, reaching behind themselves. Eddie sprinted a few more steps, stopped, and opened fire on them. Both dashed behind the vehicle they came in. Eddie moved closer and fired off a few more shots. He was smart. With Bruno's men pinned down, Eddie aimed for the tires and popped the two rear ones. It eliminated one of the SUVs from any pursuit.

He emptied the magazine as he reached the passenger's side of the car. Eddie got in, and I mashed the accelerator before he finished closing the door. We peeled out of the parking lot, a couple bullets chasing us, as I pondered how the hell we were going to escape.

* * *

DISABLING one SUV was good but not enough. Four guys piled into the second one and took off after us. I felt glad I brought the Caprice. A couple years ago, I'd acquired it from a chop shop owner who owed me a favor, and over time, he'd swapped in a new powertrain and fortified the car to resist most handgun fire. The car wasn't much to look at, so I only drove it when I thought I might need its special capabilities.

"What the hell is this thing?" Eddie said as I swung it from the lot onto Crain Highway.

"Late-'eighties Caprice Classic," I said. "It has the previous-generation Corvette engine and transmission, and it's pretty good at resisting most bullets."

He shot me an askance look. "This thing is bulletproof?"

"There's a technical term for the level of protection, but I can never remember it. More or less, yes."

Despite the newer transmission, the automatic's shifter remained mounted on the column. Maybe I could replace it with a newer console version if we got out of this. The SUV turned out of the complex and remained in pursuit. It looked like a GMC Yukon, which had its own powerful V8. The bodywork on the Caprice added weight to the point it may have been the heavier of the two. We weren't going to make a speedy getaway on open roads.

I flipped on the aftermarket GPS and looked at what lay ahead. A network of side roads ran on each side of Crain Highway. Going to the left, however, would allow me an easier drive to Baltimore if I could lose our pursuers. As a light switched to yellow, I swung the wheel hard, the tires screeching as the Caprice made the turn. Despite the red light facing them, the SUV made the same turn behind us.

On a smaller road, there was less traffic. The enforcers to

our rear decided this would be a great time to lean out the windows with a couple of guns and start shooting. Most of the bullets whizzed past us, but one or two struck the rear body panels somewhere. The blue car surged onward undeterred. We came to another intersection, and I took another ninety-degree turn to the port side, this time trying to recall how to drift from my time in Hong Kong. The car slid later and more than I expected, bouncing off a motorcycle—which toppled to the asphalt—before straightening.

"You trying out for a *Fast & Furious* movie?" Eddie said.

"You're pretty critical for someone I could've let get killed back there."

In my mirror, the SUV couldn't make the turn as well, and it ran over the poor motorcycle before bounding ahead. I glanced at the map. So many side streets. So many turns we could make better than they could. I merely needed to keep them going in circles long enough to confuse them, and then Eddie and I could floor it and get out of here.

I remembered how to drift a lot better the second time, yanking the wheel at the right moment and letting the rear-wheel drive car slide. The Caprice straightened at the proper time and took off down another new street. The Yukon was forced to slow, and its all-wheel drive prevented it from drifting. We gained some ground each turn. More bullets boomed behind us, but none hit the car this time. As the gap widened, the pistols would become less effective.

Exactly when I was feeling good about our chances, a kid chased a dog into the street.

This is the danger of driving fast on residential roads. The child halted as I stomped on the brake, wondering with a pounding heart if the Caprice would stop in time. He scampered away after the dog, leaving the road empty. I got back on the gas, but slowing so much cost us a lot of our lead. At least the goons behind us didn't resume firing until we were well clear of the boy.

With our pursuers being so much closer now, most of their bullets found the mark. They thudded off the rear of the car and its back window. So far, none breached the exterior and found their way inside, but I didn't want to press our luck. At the next intersection, I swung a hard right to drift around a tight curve, then took a sharp left. The Caprice was no sports car when it came to handling, but it also wasn't a Yukon. We regained the lead we'd lost a few moments ago.

I tried to be unpredictable as I wove through the secondary streets. The SUV could've had navigation, but the occupants may have presumed I didn't know where I was going. At one point, spying a green light, I gunned it across Crain. "What are we doing over here?" Eddie said.

"Trying to lose them."

"You don't think they'll come over here?"

"You're one snarky question from getting out and walking," I said.

Eddie harrumphed like a man twice his age but kept quiet. I angled the Caprice down a narrow road, hopped back onto Crain Highway briefly, then made a left on red onto Baltimore-Annapolis Boulevard. If we didn't have to make a goon-induced detour, B-and-A Boulevard would take us into the city.

My eyes flicked to the rearview mirror frequently. I didn't see the Yukon, but I also didn't ease off the accelerator. We set a good pace. A few miles later, the road dumped us onto 295 before it became Russell Street. "Where are we going now?" Eddie asked.

"You're welcome."

He sighed. "You're right. Thanks for getting me out of there. What do you think happened to Derek?"

He must be the guy we left in the room. "I doubt they would kill him," I said. "My guess is they left him alone as long as he wasn't a threat."

"Good."

"And I'm not doing his for you," I said. "If you were just some asshole holding money over Calvin's head, I would've abandoned you to your fate. Lucky for you, you're an asshole who knows where he's stashing a missing girl."

Eddie didn't say anything for a few minutes. I didn't much care for him, so I enjoyed the silence. Soon enough, he ruined by asking, "So where we going?"

"Out of the city," I said. I hung a right on Pratt, working my way over to I-83 North.

"Then what?"

"Then you'd better start talking."

WE CROSSED INTO THE COUNTY. I pulled the Caprice to a curb in Towson near the university. "All right." I stared at Eddie. His expression was sour, and he had trouble meeting my gaze. "We got away from Tony's men. Tell me where Iris is."

"She's safe," he said after a moment.

"You're going to need to come up with a lot more," I said.

"I lose all my leverage."

"Want to ride to a certain Italian restaurant in Baltimore?" I asked.

Eddie frowned. "Of course not. How'd you know those were Tony's men, anyway?"

"I told you . . . I heard he was on to you."

"You just happened to hear." Now, he met my gaze, and he looked angry. Eddie was no fool. I needed to play this carefully if I were going to get him to spill the beans on Iris' location.

"For one thing, I'm sort of in the information business. For another, I know Tony, but I didn't put him onto you." Which was true—I dimed Eddie out to Bruno. "I wanted to find you myself, and I did. If I'd wandered into your old company twenty minutes later, you'd probably be getting tortured right about now. Which could still be arranged if you keep Iris' location from me."

Eddie lapsed into silence. He stared ahead. I watched cars and pedestrians go by. The numbers of both were light. The temperature dropped as the day wore on, and people walking the Towson streets wore heavy coats and hats to keep out the winter cold. Finally, Eddie said, "I need a guarantee."

"Sure. I guarantee I'll drop you off in Little Italy if you don't start talking."

He shook his head. "You know what I mean. I need to be sure Calvin is still going to uphold his end of the bargain. Can you negotiate it as his agent?" A smirk turned up the corner of his mouth.

"I can make a suggestion," I said. "If Calvin gets Iris back, I think he can give you another game."

"I wanted another year."

"The Stones did a song about this."

Maybe it was my sense of humor, but Eddie went quiet again. After a minute or so, he rejoined the conversation. "I'll think about it."

"This is your best offer?" He nodded. "Fine. Think about it in jail." I produced my phone.

"What are you doing?" Eddie said.

"You'll be safe in a county jail. Tony can't get to you, and you can tell the cops where Iris is."

"I don't deal with county cops."

"You're about to," I said. "The door is locked, and the window is reinforced. You're not going anywhere." Eddie sized me up. "You're welcome to try, but you should recall I've taken out everyone you've sent against me."

He fell silent again and looked as sour as before. I called Gonzalez. When I hung up, I said, "Is this whole thing bigger than basketball?"

Eddie sulked for a moment before replying. "What do you mean?"

"Just an impression I got from Coach Baker."

"I'm a data guy," Eddie said. "I found a way to do point shaving. Period. The end."

I wasn't sure he was telling me the truth, but he didn't seem to be in a mood to continue talking. We waited for the sirens in silence.

CHAPTER 22

GONZALEZ AND A COUPLE UNIFORMS ARRIVED. EDDIE scowled at me but accepted his fate. Once the cops led him away and I answered a few of Gonzalez's questions, I drove home. As usual, I parked the Caprice on the street near my house. I went inside to find Gloria in the living room watching TV and chowing down on a pizza. She said something with hot food in her mouth sounding like, "There's more on the table."

I fetched a plate from the kitchen, added two steaming slices to it, and joined her in the living room. She smiled. I tried to give her one in return but couldn't summon it. "Long day," I said in explanation. "And frustrating."

"Seems like we've both run into that recently."

"I think pizza is an excellent elixir. There's a missing component, however." I left my plate on the coffee table, walked back into the kitchen, and surveyed the beer status of my fridge. I tended to keep it well stocked. The food situation could be dire, but I would always be able to wash down even a meager meal with a brew if I chose. I grabbed an IPA for me and a blonde ale for Gloria. She grinned when she saw the bottles.

"I should have known," she said.

After we'd each finished what was on our plates and gone back for seconds, Gloria asked about my day. Earlier in our relationship, I would gloss over a lot of the details of my cases. I still tried to avoid getting bogged down in technical stuff, but she was genuinely interested in my work. It surprised me at first, but I've gotten used to it. This also meant I didn't hold back the more interesting—and potentially scarier—details. We were honest with each other, and if a couple assholes shot at my car from an SUV, I wasn't going to hide it from Gloria.

After I told her the tale of discovering Eddie's old office and our harrowing escape from it, she blew out a deep breath and said, "Holy shit."

"Yeah. Not every day you end up saving the guy you're trying to take down."

"You think Tony's men would've killed him?"

"Eventually," I said. "They probably would've beaten him first . . . maybe outright tortured him." Gloria winced. "Tony's mostly a nice guy, but there's a streak of sadism in some of the guys who work for him. I still needed to know where Iris is, so I couldn't leave Eddie to them."

"He didn't tell you where she is?"

I shook my head and bit off a hunk of pizza. It didn't taste like it came from any of the usual delivery places. The sauce carried a subtle heat rather than simply being sweet. "I hope he'll tell Gonzalez. He's the county's problem now."

"What are you going to do?"

"I'll probably wait to hear what the cops get out of him." I drank some beer. "If I need to do some more investigating, I will."

My phone buzzed. It was a text from my father inviting me to watch the NCAA tournament selection show where the teams and their seedings were announced. I declined but promised to watch some games with him once they got going. My appetite for basketball was down this year because of my current case.

"You think he'll tell the cops anything?" Gloria said after finishing her third slice.

I shrugged. "He seemed pretty salty at getting arrested. I guess he thought I'd just let him go or drive him back home."

"Why didn't you?"

"Tony's men are onto him. If they could find him at an office he hasn't used in a year, they could nab him at home. He's safer in county lockup."

"I hope he tells them where to find that girl."

I stared at the last few ounces of my beer. "So do I."

* * *

THE NEXT MORNING, I left a snoring Gloria in bed and went out for a run. As I'd been doing of late, I kept a .38 banded around my waist as I did my laps around Federal Hill Park. I took in the spectacular view of the harbor, admired the cannons, and chased away the eight-thirty chill with four miles of pavement pounding. I sprinted down Riverside Avenue to my house, went inside, and slipped upstairs.

I managed to shower without waking Gloria, but of course, she stirred while I got dressed. She came downstairs while coffee brewed and I worked on breakfast. I didn't feel extravagant, opting for simple toast, sausage, and some berries. While we ate, I checked the sports news for Hanson's tournament seeding.

Not long after we finished eating, Gonzalez called. "We can't find the girl," he said.

This didn't sound good. "What do you mean?"

"The little girl. Iris. We don't know where she is."

"Eddie wouldn't tell you?"

"He talked. Took him a while. The asshole needed to sleep on it, but he told us where she was. We go, and she ain't there."

"I didn't think he'd lie about her," I said.

"Honestly, I don't think he did. When we came back and said there was no girl, he was legit surprised . . . maybe even scared."

"Did he offer an opinion on where she might be? Or who might have her?"

"Nope," Gonzalez said. "Told us he's got no idea."

"You believe him?"

"Much as I don't want to, yeah."

We hung up. Gloria must have seen my expression because she frowned and asked what was wrong. I told her. "What are you going to do now?" she said.

"I don't know." I'd been counting on Eddie talking, and the BCPD collecting Iris. Then all would be as right with the world as I could make it. Only the first part happened. If Eddie really was shocked at Iris' disappearance, I was back to square one.

Maybe square two. My earlier chat with Lou Baker planted the idea this whole mess was somehow bigger than basketball. I wondered if Eddie answered to someone higher in the grand scheme of things. "Actually, I think I'm going to talk to the coach again," I said.

"You think he knows what's going on?"

"At this point, it's about my only hope."

* * *

WITH JHC's spot in the big dance confirmed, the school proved very open about their basketball team and its practices. The players would leave Thursday afternoon for their Friday game in North Carolina as part of the East Region. For the three days leading up to this, they'd be practicing from ten until one. Sessions would be closed to the public but open to students and the press.

I arrived on campus a bit after one-thirty. After parking my car near the athletic offices, I texted Calvin. *Eddie is in custody. Still working on Iris. Stay strong.* I hoped he would reply as I walked into the building and found Lou Baker. No such luck. I found the coach in his messy quarters, squinting between a TV and a piece of paper. "There's an app for that," I said.

He leapt a few inches in his chair when I interrupted him. Baker raised his head so he could look through his glasses at me. Once recognition dawned in his eyes, he scowled. "What the hell are you doing here?"

"I'm still trying to help Calvin." I walked into the office uninvited, navigated my way through the chaos, and sat in a guest chair. "I'm going to guess you're still in my way."

"What are you talking about? I should call the cops." He picked up the receiver from his desk phone. The whole unit looked like it should have been upgraded and incinerated a decade ago.

"Go ahead," I said, giving an approving wave toward his ancient phone. "I'm sure they'd love to hear about how you conspired with a criminal to shave points. Plus whatever else is going on here." Baker's eyes narrowed. "I think something bigger than basketball is the driver."

"You're crazy."

"I'll tell you what's crazy." I leaned forward in the chair so I could point at Baker and almost poke him in the face. "Calvin's cousin took a few bullets, his girlfriend caught a beating, and his daughter is missing. Does all this happen over some goddamn basketball games?"

"I . . . I didn't know any of what you're saying." Baker's glare contorted into a concerned frown. I didn't have a good enough read of the man to know if he was sincere. "I'm sorry to hear about all of it."

"Don't be sorry, Coach. You can help me, and you'd be helping Calvin and Iris, too. Tell me what's really going on here."

"Why are you so convinced something else is happening?" he said. "Large bets on basketball could make a man do strange things."

"Just a hunch," I said. "Something I picked up when we chatted at your house."

Baker fell silent as he regarded his desk. The mess made it a lot to take in. "I never wanted my part in any of this," he said after a moment, shaking his head. "The promotion to assistant AD, all the shit going down with Calvin . . . none of it."

This was easy to say after the fact. I didn't want to push the coach away now, however. We were finally getting somewhere. "I'm sure you didn't. It would be a lot for anyone."

"Tell me something," Baker said. "Did his cousin make it?"

"No. Died at the scene."

Color drained from Baker's face. He brought his hands and arms in tight. I could almost feel him withdrawing into himself. The man who was about to tell me what I needed to know was retreating inside a coward. "I'm afraid I can't help you." Baker's voice was quiet, and I picked up a tremor in it.

"Sure you can."

"No. You should leave. I can't help you."

"Dammit, Coach." I stood and walked around the desk.

Baker grabbed the phone and started dialing. I swatted the handset away from him. "Don't turn into a coward on me now. Something's going on here. It's swallowed you up, and it's doing the same to Calvin. His daughter is missing. She's an infant. We don't even know where she is. Are you really willing to let this happen to a little girl?"

"She . . . she's not my little girl."

I punched him in the face. The chair upended, and Baker spilled onto the floor. His glasses fell off his nose, and he felt around for them. He slipped them back on and stared up at me. A bruise already formed next to his mouth. "Tell me what I want to know," I said.

"No."

I kicked him in the solar plexus. As close as I stood to him, it wasn't a powerful blow, but the result was good enough. I didn't want to pummel him, but how could he be so callous about Iris? Baker sucked wind. His eyes grew wide as he gasped. I drew my first back, but he held up his hands and shook his head so hard his second chin vibrated at its own frequency. "Talk," I said through clenched teeth.

"Okay . . . okay." He put his hands on the floor and looked up at me. When he realized I wasn't going to help him to his feet, he set his chair upright again and hauled himself into it. The coach put the receiver back into the cradle and took his first deep breath since I'd kicked him. "About a year ago, maybe a little more, we had a big party on campus. We do it every year. The basketball and football teams get together and do a celebration every March."

"An annual tradition."

"At least the last few years . . . since both teams have been good. You know football and men's basketball are the only two college sports which turn a profit?" I nodded; we heard this every time someone broke a lacrosse stick at Loyola.

"Anyway, we started doing it in March because of the tournament. It's a popular event. Lots of students who don't even care about sports turn up."

"Get to the point," I said.

Baker held up his hands. "Last year, a girl—a student—was . . . uh . . ."

"Raped?"

"Sexually assaulted," he said.

"A distinction without a difference."

"She was . . . assaulted by members of both teams." I sighed and rubbed my temples. How many problems in college athletics began with athletes behaving badly? "If word of this got out, it would ruin both programs, never mind the damage it would do to the school."

"Good," I said. "Sounds like exactly what should happen."

"We needed to make it go away. So I turned to the boosters. Eddie's one of them. He had a . . . creative solution. The girl got paid off, the investigation never went anywhere, I took on more oversight, and both programs were in hock to him."

"And Calvin got farther in the hole when he needed money for his mother." Baker bobbed his head. "Was he one of the—?"

"No."

This time, I believed him. Calvin didn't seem the type, anyway. "Did you put him onto Eddie?"

"Yes," the coach said. "I . . . never thought it would get this far. Kidnapping a child." He blew out a short breath.

"It has." I took out my phone. "Now, I need you to help me fix it."

Before Baker could answer, the door burst in, and four JHC police stormed the office with guns drawn. Baker backed away from the desk and threw his hands up right away. I remained sitting. His call must've gone through before I knocked the phone away from him. "Don't move," one of the cops hollered at me. None of them were the two I saw in the tavern with Eddie.

My phone vibrated. I glanced at the screen. Calvin. *I'm still getting the squeeze.* "Put down the phone!" another cop said.

Instead of following his instructions, I dashed off a quick text to Gonzalez, contorting myself away from the officer trying to snatch my mobile. I pressed send and powered the device off before he wrestled it out of my hands. He looked down at the dark screen. "Unlock it!"

I shrugged. "Forgot my password."

"Unlock it," he said again, leaning closer for emphasis.

"No."

"We can make you."

"This school have a pre-law program?" I asked. "If so, you might want to audit a class. The college may even give you a discount."

Another officer stepped forward. "You're under arrest," he said, and he read me my Miranda rights. He patted me down, finding only my wallet and a pocket knife. At least I'd left the gun at home. "Come on." The four of them escorted me out of the building, and I cooperated as the one who insisted I unlock my phone shoved me into the back of the car with more force than required.

CHAPTER 23

AFTER A SHORT DRIVE ACROSS THE CAMPUS, THE TWO officers herded me from the car and toward their headquarters. It was a squat single-story building with a brick front and faded white siding on the wall nearest me. I'm certainly no maven of home improvement, but the windows looked like they should have been replaced two presidential administrations ago. I wondered what this building had been before it got pressed into service in its current role. It seemed ill-suited to the task and looked out of place with every other building on campus.

Inside, the view didn't improve. Linoleum covered what felt like a concrete floor. Calling the office furniture shopworn would have been too complimentary. Cubicle walls dotted the landscape. Old whiteboards hung on ill-painted drywall. It all looked bad enough for me to ask one of the cops, "Is this your permanent building?"

"Yes," he said as he walked with me. "Not up to your big-city standards?"

"I'm not sure it's up to building code standards."

He didn't say anything else. After they fingerprinted me and snapped a few photos, we ended in the back corner of the place. I sat to the side of a pair of desks pushed together. From across the room, I saw the two cops who accompanied Eddie to the Final Score. They stared me down before turning away when I didn't express interest in their game. The two I rode with took seats at the desk. Both were white, probably about five years older than me, and built like they might've played football a dozen or so years before.

"Found your car," the blond one said. His name tag identified him as Jackson. "I wonder what we'll find inside it."

"Maybe the warrant allowing you to search it?" I offered.

Jackson didn't react, but his black-haired partner—Meadows—snorted. He shrugged when Jackson glared at him. "You think we need a warrant?"

"I guess it depends. Is it illegal for a Maryland resident to park his car on this campus?"

Meadows tried a different tactic. "What were you doing to the coach?"

"Talking."

"About what?"

"The benefits of a zone defense versus man-to-man."

"Which defense gave him the bruise on his face?" Jackson said.

"You'd have to ask Baker how he got it."

"We did," Meadows said. "He told us he bumped into a cabinet handle fixing something in his kitchen." Jackson scowled at him again. He probably wanted to lie to me there. I figured Baker wouldn't give me up. He'd want as little scrutiny on himself as possible. The faster he could get rid of the police, the better for him. You can't press charges against cabinetry.

"There you go," I said. "I'd spread my hands for emphasis, but you still have me cuffed."

"You're gonna stay in bracelets until we get some

answers," Jackson barked. Eddie's two friends sat nearby. I didn't care for the predatory looks on their faces. For the first time, I felt nervous being here. Those two assholes could decide I needed a beatdown—or worse. Jackson seemed like enough of a prick to go along with them, and Meadows' objection wouldn't matter against three of his colleagues.

"I've been nothing but truthful so far," I said.

"We'll see." Both Jackson and Meadows fired up their computers. I cast my eyes around the area. For as dilapidated as the building and its furnishings were, the IT equipment appeared new. Sleek widescreen monitors with thin bezels sat on the desks. The laptops looked new with USB-C ports visible on the two closest to me. The department certainly spent its budget in strange ways. What good were fancy new computers if your station house crumbled around you?

To my left was the break room. In addition to the compulsory employment posters, I noticed signage for the various services and vendors to call in case of problems. The copiers and office equipment came from Digital Sales, a company I encountered on my first case. The company which serviced the cloud storage and networking equipment? None other than Fast Eddie's Data Warehousing.

The investigation never went anywhere. I remembered Lou Baker telling me this a short while ago. I believed him at the time. In a way, I still did. However, now I figured the investigation may not have come to a satisfying conclusion, but officers still performed work on it. If they used the cloud for data backup, it would still exist. I smiled.

"What are you happy about?" Jackson asked.

"I'm just pleased to be surrounded by such dedicated public servants," I said.

"The hell do you mean?"

"I'm sure no one here would ever do anything like . . . I

don't know . . . scuttle an investigation for political purposes. And I'm sure all these brand new computers went through the proper contracts and acquisition."

"You saying we're on the take?" Jackson glowered at me. Meadows eyed him warily.

"Maybe not you directly," I said. "Somebody is, though. Before I'm done, I'm going to figure out who." Eddie's two pet cops stood and walked closer. Behind them, the door opened. Gonzalez led two other plainclothes county officers into the squad room.

"Who's in charge here?"

"The captain's out on a call," Jackson said.

"You'd better get him," Gonzalez said.

Jackson marched to the new arrivals. "Who the hell are you?"

Gonzalez shoved his badge in the taller man's face. "You're out of line here. As part of our oversight duties, Baltimore County is taking over this investigation. We're going to start by uncuffing your prisoner."

Meadows took out his keys and freed my wrists. I flexed my hands and rubbed my lower arms. Gonzalez approached, ignoring the daggers glared at him by Jackson and the other two. "You all right?" he said.

"I've been treated worse." And I had, though not in this country. "I presume you got my text."

"Yeah." Gonzalez took out his phone. "'At JHC. I know what happened. Cops arresting.' You could be a little more specific."

"You try sending a long text with a guy hanging off you," I said. All the Hanson cops except Jackson were sitting. Gonzalez's two comrades pulled up chairs near them.

Gonzalez pointed at Jackson. "You call your captain yet?"

"I will," the other man grumbled.

"Tell him to hurry," Gonzalez said. "We're going to have a conversation, and he's not going to like it."

* * *

THE HANSON POLICE CAPTAIN, a middle-aged ginger named O'Hearn, arrived about ten minutes later. He seemed unperturbed for someone whose career teetered on the edge of a grave he'd dug himself. Gonzalez and I joined him in his office while the other two county cops babysat the rest of the JHC force.

O'Hearn's bachelor's and master's degrees in criminal justice—the former issued by the school he worked for—hung framed on the wall behind his desk. Like most police commanders, he owned a bookshelf stuffed with dusty old tomes covering a boring swath of the law enforcement spectrum. The captain's full head of red hair showed gray above the temples. It might spread after our conversation today.

"You're Gonzalez?" O'Hearn asked.

"Yep." He showed his badge.

"And you're a PI?" he said to me.

"I am."

"Get lost."

"He stays," Gonzalez said.

"Why should I let him?" O'Hearn asked.

"Because I'm telling you to, and you're not really in a position to make demands."

O'Hearn glanced between Gonzalez and me. He dismissed the whole thing with a wave of his hand. "What's this all about?"

"The cover-up of a rape on campus about a year ago," I said.

"Jesus," Gonzalez whispered. I would've liked a chance

to catch him up on what I knew and suspected before this *tête-à-tête* with the captain, but we didn't get the opportunity.

"Serious accusation," O'Hearn said as if confirming the grass was, in fact, green. "What's your proof?"

"You're not even going to deny it?"

"Do I need to?"

"I don't know if it would help," Gonzalez said.

"Captain, you have two options here," I said. "You can admit to what happened and your role in it. I'm sure Gonzalez will have to strip you of your command, but it's the best outcome for everyone, especially you."

"What's my other choice?"

"Sit there like an overgrown leprechaun and deny everything. I'll find the proof I need, and when I do, I'll be here when they drag you out in shackles."

O'Hearn steepled his fingers and didn't say anything. He looked between me and Gonzalez again. "Let's presume you're right. Now what?"

"Now we need to see all your notes," Gonzalez said.

"No notes. The investigation didn't lead to anything. We don't keep those kinds of files on the network."

"Do they get archived?" I asked.

"Before they're deleted, yes."

I gave Gonzalez a thumbs-up gesture before he launched into his next question. "Pretty convenient. Anybody comes around asking for the records, and you don't have them."

O'Hearn shrugged. "It's in our policies. You guys audit them every year, don't you?" He had the gall to show a small smug smile.

"It's part of our oversight," Gonzalez said. "I'll point out the people doing the auditing are civilians, not cops. I'll also point out you shouldn't look so fucking satisfied considering your department looked the other way while a bunch of athletes raped a student." The captain's mirth vanished. "You don't have the notes. Fine. Tell me who worked the case."

"I don't—"

"You'd better remember." The two men engaged in a staring contest. O'Hearn looked away first.

"Jackson and Bradley," he said.

"Jackson is the blond asshole who had me cuffed at his desk," I said.

"Send them both in here, along with my men," Gonzalez said.

A minute later, four officers entered. The office wasn't built with this kind of crowd in mind. It was narrow, and taking the occupancy from three to seven made for cramped quarters. The two JHC cops stood as close to O'Hearn's desk as they could get. Gonzalez's compatriots from the county flanked him behind his chair.

Sometimes, the universe is fair and just. Bradley was one of the two cops with Eddie Ferrugia in the tavern. I smiled at him. He did not look amused. "Been to any good watering holes lately?" I asked him. He didn't take the bait.

"You two are leaving," Gonzalez said to them. "Mitchell, Fields—get these two to tell you everything about a sexual assault they helped cover up. I want names, dates, times, witnesses . . . all of it. If they don't want to talk, throw them in jail for obstruction."

"You got it," one of the county cops said. Jackson glared at everyone. I wondered if he would put up a fight.

O'Hearn must have reached the same conclusion. "Stand down, Jackson. Go with them. Answer their questions."

"But Captain—"

"Go!" O'Hearn pointed sharply toward the door. "We're done hiding this."

"You're going down, too," Jackson said, leaning over his

commander's desk as best he could.

"If it happens, it happens," O'Hearn said. "We were all following orders. Now get out of here."

Jackson grumbled some more, but he and Bradley left with Mitchell and Fields. When they were gone and the door closed behind us again, I said, "Whose orders were you following?" Gonzalez shot me a sidelong grin.

"I'm an employee of John Hanson College," O'Hearn said. "Who do you think bosses me around?"

"The president and the board of regents." He nodded.

"You're saying they all knew about what happened?" Gonzalez asked.

"Yes."

"University management knew about the rape of a student by several athletes and directed its cover-up?"

"Yes."

Gonzalez released a deep sigh. He turned to me. "You have any idea it was this big?"

I shook my head. "It makes sense, though. Institutions rot from the top down." I posed a question to O'Hearn. "Have you been in contact with Eddie Ferrugia recently?"

"No," he said.

"You don't know where he might be holding a kidnapped young girl?"

He blanched. "Jesus Christ." He crossed himself to atone for his blasphemy. "I had no idea. I wouldn't have gone along with kidnapping a kid."

"But you'll gladly participate in covering up a rape."

O'Hearn started to answer, then stopped. "Probably best you don't say a lot more," Gonzalez told him.

"I'm going to need to talk to Eddie," I said.

"Good thing I know someone who can take you right to him," Gonzalez said.

CHAPTER 24

GONZALEZ AND I TOOK HIS CAR TO THE COUNTY LOCKUP. It was an unmarked Dodge Charger with the usual police bells and whistles--literally in some cases--inside. The crackling of the radio frequently interrupted the satisfying sound of the V8. "How can you make heads or tails out of what people are saying?" I asked when someone finished a sentence sounding like gibberish to me.

"You get used to it."

"I don't see how. It all sounds like the adults talking in the Charlie Brown cartoons."

Gonzalez grinned. "Figured you'd be too young for those."

"They're classics. When I was a kid, the first song I learned on the piano was 'Linus and Lucy.'"

"The song Schroeder always plays. Right?"

"Yep."

"Why am I not surprised you played piano when you were young?" Gonzalez said.

"My parents basically made me." I shrugged. "I didn't mind it. Haven't played in years, though."

We fell into silence. Our destination was in Towson, not far from his station house. We entered through a side door, took a set of stairs down, and ended in the area reserved for holding cells. Each could house multiple miscreants at a time, though at the moment, only about half were occupied. Two large desks pushed side-by-side dominated most of the floor space in the front of the room. Eddie Ferrugia enjoyed one to himself toward the back. Gonzalez and I both showed our IDs, and then we adjourned to a small interview room.

Eddie, escorted by one of the officers manning the desk, joined us a couple minutes later. He wore handcuffs, which no one offered to undo as he sat across from us. For a man who normally looked in control and upbeat, Eddie now looked glum and resigned to his fate. Dark circles under his eyes highlighted his lack of sleep. He retained enough clarity to glower at me, however. "I can't believe you put me here."

"I offered to drop you off in Little Italy instead."

"Screw you. You know what they would've done to me."

"Then, this seems like a much better alternative," I said. "You might try being grateful."

"You two measure your dicks later," Gonzalez said. "We're here for a reason. Where's the girl?"

"I told you where she was." Eddie leaned back as much as the metal chair would allow him and turned away from us toward the door.

"We've been over this, Eddie. She ain't there."

"Then, I don't know where she is."

"Not good enough," I said.

"Why should I help you?" he said, giving me the side-eye. "You put me in jail."

I could've pointed out how behind bars was the correct destination for a criminal, and I could've reiterated how much worse the alternative would have been. Neither of those would compel Eddie to help right now, however. He was the only one who might know where Iris went. I couldn't even begin to speculate. "You left Iris with someone," I said, trying to purge my voice of hostility. "She's a baby, and she'd need someone to take care of her."

He nodded. "I'm not trying to hurt a kid. It was all to motivate Calvin."

"It worked. If we don't know where Iris is, though, this can't keep working. How do we know whoever has the child will give her back?"

"Have you been listening? I don't know where she is."

"Who'd you leave her with?" I said.

He didn't answer my question. "I knew there was money in this. I've been an entrepreneur. A couple of my guys, though . . . they see a little cash, and it totally changes them. They're trying to make all the money all the time."

"You're saying they could've gone overboard?" Gonzalez asked.

"I left Iris with one of my guys, Arash. He lives with his sister, and she knows how to look after a kid."

"He one of the zealous ones you mentioned?" Eddie's head bobbed. "What's Arash's last name?"

"Shirazi."

My mouth fell open. Gonzalez must have seen me gaping because he turned to me and said, "What? You know him?"

"'I'm pretty sure I met him," I said after the shock wore off. "Not too far from here, actually. A couple of guys were going to beat his ass in a bar fight, and I saved him." I couldn't be sure Eddie and I referred to the same guy, but how many men named Arash could work in sports analytics in this area?

"You didn't know he was involved in this mess?"

"No. This was before I started working it. He told me he did predictive modeling on basketball and football. I never associated it with this."

"Where's this Arash live?" Gonzalez said, turning back to face Eddie.

"I don't know. In Baltimore somewhere, I think."

"Don't you send him a paycheck?"

"I hired a payroll company. Ask them."

"What about his job application?" Gonzalez said, his tone getting more clipped with each new question.

Eddie had the nerve to laugh. "Who fills out job applications? I'm not running a Burger King. Either you get recommended for jobs like this, or people already know you."

"We'll find out where he lives," I said before Gonzalez could launch into a tirade. We both stood. Gonzalez walked to the door. I stayed at the table, leaned over it, and got in Eddie's face. The proximity made him scurry back in the chair. "You'd better hope nothing happens to Iris, you asshole."

"I'm ready to return to my cell," Eddie said, looking past me to Gonzalez for help.

"Get used to being in one," I said as I left.

* * *

Arash's picture stared back at me from his Facebook profile.

In it, he showed a smile projecting confidence. It was a far cry from when I met him outside a bar in Towson with two drunks about to beat his ass over a sports argument. This was definitely the same guy, however. Another picture highlighted his white Persian soccer jacket.

"He doesn't seem like your type," Gloria said from behind me.

I heard one of her footsteps, so her sudden appearance

didn't startle me. Her comment made me grin in spite of my current mood. "Is he yours?"

She walked into my home office, sat on my lap, and peered at the screen. "I'll pass." She leaned against me, and I slipped an arm around her waist. "I usually go for smart guys who are good with computers, really driven about what they do, and who can beat up three football players at a time."

"Pretty specific type," I said.

"I know." A smile played at the corner of her mouth. "What about you?"

"I favor beautiful women who play tennis and who have much bigger hearts than they give themselves credit for."

"Pretty specific type," she said.

"I know. It's like we should start dating or something."

She cupped my face with her left hand and pulled me into a long kiss. "Or something," she whispered, her breath hot on my face.

"Later," I said. "I'm still trying to find Iris."

One of the many things I loved about Gloria was her ability to turn off vixen mode when confronted with a serious situation. She sat up again. "Do you know where she is?"

"I'm working on it."

She inclined her head toward my monitor. "Does he have her?"

"As far as I know," I said. "According to Eddie, this guy is zealous enough about collecting cash to freelance in an already messed-up situation."

"I hope you find her." Gloria gave me a more sedate kiss this time, stood, and walked toward the door. I half-turned to watch her leave.

Then I got back to work.

* * *

ARASH LIVED in the Reservoir Hill section of Baltimore, south of the Maryland Zoo and Druid Hill Park. As the crow flies, it wasn't too far from where Calvin's cousin Ben got shot keeping watch over Iris and Tamika. Greenspring Avenue, cutting through the western side of the foliage, meant it wouldn't be too far as the car drives, either. I pondered these things as the Caprice kissed the curb on Newington Avenue.

The homes here were brick-front rowhouses but with a twist. Each featured a rounded protrusion past their main doors and extending to the top of the house. It lent them the appearance of small towers. Overall, I liked the look. A rounded interior wall with built-in bookshelves would be perfect on the top floor.

Enough cars lined the street to make me park a couple units down from Arash. Rollins, currently on his way, would discover even fewer spots for his obnoxious pickup. Speaking of which, I heard its distinctive growl as it approached from the top of the street. For someone who could be so stealthy, Rollins chose a vehicle which was the exact opposite. Of course, my Caprice with its decade-old Corvette engine was not the most quiet of vehicles, either.

Rollins padded from his truck and sat in my passenger seat. "He home?" Never a greeting—always right down to business.

"There's a light on upstairs," I said.

"Doesn't mean he's home."

"I know. I just figured it would be bad form to break in and look around before we break in and look around."

Rollins grinned. "Work smart, not hard. Let's go." We walked to the end of the street, made a quick right, and picked up the alley running behind the houses. More cars were parked here, some on pads and others far enough out to make driving down here treacherous. We kept low and made our way to the back of the house. Hopping the three-foot chain-link fence was simple. From there, a short walkway took us to the rear entrance.

"I'll go in first," Rollins said as I crouched to work on the lock.

"Right," I said. "I don't want to shoot anyone unless we have to . . . especially because we're not supposed to be in there."

The tumblers lined up, the lock clicked open, and I slid back a step. Rollins moved past me, nudged the door open, and walked inside the dark house.

I drew my pistol and went in behind him.

CHAPTER 25

THIS BEING A BACK DOOR IN BALTIMORE, WE ENTERED into the kitchen. Fading sunlight streamed through the windows on either side of the sink to show a neat room. The counters were clean and free of clutter. No dishes piled up anywhere. I've walked into many houses with kitchens better classified as disaster zones. A well-maintained one took me by surprise.

Rollins cocked an eyebrow at me. "Want to stop to make a sandwich?" he whispered.

"We could eat off these counters."

"Let's save it for later." He crept into the next room. The illumination behind us faded. Linoleum yielded to wood flooring. We entered a small dining room large enough for a narrow table, four chairs, and nothing more. A hallway exactly the length to accommodate a door on each side led onward. Rollins opened the one on the right. "Powder room."

"This one's probably the basement, then," I said, keeping my voice low. I opened the door. A slim wooden staircase went down into darkness. "I'm going to check it out." Rollins nodded and took position in the short corridor. I found a switch on the wall and flicked it on. A light flickered to life somewhere below. It afforded me a great view of the rickety steps as I descended them. I didn't expect to find Iris or anyone else down here, but we needed to investigate.

Many basements in Baltimore are unfinished, and this one was among them. Like in mine, exposed beams compromised the headroom. I would have needed to duck a little without them regardless. Storage shelves, some plastic and others metal, lined the walls. A few strained under the weight of the boxes stacked on them. There was nothing else down here. I'd figured the basement would be a dud, and it was. I padded back up the stairs and gave Rollins a thumbs down as I reached the top.

We moved on to the living room. Like most houses I'd been in, this one featured a flatscreen TV mounted on the wall. A Playstation 4 and an impressive collection of games occupied a horizontal bookshelf. The rounded front of the house manifested itself in a large window affording an excellent view of the street. Rollins flipped through a stack of papers on an end table, but the single shake of his head told me he found nothing.

As quietly as we could, we ascended the stairs. They were also wooden and creaky in a couple spots. Despite our best efforts, anyone up here would have advance warning we were coming. The landing opened into a bathroom at the back of the house and a large bedroom at the front. Considering its size, this was likely the master suite. Rollins and I searched both areas and found no people or items of interest save a laptop on the bed. Computers were always of interest to someone like me.

The third floor held another bathroom and two more bedrooms. All were empty. We trudged up the final set of steps. At some point, this was probably a converted attic. The ceiling was lower here to the point I could barely stand and move around. A couple full bookshelves and an empty desk occupied the floor space. "Somebody's office," Rollins said. "This guy lives with his sister?"

"Yeah. Room is probably his. His job would allow him to work from home."

We went over everything but didn't turn up a single useful thing. Not even a clue where Arash had gone. I followed Rollins down to the third level. We walked into the bedroom facing the street, the larger of the two. He opened the closet door. It was full of women's clothes. Rollins looked behind the garments. "Don't see a suitcase," he said. "Doesn't mean they went anywhere, but there's enough room in there for one."

I checked the closet in the other bedroom. Apart from hangers and a bin of cleaning supplies, it was empty. This must have been the guest room. We went to Arash's quarters and conducted the same search. No luggage. "You didn't see any in the basement?" Rollins asked.

"No. The lighting wasn't great, but I didn't notice any. It was kind of musty down there, too. Not the best place for your Samsonite."

"What do you want to do?"

I looked at the laptop on Arash's bed. "Let's grab the computer. If he did something to prepare for wherever he went, I'll find it."

We snagged the Lenovo and left.

* * *

I MAINTAINED enough equipment in my home office to do a fair bit of work. Rollins powered on the laptop. It displayed a

standard Windows 10 login screen. Lacking Arash's credentials, I turned it off and closed the lid. Following my instructions, Rollins used a small screwdriver to open the case. He
extracted the hard drive and handed it to me. I'd connected a
reader to my PC and plugged Arash's drive into it.

"What are you looking for?" Rollins said as he leaned
back in a guest chair.

"Anything, really. I'm going to start with recent documents and Internet browsing history, though. Those are most
likely to tell us what he's up to."

"If he made whatever arrangements on this laptop."

"Sure," I said. "We're hoping for the best here. If he did it
all on his phone, I guess we're screwed."

My mobile buzzed in my pocket. Calvin texted. *What's
going on? You have Iris back yet?* I rolled my eyes. "What is
it?" Rollins asked.

"Calvin wants an update." I put the phone down and
setup the purloined drive in Device Manager. A moment
later, I browsed its contents, opening an old spreadsheet to
test for encryption. The file opened in human-readable
format. "No crypto. We caught a break there."

"Is yours encrypted?"

"Have we met?"

Rollins smiled and went back to watching me work. My
cell vibrated again. I looked at Calvin's latest message. *Come
on, tell me. What's going on?*

I fired off a reply. *I'm working it. Have a line on the guy
she's with. Leave me alone so I can get to it.*

Radio silence ensued. I ran a search for anything created
or modified in the last week with popular document file
extensions. Over a dozen results popped up. I didn't want to
eliminate any without reading them, so I opened each one,
even the boring spreadsheets talking about the latest trends in

basketball analytics. I wasn't sure I'd learned anything after skimming it. Perhaps a career in sports data was not in my future. I would survive.

I closed the last file and sighed. Combing through browsing histories is never a fun task. On rare occasions, it could be interesting, but the reality was regular people searched for regular things. Arash was likely to disappear after the abduction of Iris, but he could have made the arrangements first. I went over everything from the last four days.

Arash visited a lot of websites related to his job. It was too bad he decided to usurp Eddie because he was a diligent worker. Maybe he felt himself to be the real power behind the throne, and when Eddie enjoyed a stay as the guest of the Baltimore County Police, Arash pounced. "Nature abhors a vacuum," Eddie told me when we met in the Final Score tavern. I wondered how he'd feel about his own sentiment being used against him.

Once I came across non-work sites, I took notes. After going through four days' worth of records, I had a crick in my neck and a page of scribblings. "Anything we can use?" Rollins asked while I rolled my head from side to side.

"I think so," I said. "I want to review this first." I scanned the list, putting a priority on anything related to travel. If Arash hopped on a plane, we needed to know where and when. If he rented an Airbnb somewhere, I would find it. I crossed off the less relevant results and focused on a site touting discounted vacation rentals.

The website alone didn't provide a clue where Arash went. For this, I examined his temporary Internet files. Microsoft makes the main folder easy to find, then turns everything below it into a mess. I dug up the most recent entries and sifted through them. A photo corresponding to the vacation site popped up. It showed a cabin likely to be favored by campers and other fans of the wilderness. Thankfully, it was captioned.

The property belonged to a community in Frederick County.

* * *

I DIDN'T KNOW anyone in Frederick County. Having a law enforcement contact could be useful if we needed to kick in a door or shoot an aggressive legbreaker. Hoping for the best in this rather narrow circumstance, I called Rich. "You know anyone in Frederick County?"

"Define 'anyone.'"

"A person. *Homo sapien.* In this case, somebody in law enforcement."

"Why do I feel you have something reckless in mind?" Rich asked.

"Probably because it's my default plan."

"Maybe you should come up with a better one."

"Rich. Frederick County—yea or nay?"

"Yeah, I know a deputy out there," he said. "You looking for some official support?"

"Only if this goes off the rails. I think you, Rollins, and I can handle it."

"What if this guy has a building full of men?"

"Good thing we have a recon expert," I said. "If it looks like we'd be walking into superior numbers, we can summon official backup."

Rich sighed. He did this often when we talked. "I'm not

sure I like this. I know why you're doing it, though." He paused, and I could picture his frown and pursed lips as he stewed over what to do. "All right. I'm in."

"Thanks, Rich. Can you meet us here in an hour?"

"I'll be there," he said and hung up. Rollins left to gear up. An hour later, both of them sat in my living room with an olive military duffel at their feet. Rich packed lighter, probably not wanting to strain his unofficial participation in this rescue operation . . . or whatever it was. I knew Rollins was good for an array of tactical gear.

"Here's where they're staying," I said, showing each a printout of the cabin. "I called the management company, and they're staying in one-fifteen." I passed Rich a double-sided printout. "There's a map of the area. None of the cabins are really close to one another, so we shouldn't attract a lot of attention. The other side is a floor plan I found online. Pretty simple layout." The bottom level consisted of a living room, dining room, and kitchen. Upstairs were the three bedrooms. Each story housed a bathroom.

"Only one way up and down the stairs," Rollins said. "An adult could jump from a second-story window, but I don't think they'd risk it with a child."

"Unlikely," Rich said in concurrence. "There's a back door, though. We'll need to breach both. If everyone is on the second level, we keep containment by putting someone at the bottom of the stairs. I'll do it."

"You sure?" I asked.

"It's my day off. I don't want to raid the second floor and maybe get into a shootout."

I grinned. "Fair enough. Everyone ready to go?"

"We'll take my truck," Rollins said. "Might need it in the woods."

I checked my .45 and two spare clips. Then, I slipped a

bullet-resistant vest over my head. It had been a while since I last wore it. One of these years, I might actually get used to storming buildings. Until then, I felt glad for the company of two professionals. "Let's hit the road," I said. "We have a little girl to rescue."

CHAPTER 26

We rode in Rollins' truck to Frederick County. It's a scenic and rural part of Maryland, with its eponymous town being the largest city. We drove through a fast food restaurant for a quick dinner, eating while we continued along the Beltway and I-70. Civilization yielded to trees as the landscape sped by outside my window.

Rollins' GPS took us to the wooded community. It billed itself as a campground, but it only featured cabins. No tents or RVs. I loathed camping, but wasn't it supposed to be a sleeping bag inside a tent? Spending time in a building in the woods seemed a lot like spending time in a building in the city to me. All you did was change the background and subtract a few creature comforts.

With night having settled in, we didn't see many people milling about. This would make our job easier. A family of stargazers enjoyed the lack of ambient light as they looked up at the black sky. The son peered through a telescope and pointed excitedly at something far above in the heavens. I recalled doing something similar the one and only time my parents took my sister and me camping. Whether my mother or I hated the weekend more was still a subject of occasional debate.

Without proper roads, units tended to be in sequential order. We drove past 113 and 114. Our destination loomed ahead on the left. The nearest cabin must have been a hundred yards away. Rollins killed the lights and brought the truck to a stop behind a large bush and tree. It would be difficult to see from the dwelling.

We got out and shut our doors as quietly as we could. While we lingered to detect if anyone noticed us, Rich and Rollins conducted a weapons check. Never one to be excluded from such fun, I followed suit. "I'm going to scout around," Rollins said. "You two stay out of sight as best you can. We'll firm up our plan when I get back."

"All right," I said.

"You're supposed to say, 'Roger that,'" Rich told me.

"I'll leave it to you professionals." We slipped Bluetooth earpieces in our ears, and Rollins established a three-way call. Then, he padded away. Even standing a few feet away, I couldn't hear him as he moved over the forest floor. I knew I had my uses in situations like this, but Rollins possessed training and skills I could never hope to match. I felt glad he was willing to work with me so often.

Rich and I took up positions on either side of a large oak tree. We were about fifty feet from the front door. Rollins long since disappeared into the foliage. "What kind of numbers you think we'll see in there?" Rich asked, his voice quiet above the breeze.

"Pretty low," I said. "These places aren't big. You can't sleep an army inside. Besides, Arash doesn't strike me as the type to inspire a lot of loyalty."

"He's right," Rollins said from somewhere behind me. I about leapt into the tree, and it took all my self-restraint not to swear at the top of my lungs. "I didn't see anyone on the ground level. I estimate three or four hostiles upstairs, plus the child."

"There's a back door, right?" Rich said.

Rollins nodded. "Jeep parked nearby."

"I guess they're not trying to advertise their presence," I said. "With as far as it is between units, I doubt anyone's even heard Iris cry."

"Let's get her back," Rollins said. He pointed to the cabin. "Rich and I will go in the front. You take the back. If there's no one on the ground floor, we meet at the stairs."

We all skulked off. I broke from Rich and Rollins, stayed in a crouch, and moved to the rear of the cabin. A Jeep Grand Cherokee sat about fifteen feet away. It could hold four adults plus Iris. I checked the knob and found it locked. "Have to pick my way in," I said over the connection.

"Same here," came Rollins' reply. I knew Rich didn't know anything about massaging the tumblers. Chalk up another skill to Rollins. One day, I would find something he couldn't do, but it wouldn't be this day.

Everything clicked into place a minute later. "I'm in." I drew my pistol again.

"Need a few seconds."

"I can pick a lock faster than you?" I said. "I'll take it."

"Everyone has to be good at something," he said. "I think I got it. Let's go in three . . . two . . . one."

I turned the knob and pushed the door open. A woman walked from the stairs into the kitchen. She wore jeans and a hoodie and managed to make it look good. Her hair and complexion reminded me of Arash, and her dark eyes widened when she saw me. She didn't turn around. I put my left index finger over my lips. She stared at me, giving no indication she saw or understood my gesture. Rich and Rollins possessed enough sense to stop and do a couple of mean statue impressions. The woman whispered, "Did Eddie send you?"

"We're here for Iris."

"We?" She half-turned, saw my two companions, and took a step toward me.

"What's your name?" I said, hoping to keep her calm and focused on me.

"Sarah." She was barely audible, and her eyes threatened to pop out of her head.

"You're named after Abraham's wife." She offered a tentative nod. "Are you Arash's sister?" Another head bob. "Iris' parents are worried sick about her. We're here to take her home." She didn't say anything. "Sarah, I don't think you're a kidnapper."

"I'm just trying to help my brother."

"I get it. I wish your brother were doing this the right way, but he's not. The Jeep yours?"

"Yes," she said. "I drove us all here."

"Drive yourself out of here, then," I said. Sarah stood rooted in place. "You have your keys on you?"

"Yes."

I jerked my head toward the back door. "Go. Walk outside, give us a couple minutes, leave the carseat, and then drive away. Don't call anyone."

Sarah pivoted to Rich, who gestured toward the back door. She fished a set of keys from her pocket, shook her arms into a jacket, and scampered out the rear. I walked toward the stairs. No one on the second level gave any indication they'd heard our exchange. The sounds from a TV made their way down to us. "We ready?" I said, looking between Rich and Rollins.

"Let's go," Rich said, and we ascended the steps.

* * *

THE STAIRS DIDN'T BETRAY Rollins or me with any squeaks or cracks. As we stepped onto the second level, the sound of the TV came from ahead of us. A door stood slightly ajar. Rollins checked the room behind us and emerged shaking his head. We crept onward. From inside the room, someone called, "Sarah, are you ever coming back?"

I nudged the door open with the muzzle of my .45. Arash was the first to see me. Recognition and horror crossed his face at the same time. He and one other man sat on the bed with another in a chair and Iris in a small crib. Rollins entered behind me when I moved to the side. I trained my gun on Arash. Rollins covered both of the other two. "I don't think she is, Arash," I said.

Three sets of dark eyes glared at us. Iris lay quiet, probably asleep, amid this den of kidnappers. The guy in the chair held a revolver in his hand. So far, he possessed the good sense not to raise it. "How did you find us?" Arash said.

"You should've taken your laptop."

He closed his eyes and blew out a long breath. "You want the girl?"

"We do."

"And if we give her to you?" the fellow on the bed said. I didn't recognize him, but he was built like the enforcers Eddie kept around.

"Then, you get to go to jail quietly."

He scoffed. "What if we don't?"

"Then, you go to the morgue quietly," Rollins said.

"Just two of you."

"You can count," I said. "Impressive. There's only two of you, too. Arash doesn't count." He opened his mouth, but I cut him off. "Shut up, Arash. If you cowered from a couple of drunks in a bar, you're not finding your spine now."

"Raise your gun one more inch," Rollins said, "and you're dead."

The guy in the chair cast his eyes between us. He'd lifted the revolver an inch or two. I hadn't even noticed. "Why don't you throw it away?" I suggested. His eyes narrowed as he sized me up. He did the same to Rollins, then held the revolver at arm's length and tossed it into the far corner of the room. "Good decision. Rich, call the sheriff's office."

"I'm on it," his reply came into my earpiece.

Rollins kept his gun trained on the trio. They all glowered at us. The guy who could do math frowned as he realized we brought a third. I checked on Iris. She lay on her back in the small crib, her eyes closed and her breathing steady. I felt absurdly unqualified to care for a child, even for a limited time. Hopefully, Sarah left us the carseat.

The .45 grew heavy in my hand, but I didn't want to lower it. The two guys with Arash might find some courage if I did. Then, Rollins would shoot them both, and I'd prefer it if no one died before we left. Despite the growing pain in my arm, I kept the gun trained on Arash and his friend on the bed.

A minute later, sirens pierced the night.

RICH'S DEPUTY FRIEND, a woman named Hendricks, arrived a few minutes later along with four of her closest uniformed friends. Arash and his hired help got herded into police cars. Hendricks and another deputy stayed and posed some questions to our group. First among these, of course, was why we didn't call for support as soon as we went in.

"It was a fluid situation," Rich said. "We didn't want to do anything to tip them off or put the baby in danger."

I found his explanation acceptable. It took a few follow-up inquiries, but the deputies eventually did, too. Because of Rich's official status, they allowed us to leave with Iris, who was awake and unhappy to be surrounded by so many people she didn't know. Sarah left the child seat as promised, and Rollins set it up in the second row of his truck. I raided the fridge inside and found a full baby bottle and a gallon of milk. I grabbed the former.

Rollins fired up the obnoxious pickup, which rumbled in the woods much like a fleet of chainsaws. Neither Rich nor I wanted to sit with a fussy baby. We played rock, paper, scissors, which I won, and then won again when Rich insisted on best-two-of-three. "You're much more paternal than I am," I said in mock consolation. Rich's sour expression told me what he thought of this sentiment.

We piled into the truck, and Rollins took off for Baltimore. Once we were out of the camping community, I called Calvin. Despite the late hour, he picked up right away. "You know where Iris is?"

"I do," I said. "She's sitting in the back of the pickup I'm riding in." I considered adding a barb about Rich here but thought better of it. Thirty years old, and I was already getting soft.

"Oh, thank God," Calvin said. He fell silent, and it took a few seconds for me to realize he was crying. It was understandable given the events of the last couple days. I gave him the time and space he needed to compose himself. After a minute, he came back on the line. "Are you bringing her here?"

"I'd rather take her to a hospital to get checked out. Even though she wasn't gone long, we don't know how well they took care of her." For her part, Iris cried in the rear seat. Rich removed the bottle from a cupholder and gave it to her. She put the nipple into her mouth and quieted down. "You have a preference for where she goes?"

"We're on the Hopkins network."

"All right," I said, "we'll take her there."

Calvin gave me the name of Iris' pediatrician, and we hung up. I searched for any Hopkins-run urgent care or similar facilities, but none were nearby, and any we could drive to would be closed by the time we arrived. "Guess we're going downtown," Rollins said. He glanced at his rearview mirror. "How you making out back there, Dad?"

"Fine," Rich said. He flicked his eyes to me. "How'd you beat me at rock, paper, scissors?"

"I can't divulge all my secrets," I said.

"Tell me. I want to know."

I shrugged. "All right. I figured you'd go scissors the first time. Most people, for whatever reason, consider it the safe middle choice. Once I beat you with rock, I guessed you'd go paper the second time."

"You play a lot?"

"No. It's a game about people, though. It's not random."

"I'm glad I could be so predictable," Rich grumbled.

"Me, too." I grinned at him, and he smirked in spite of his mood.

When we got to Hopkins, Rich and his badge handled the check-in and explanation. The on-duty nurse in pediatrics, a redhead who looked like she brooked no foolishness, told us Iris' doctor wasn't in, but a pediatrician working would give her a complete checkup. We took seats in the waiting room. Thankfully, it was empty. I doubted many people in tactical gear plopped down in their chairs.

A few minutes later, Calvin and Tamika arrived. The

first time I met Tamika came under trying circumstances. Tonight, she was pleasant, though obviously amped up to see her daughter. The bruises on her face were healing nicely. After a moment to make sure everyone was acquainted, Tamika wrapped me in a tight embrace. "Thank you, thank you, thank you," she whispered.

"It was our pleasure." I inclined my head toward the entrance to the pediatrics wing. "Go see your daughter."

They both bolted through the door.

* * *

By the time I arrived home, the clock was ready to strike midnight. Gloria must have departed for the comforts of her own bed, so I had the run of the place. I capitalized by enjoying a snack of tortilla chips and guacamole and then going to bed. We millennial detectives lead very exciting lives.

I checked my phone and saw Gloria texted earlier when we were at the hospital. She drove by, saw I wasn't home, figured I was off rescuing a baby, and went to crash at her own place. I sent a reply telling her I was home after a long evening, Iris was safe and sound, and I was going to sleep. Then, I did.

A dream of babies in the woods roused me from my slumber around eight-thirty. Groggy though I felt, I knew I was awake. I trudged downstairs, brewed coffee, and whipped up a quick breakfast of an omelet and toast. I ate it at the kitchen table, alternating between taking a bite and rubbing sleep from my eyes. Once I finished eating, I robotically drank my second cup of java and waited for the caffeine gods to jolt me awake. They must have needed their own morning beverages.

After a shower, I drove to the office. Standing under the hot water and then cruising into Canton with the windows cracked got my blood moving and made me feel like a living person again. I sat at my desk and pondered what transpired yesterday. Iris was back with Calvin and Tamika, and anyone who could try and take her away again was in jail. By any reasonable measure, it was a win. I should have felt good about it.

I didn't.

The whole thing felt incomplete. I'd been able to get Calvin out from under Eddie's thumb, but what if Denise needed treatment before the NBA check cleared? The point-shaving issue was in the rearview, but powerful people at John Hanson College enabled the whole situation by covering up a terrible sexual assault.

Eddie Ferrugia was small potatoes. The school's power brokers were the real villains. I figured most of the administration knew and at least tacitly approved of the whole thing. Wherever college and money intersected, boosters were always there. Eddie had been one of them. How many more were involved? How deep did this scandalous rabbit hole go?

I needed to find out. JHC's website told me who the administrators were, and a couple Google searches turned up an organization chart. I crafted an email in the form of a survey, asking recipients to answer a few questions about their school. When they visited the page, they would also receive a little bit of code I could then exploit. I sent this to every logical recipient based on the org chart and waited.

Sometimes, things turn out well. About twenty minutes after my message went out into the world, someone opened it. I checked the name—Ken Georgealis. He served as the chief technical officer of the college. Not a bad get. I figured Ken, like most C-level executives, thought he was Very Important and could not abide with a plebeian user account. Especially as the CTO. No, he would insist his position required an administrative account, and anyone who could refuse him worked for him.

My trojan allowed me to peruse his files. I soon found a list of production servers. Because Ken Georgealis was a buffoon, his document also listed an account he could use to login with administrator privileges on each. It's always nice to see an overpromoted idiot out himself. Pity it couldn't be more public. I scanned the list, found the Exchange server, and opened a remote connection to it.

Exchange is Microsoft's corporate email manager. If Ken was dumb enough to keep a list of privileged credentials on his desktop, then he and others were probably dumb enough to discuss the cover-up via the college's email system. Once logged in, I conducted several searches. To my surprise, I came up empty. At least the people involved in this little conspiracy possessed the good sense to talk about it out of band.

Or did they? Outlook, the client-side application which connects to Exchange, allows users to save messages into PST files. These could be stored anywhere; most people keep them on their local drives. I took up my search of Ken Georgealis' system again. After a minute or two of crunching, it showed no results for PST files.

This left means like personal emails, texts, and encrypted messaging apps. I figured administrators weren't smart enough to use the latter. I could find the trail if it existed, but it would take time. The young hacker in me wanted to deface the JHC homepage and broadcast the accusations to the world. This might alert the guilty parties someone was on to them, however, and then whatever evidence existed would disappear. I needed a more mature approach.

Being thirty sucked.

I texted Gonzalez and asked if they were moving on the administration. He said they were working on it, and these things took time. I let it go, passing on the chance to take another shot at the system Gonzalez served and I skated around. Instead, I reached out to someone who might be able to get the whole thing moving a little faster.

On my first case, local reporter Jessica Webber chronicled my history—a sanitized version—and travails. She was the first person to get the word out about me, which is an unfortunate necessity when running a free detective service. I hadn't spoken to her in over a year, but I fired off a text to gauge her interest.

Jessica, I have a scoop for you.

CHAPTER 27

AN HOUR LATER, THE ELEVATOR DOOR DINGED, AND footsteps approached. The clack of heels on tile echoed from the hallway. The outer door of my office swung open, and Jessica Webber walked in. She looked just like I remembered —tall, blonde, and gorgeous. Memories of our times between the sheets flew into my head. I took a deep breath and summoned my most professional smile. "C.T., it's so good to see you," she said.

I stood, she opened her arms, and we hugged. The smell of her hair and the feeling of her pressed against me brought back even more memories. It was all they would be. "It's great to see you, too," I said. "How have you been?"

Jessica sat in a guest chair, and I plopped back into my leather executive number. "Really well. I'm still with Channel Thirteen." The local news channels bounced between network affiliates with some regularity, and I had no idea which mapped to what anymore. They all reported the same stuff, anyway. "I did some national work, but I'm back to local stories. I like it better."

"I think I have one of those local stories for you." Jessica took out a notepad, and a diamond on her left hand caught the light. It was a nice engagement ring. Good for her. She looked at me expectantly. I inclined my head toward her bedazzled finger. "Who's the lucky guy?"

A wide smile overtook her face. "His name's Jonathan. He's in IT. I guess you could say it's his job to keep people like you out of systems."

"A fool's errand," I said.

She grinned. "He likes it. We met . . . almost two years ago now, I guess. We've been engaged for four months."

"Congratulations."

"Thanks. What about you?"

"I'm not the marrying type."

"I remember that about you," she said, and a smirk appeared and disappeared from her features quickly. "You seeing anyone?"

I nodded. "She's in fundraising. We've known each other since I got back from Hong Kong but just made things official last year."

"Official, huh? Like with a ring?"

"No."

"You know what Beyoncé sang, right?"

I chuckled. "I don't think she's the marrying type, either."

"You've talked about it?" We hadn't, actually. I made an assumption, though I based it on hints Gloria dropped over time. Both of us were happy the way things were now. No ring or piece of paper would make it better.

"I'm not the story this time," I said.

Jessica smiled. "Sorry. It's hard not to be a reporter sometimes." She held her pen ready to take notes. "What's the scoop?"

"You've heard of John Hanson College?" She bobbed her head. "About a year ago, a woman was sexually assaulted by several athletes."

"Jesus." She blanched. "I don't remember hearing anything about it."

"You didn't. They managed to keep it under wraps. The athletic director got fired, the assistant AD moved up, the basketball coach took on some of those duties, and the campus police dropped everything. They were probably directed by the administration, but I can't find a record of it. The whole thing got swept under the rug."

"The victim never came forward?" Jessica asked.

"No. I don't even know her name, and I haven't pried. They've gotten away with it so far." I sighed. "There's an issue, though. I mentioned the basketball coach. To pay back one of the boosters, the basketball team has been . . . fixing games."

Her pen stopped moving. "Point shaving?"

"I'm impressed," I said.

"I grew up in a house where some sport was always on TV. What's the issue with the team?"

"One of the players, Calvin Murray."

Jessica's eyes widened in recognition. "*Calvin* was shaving points?"

"The booster paid for his mother's medical care. It's all a rat's nest of cause and effect. When Calvin wanted out, they kidnapped his baby daughter." She stopped writing again and regarded me with concerned eyes. "She's fine. I got her back. Still, I'd like to keep him out of the story if possible. He's a good kid who got swept up into a shitstorm."

"I'll do my best," Jessica said. She jotted a few more things down. "Any other information?"

"This should be enough to get you started. If I uncover anything else, I'll pass it along."

"Are the police looking into it? Not the Hanson cops, obviously."

"Yes," I said. "The county's taken over. Detective Sergeant Gonzalez is lead investigator."

Jessica flipped her notebook shut. "Thanks, C.T. I'll dig around and see what I can find."

"Be careful," I said. "These assholes brought in a bunch of criminals."

"That sounded dangerously close to concern, Mister Ferguson," she said, flashing a smile I remembered well.

"I wouldn't want to see anything happen to you, Miss Webber," I said.

"It'll be Missus Weston sometime soon."

"You'll still be Jay-Dub, then."

Jessica laughed. We stood and hugged again. "Good to see you," she said. "I'll keep you in the loop."

"Same." She left, and I fought the urge to watch her leave.

I didn't like passing this off, but I put it in very capable hands. Even if the Hanson administration somehow snowed Gonzalez, the story would come out.

* * *

Not long after Jessica departed, Denise Murray walked through the door. Her smile showed more strength than I'd seen from her recently. She still looked thin and weary, and I hoped she would be all right long term. Calvin and Iris needed her. She sank into the chair Jessica recently vacated. "Thank you."

"I'm glad we were able to find Iris," I said.

"Not just Iris. You helped Calvin, too. He's free to do what he wants now."

"What's he going to do?"

"He wants to turn pro," Denise said. "He don't have

anything to prove in college anymore. Even if they lose their first game."

She was right. Calvin was a hell of a player and would be picked near the top of the NBA draft—so long as the point shaving didn't make it into the news. I hoped Jessica could keep it tamped down. An administrator could still leak it in the hopes of deflecting criticism, of course, and we couldn't do anything about it. Denise didn't need to be burdened with this, however. Enough was piled on her plate. "How are you doing?"

"Day by day. I'm all right for now. I know I'll need another round of treatment. Doctor Cheng is confident one more is all."

"When will you need it?"

"Probably in a couple months." Sometime in May. The NBA draft was usually in late June, and contract negotiations could go on from there. Calvin's rookie deal wasn't in Denise's timeframe. She must have seen me fretting because she gave me a gentle smile. "Don't worry about me. I'll be all right."

"Calvin won't have his pro money in time, though."

"We'll figure something out," Denise said. Or they wouldn't, and she'd be dead. Calvin would bury his mother, and Iris would grow up with no memories of her grandmother.

I couldn't let it happen.

* * *

EDDIE TOLD me he used a payroll company to dispense wages to his workers, despite the size of the company. It was an unwarranted extravagance, but I figured he could afford it as long as the basketball money rolled in. There wasn't a wealth of local options, and after a few minutes of clever searching, I found the right one. Paychexperts, a miserable portmanteau of paycheck and experts, handled the money. I had no idea who founded the company, and I already hated him. It would definitely be a him, too—no woman would be so unfunny with a business name.

Any company processing payroll must contend with sensitive information. Specifically, they needed to worry about bank accounts and social security numbers. These were high-value targets for people like me. I began by doing some research on the company and performing a basic, unobtrusive scan to map their network. Like most small businesses, Paychexperts' network reflected the size of the company. They owned four Internet-facing servers.

I deepened my research. Google is a much more powerful tool than most people think it is. In addition to looking up the dankest of memes, it responds to certain commands and operators to run very specific searches. For instance, I launched searches of the company's site for documents ending in common Microsoft Office file extensions. These weren't hidden per se, but a casual browser would be unlikely to stumble upon them. Clever use of Google revealed them.

I downloaded the files and perused them. A few were boring legalese about terms of service, contracts, and the like. It was almost enough to make me need another cup of coffee. Next was a spreadsheet of IT assets. Bingo. I cross-referenced it to what my scan showed. One of the Windows desktops served as a conference room PC. Like many similar computers, this one was older and missing updates. Guests and visitors need to make presentations, and this led to lax security. The PC designated for recycling finds a new home with a projector cable coming out the back of it, and no one gives any thought to how it affects the company's defenses.

Almost no one.

This particular machine still ran Windows Vista, deprecated several years ago, as well as vulnerable versions of many common applications. Why it was even on the network with a public address mystified me. I would take advantage of it, however. I fired up Metasploit, a tool used by many people on the spectrum of white to black hats. A wealth of Vista and other exploits greeted me. I crafted a payload, fired up the exploit, and sent it at the poor machine.

It knuckled under right away.

I was now the proud owner of a file explorer window showing me everything on the PC. Someone remained logged in, also allowing me to see network-connected drives. I hunted around for a while until I came across the treasure trove. Copying the files across my exploited connection was simple. I covered my tracks and killed the exploit, severing my link to the poor old machine.

The only info I needed was Arash's, so I flipped past all the rest. I found his banking information. Using Denise's records Alice pulled for me earlier, I had her data, as well. Accessing Arash's account required a PIN. I tried his birthday. No dice. I found his sister's birthday and entered it.

It worked. Arash's account swelled past half a million dollars. Either sports analytics was a far more lucrative field than I thought, or he found a way to take a cut of what Eddie brought in. Regardless, he'd been charged with kidnapping and other crimes. This money wasn't going to help him, but it could help Denise. I transferred the amount of her treatment into her account.

I'd been about to lament my inability to resolve the coverup so neatly when I realized I was an idiot.

When the Hanson police detained me, I saw a sign in their headquarters: Fast Eddie's Data Warehousing. I'd forgotten about it in my quest to return Iris to her family. The electronic trail of many people on the JHC campus conspiring to cover up a gruesome sexual assault probably resided on Eddie's systems. No wonder he'd been able to setup the deals he did. He owned all the leverage in negotiations. Buy these new computers, or I'll go to the press. Let's shave points, or I'll release these documents. It was brazen but brilliant.

I wanted to investigate Eddie's data scheme in person. In the meantime, I called Denise Murray. "Check your bank account later today," I said.

"Why?"

"I think you'll find your next treatment has been paid for, too."

She didn't say anything for a few seconds. "Did you . . . "

"The Ferrugia organization wishes to apologize for how things have gone recently. They'd like you to undergo your next round of treatment with their compliments. Or something . . . I'm not a spokesman."

"I don't know how you got that money," Denise said, tears making her voice shake. "But thank you."

"Thank me by living a long life," I said.

* * *

I DROVE BACK into Glen Burnie to the erstwhile home of Fast Eddie's Data Warehousing. Before venturing inside, I circled the building and looked for goons or police. I saw neither. After parking the Caprice in a prime spot to make a hasty retreat if necessary, I went in and took the stairs to the third floor.

On the third landing, I peeked out the window in the door and saw no one. I inched it open, looked east and west down the hallway, and found it empty. Eddie's door remained locked. I did the same thing as before, timing my picking with the sweep of the camera. When the tumblers open, I waited for the electric eye to turn away, slipped inside, and flipped the light on.

Tony's men did a number on the place. They'd knocked over all the chairs, broken every monitor, and stomped the laptops to bits. The important parts remained in a locked metal cage, safe from the random rage of unqualified hoodlums. Dents and scratches near the lock indicated they tried to bash it open, then probably took their frustrations out on the more accessible equipment when their crude method failed.

The tools on my special keyring got me inside the rack in about a minute. Everything appeared intact. I walked to the back and verified all the power and networking cords were still good. They could have cut the exposed parts of those but didn't. With the general state of the place, I didn't think many replacements lay waiting to be deployed.

In most server racks, the keyboard sits on rails, and this one was no exception. I slid it out and lifted the console screen. A login prompt greeted me. I had no idea what credentials would get me in. The contents of my flash drive could help, though I figured it would take a while. I looked at the equipment. How often did someone come here to login? Most administrative work could be done remotely. People frequently wrote down passwords and left them in easy-to-find locations. I wondered if Eddie or his people took the lazy way here.

Peering into the rack, I saw no Post-it notes or papers slid beside, atop, or behind anything. I stepped back, crouched, and looked at the bottom of the keyboard. Taped to the bottom was a small piece of paper with a single string of characters on it. *Mınn3sotaF@ts!* I smiled. Sometimes, the universe made things a little easier. I noted the strong password, which was good but completely defeated by leaving it someplace a scofflaw like me could find it.

Whoever left the note didn't record a username, but these are usually standard. I tried *root* and *Eddie* without success before the system accepted *admin.* From the home screen, I had access to all attached storage, which added up to over a hundred terabytes. I wondered how many companies' data still resided here. When Eddie's business shuttered, did he simply keep it all? Businesses have grown much smarter about the cloud and information management over the years, but some outsourced it and forgot about it. Was Eddie—or now Arash—trying to make money from something else on a hard drive here?

I pushed those thoughts out of my head. I came here for specific data, and I went about searching for it. The top menu was organized by storage device ID, but subsequent levels showed a more conventional file manager. Presuming Eddie and his crew organized the information competently—and considering what he used it for, I felt confident they did—it shouldn't take a lot of effort to find it.

It didn't, but it did take time to comb through all the various media. I found what I wanted in a folder called *JHCPD.* Inside were investigative notes from incidents minor and major, including a sexual assault with several alleged perpetrators which ended up going nowhere. A dedicated email subfolder revealed messages from the administration to the police, telling them this needed to go away, and the whole thing would be taken care of.

I connected my flash drive, configured it via the console, and copied the data I needed. Once completed, I disconnected, returned to the main menu, and changed the password on the admin account. Screw Eddie and Arash. If they or their minions wanted to make money off data they were holding hostage, let them work for it.

* * *

BACK AT MY OFFICE, I copied the contents of the flash drive to my PC's hard drive plus a couple different online repositories I use. It would be too melodramatic to automate delivery in the event I died, but the ham in me thought about it for a second. I looked over the trove of information when the elevator bell sounded from down the hall. The footsteps approaching were heavier than my last visitor's. I unholstered my gun and held it, resting my hand on the desktop.

Eddie Ferrugia edged his head through my outer door. I raised the gun, and he disappeared. "I came for help," he said.

"I helped you already."

"I think I could use someone like you right now."

"Too bad," I said. "I'm still cleaning up the mess you and your asshole friends made at Hanson."

His face appeared in the doorway again, and he showed me his empty hands. "Can I come in?" He paused when I didn't say anything. "I'm unarmed."

"I'm not."

"I told you . . . I need your help."

"What are you doing out of jail, Eddie?"

"I made bail," he said. "Can we talk about it in there?"

I set the pistol on the desktop within easy reach if I wanted it again. "Fine." I closed the lid on my laptop. Eddie walked in and sat in a guest chair. He looked around, including over his shoulder a couple times. His knee bounced up and down.

"I need to get out of town," he said after a moment of silence.

"So go. I'm sure you have a GPS on your car. You don't require my help."

He shook his head. "I need to get away. Start over."

"How'd you make bail?" I said.

"I told the truth. Sure, I did some shit . . . helped the college cover up the rape. It's my alma mater, y'know? I couldn't watch the athletic department get destroyed."

"Yeah. Heaven forbid we have some accountability for a terrible crime." He frowned. "You're not endearing yourself to me, Eddie. Considering everything you've done, I'm pretty sure I could shoot you and only have to pay to get the carpet steam-cleaned."

"I heard Arash got arrested." I said nothing and confirmed equally as much. "He was always pushing me to do more. Said we could get another college involved, too. He was working on ways to shave points in football. Arash mighta looked like a wuss and a geek, but he wanted to go after the money hardcore."

"You didn't want to kidnap Iris?"

"No." His head wagged side-to-side. "No way. I didn't want to take the chance of hurting some kid."

"You seemed pretty committed to the cause on the phone." I leaned back in my chair and studied Eddie for a reaction.

His eyes drifted to the gun, which still lay a couple inches from my hand. Considering the width of the desk, he wouldn't have a chance to grab it before I could. I also didn't think he'd try. Eddie was in a bad spot. He wouldn't risk whatever I could do for him by shooting me. He looked up at me. "Can you get me out of town?"

"I already gave you some advice there," I said. "You just

need a car, a phone, and gas money, and I'm not helping you with any of those three."

"I told you . . . I gotta start over." He ran a hand through his hair. Eddie's knee, which had been still for a few minutes, bounced anew. "Look, I know you're tight with Tony Rizzo." I offered no reaction. "You tried to play it coy, but I figured it out."

"You're worried Tony's going to come for you?"

"He already tried once."

By now, Tony probably knew Eddie was back on the street. I wondered if Bruno and an SUV full of goons would be rolling up any minute. "You weren't followed, were you?"

"No. I was careful."

I couldn't help Eddie disappear, but Joey could. My concern was Tony finding out. Like me, Joey wanted to stay on the good side of Tony's ledger. After our chase through Glen Burnie, I wasn't sure of my standing. One of these days, I would go face my family's old associate. I would not, however, involve my best friend in this. "There's a guy I hear can help you," I said after some consideration.

Eddie smiled for the first time since he arrived. Probably the first time in a while. "Great. When can he start?"

"It's up to him." I pointed at Eddie for emphasis. "I know someone who's an expert at this sort of thing, but I'm keeping him out of it. I don't trust you as far as I can dropkick you. If Tony's goons shoot you, it's no loss, but I'm not bringing my friend into this."

"I get the scraps, then?"

"You're lucky you're not getting a bullet," I said. "There's a guy on Howard Street. Runs a small photo studio near the Arena. He makes fake IDs . . . good ones, from what I hear. They'll get you out of town."

"Thanks. I owe you." Eddie stood and offered his hand.

I looked at it but didn't shake it. "Yeah. You do. Repay me by fucking off and never coming back."

Eddie smirked and left. I texted Joey and gave him a heads-up. Hopefully, this would be the last time I would need to deal with Eddie Ferrugia.

CHAPTER 28

ONCE I BANISHED EDDIE FROM THE OFFICE, I SENT Jessica a link to the treasure trove of documents I pilfered. It came from an anonymous email address, of course, and the link and repository couldn't be traced back to me. Jessica would know what to do with it all, and I trusted her to keep me out of it.

About an hour later, I got a call from an unknown number. "It's Jessica," she said when I picked up. "This is my burner phone."

"I'd like to say I taught you well, but I don't think you learned this from me."

"I didn't. I looked over everything you sent . . . and oh, my God." She paused for a breath. "The shit is going to totally hit the fan."

"You're running it?"

"I'd written the skeleton of the story already," she said. "I knew you'd come back with the good stuff."

"I do my best," I said. "When's it coming out?"

"Should hit the six o'clock news tonight."

"Have you contacted the college?"

"Someone did. Asked in general terms, I think. We didn't want to tip them off. We haven't heard anything yet."

"You have anyone on site?"

"Yeah," she said. "Not a news van . . . too obvious. We have a producer on campus keeping an eye on the administration building."

"It's going to be great. Let them all twist in the wind."

"This is a good scoop, C.T. No other station appears to be on to it."

"You're welcome," I said.

"Thanks. I'll be sure not to credit you in my awards speech."

"I think we can figure out a way to work me in by then."

"I have to go. Keep an eye on the news this evening."

"I will." We hung up. I drummed my desktop, finishing with a flourish. This was great. The Hanson administration prioritized athletics and boosters over a traumatized young woman. Let them pay for it—first in the court of public opinion, then legally. Iris was safe. Calvin didn't have anyone looming over him anymore. Denise could afford her next round of treatment.

Not bad for a few days' work.

I thought about Eddie getting out of town. Joey would take care of him. Unless Eddie did something stupid wherever he resurfaced, he wouldn't need to look over his shoulder.

Did I?

I helped Eddie get away from Tony's men. They must've known it was me. By now, word probably made its way to Tony. If he was back in town. He wasn't the type to call or stop by. I would need to go see him and hope I didn't get dragged into the kitchen and shot.

Might as well get it over with.

* * *

I parked about a block from *Il Buon Cibo*. The doors reopened for dinner about five minutes before. I got the feeling Tony wouldn't be feeding me tonight, if he were even here. Bruno might try to feed me a bullet. I didn't wear a gun, but I'd taken the precaution of putting my bullet-resistant vest on under my jacket.

When I walked in, the maitre d' gave me the same neutral expression as before. Not a good sign. Tony sat at his table again. As I walked closer, I saw he looked a little better. More color returned to his face. He stared at me as I approached. Bruno glowered with open hostility. "Good to see you're doing well, Tony," I said.

Bruno leaned closer. "You got some nerve showing your face in here."

"All's well that ends well." I gestured to the open chair. Tony offered as small a nod as possible.

"What happened?" he said as soon as I sat. "Bruno tells me you came to him with a problem. Then, you prevented him from solving it."

It was certainly one interpretation of events. Arguing about it wouldn't get me anywhere, though. I needed to spin it in my favor. "I think the solution he tried to bring about would've caused more problems."

Before Bruno could protest, Tony silenced him with an upheld hand. I noticed the prominence of the bones and liver spots. He may have improved somewhat, but he still appeared unwell overall. "Explain."

"Like I told Bruno, a young child was missing. At the time, the guy I went to visit was the only one who could tell me where she was."

"You woulda found her eventually," Bruno said. Tony glared at him. He frowned and studied the tablecloth.

"Could you have found her eventually?" Tony asked.

"Probably," I said. "It may have been a long time, though. Days. She wasn't exactly staying with an early childhood development specialist. Eddie told me who took her. From there, I was able to find her and get her back."

"What about Eddie?"

"What about him?"

"Where is he, goddammit?" Tony's face reddened. This was the loudest I'd heard him conversing at this table.

"I don't know. I dropped him off with the county police."

"He made bail," Bruno said.

I shrugged. "I don't know where he is." Which was true. If Eddie were smart, he'd be holed up somewhere no one would think to look for him. Then, Joey would set him up with a new identity far away.

"You lying to me?" Tony said.

"No." I met his stare. "I don't know where he is. I needed him alive, which is why I got him out of Glen Burnie. If you want to go after him now, I'm not going to stop you."

"Mighty nice of you."

I didn't say anything. We sat in silence for a minute. I rarely get uncomfortable in these situations, but it felt awkward, especially being across the table from two people who didn't like me much at the moment. The vest felt heavy around my torso. I forced myself to inhale, pushing my chest against the resistance and weight, then exhale. Tony jerked his head toward the door. "Hit the road. I don't want to see you for a couple weeks."

"That's it?" Bruno said, pointing at me. "After what he did?"

Tony glared at his *consigliere*. "I don't like how it

happened, but I think he had a good reason." He glanced back to me. "I think we'll be all right. For now, get out of here."

"Take care, Tony," I said. "Bruno."

Neither of them said anything as I left. The next time I remembered breathing, I sat in the Caprice.

* * *

As I DROVE AWAY from Little Italy, Melinda called and asked me to come by the Nightlight Foundation's headquarters. It was not on the way home, but it wasn't far, so I said I would. For a day where I really didn't have anything planned, this turned out to be very busy. I parked the Caprice on the street and walked inside. Melinda waited in her office. She smiled when I entered, but it lacked some of the usual wattage. "What's going on?" I said.

She turned her laptop around. A simple background stared back at me. *Davenport. Mayor. It's time for change.* I closed my eyes and rubbed the bridge of my nose. "Please tell me you're the Davenport running."

"I could," she said, "but I won't lie to you." She pivoted the PC back to herself. "It's public tomorrow."

"Shit," was all I could manage to say.

"I figured you'd rather hear it from me than see it on the news," Melinda said.

I nodded. "So his political action committee . . . the one he setup to find new leaders for the city . . ."

"Found himself."

"Convenient," I said. "And a little predictable."

Melinda nodded. "I wish he weren't doing it, to be honest."

"You involved?"

"As little as possible. I told him I believe in what I'm doing here. Helping girls who were in the same spot I was is a lot more important than being on some task force or tiger team. Whatever a tiger team is."

"He'll probably work with Gloria, too." This would make for some interesting conversations around the house. We'd probably have to declare a truce on the subject of Vincent Davenport. I'd be hoping for anyone to beat him, and Gloria would be lining up the next swanky soireé to line the campaign coffers.

"I'm sure he will," Melinda said.

"Anyone else announce yet?"

"Just a city councilman so far. He's popular in his district, but everyone in the city knows my father. He'll have the advantage."

I didn't ask, but in a dedicated blue city like Baltimore, only one party registration really mattered. With Vincent Davenport making his announcement tomorrow, other potential candidates may decide not to bother. He enjoyed the name recognition, and his personal fortune would allow him to outspend anyone else. "At least he's not corrupt," I said, trying for a positive spin. "Not in the classic political sense at least."

Melinda didn't take the bait. She understood how I felt about her father and what he likely knew and allowed to happen while she was Ruby. "I don't want to sound like I'm trumpeting the cause too much, but he's a local guy who's run a major business in the city for years. He's put a lot of people to work—people of every race, religion, and all the other factors that matter. I don't want him to run, but I understand why his committee came to the conclusion it did."

"I just wonder if the whole thing was a *fait accompli*."

"That's a little cynical of you," she said with a grin.

"Your father brings it out in me." So did some of my cases, this one included. "Any other bombs you need to drop on me?"

"One a night is enough," Melinda said.

"It is. Thanks for the heads-up." She came around the desk, and we hugged before I left.

Within a year, Vincent Davenport would be mayor of Baltimore. While the position didn't give him any direct influence over me—my license is issued by the state—whatever effect his policies and hires had on the police department would roll downhill to yours truly.

"I need a drink," I said to the empty car as I drove home.

* * *

I ENJOYED one when I arrived home. I mixed a whiskey and Coke capable of supporting a straw and spoon on its own, and I sipped it while I sat on the couch and stared at a blank TV. Gloria texted and said she would come by. I finished the drink before she pulled up. After our usual kiss and hug greeting, Gloria clearly sensed I was out of sorts, so she asked about my mood. "Been a long day," I said.

"Tell me about it," she said, sitting beside me on the couch. I recapped the last twenty-four or so hours, leaving out the part about Vincent Davenport. She'd find out on her own soon enough, and I didn't look forward to the day. "Sounds like you need a relaxing evening."

"I do."

She smiled. "I have a few things in mind," she said in a lascivious tone.

It forced me to grin. "I'm sure you do. The first thing I need to do is eat, though. Pick a place and let's get something delivered."

She opted for pizza and salad, and I don't think I would have argued if she'd suggested sweetbreads and okra. Maybe then, only because I knew what the former was from watching cooking shows. Forty minutes later, we shared dinner on the couch, each of us enjoying our beer of choice. "You want to put the news on?" Gloria said when we were well into the entree round. "By now, the Hanson story might've gotten out."

I flipped on Channel 13. The clock struck six, so the five o-clock show ended, the hosts passing the baton to a new set of anchors. We watched a couple stories about murders because these things always kicked off the broadcast. Then, they pivoted to the Hanson story. Jessica Webber, looking both dynamite and professional in a skirt and blazer, reported from the campus. "An anonymous source provided us with emails sent from officials at the college to the campus police," she said, driving a spike through the careers and futures of everyone involved.

"What do you think will happen?" Gloria asked when the segment ended.

"I'm pretty sure everyone on the hook will have to resign. There will be upheaval over there, but they'll sort it out."

She patted my knee. "You did a lot of good."

"I hope this doesn't thrust the victim into the spotlight, though. She went away quietly, and she might want to stay off the radar. I hope everyone respects her wishes."

"You think they will?"

"Some," I said. "Others will drag her out of hiding for a story."

It was a sobering thought in a case which proved full of them. After we ate and I washed the dishes, my phone rang. My parents must have watched the news, too. "Coningsby, is this the case you were working?" my mother said.

"Not at the beginning, but I couldn't ignore it. I got Calvin off the hook, but he was only there in the first place because of this whole mess."

"Were you Jessica's source?"

"If I told you, I may not be anonymous anymore," I said.

"Very well, dear. You did great work. Your father and I are very proud of you."

"Thanks, Mom." She always told me this at the end of a case, like I brought home a good report card. Sometimes, I felt better about the resolutions than others. This was a mixed bag out of my concerns for the victim's privacy.

"Your father wants you to come by and watch the Hanson game tomorrow," she said. "Richard will be there."

"How can I say no at this point?"

"Great. We'll see you tomorrow. Your father and I will transfer the usual amount into your account. Are you going to bring Gloria?"

"Presuming she wants to watch a basketball game with three guys who don't know the sport very well, sure."

"You've known Gloria a couple years now," my mother said. I didn't reply. "Do we need to go ring shopping soon?"

"Mom! No, we don't."

"Suit yourself, dear. We'll see you tomorrow."

We hung up. I asked Gloria if she wanted to watch the Hanson game in the company of three men who sort of understood basketball. "I'd be a fool to say no," she said with a grin.

I put the dishes away. Gloria slipped up behind me and rubbed my shoulders. Tension fled my body as her fingers worked their magic. "How about we go upstairs?" she said, her breath close to my ear. "You can enjoy the company of a woman who sort of understands massage."

"I'd be a fool to say no."

CHAPTER 29

John Hanson College tipped off against South Carolina at two-thirty. I knew Rich would arrive early, and the same would be expected of me, so Gloria and I snaked our way up my parents' long driveway at two o'clock sharp. My mother might faint when I walked through the front door thirty minutes ahead of schedule. Gloria and I both wore jeans with me opting for a hoodie and her for a sweater. I let Gloria walk ahead of me so I could study how her jeans hugged her hips. I wished the stroll from the car were a longer one.

We entered through the front door, moved past the foyer and unused living room to the family room. Here, my father mounted a huge TV on the wall over the objection of my mother a few years ago. Both of my parents and Rich sat on the couch. None of them acknowledged Gloria and me as we entered the room. When I saw the TV, I understood why.

"The president, vice president, athletic director, and three board members from John Hanson College resigned today," the well-dressed woman on the news told us. "More departures may be imminent, especially in the campus police force, which was also named in the sexual assault cover-up now rocking the school. The Presidents, of course, play South Carolina later today in the first round of the NCAA tournament.

"None of the officials offered any comment when asked. The school's public relations director said they would have a statement tomorrow. Meantime, the dean of students, Erin Bellagamba, will serve as acting president. The Baltimore County Police and Maryland State Police are investigating the campus force.

"Basketball coach Lou Baker, who's also the assistant athletic director, had no comment for reporters before the game."

My father muted the sound. "Quite a shakeup," he said. He offered Gloria a larger smile than he did me. I couldn't blame him. "Hello, Gloria."

"Thanks for having us," she said. "It was a difficult invitation to pass up."

My mother gave me a quick hug as she passed, bringing a fresh bowl of tortilla chips from the kitchen. Gloria and I ate a small lunch before we came, figuring my parents would outdo themselves on the snacks. The aroma of something cooking in the oven wafted into the family room. I fetched a couple brews from the fridge, plopped down on the loveseat, and Gloria sat beside me.

"This all turned out pretty well," Rich said. He raised his bottle in salute. I did the same.

"I figured they'd clean house. The question was whether it would be before the game or after the team's run in the tournament ended."

"I'm kind of surprised they did it now. It risks distracting the players."

"I'm not," I said. "Considering what happened and who was involved in squelching it, I think they needed to move as quickly as possible. You have to show the public you're taking these things seriously. It all started because some people prioritized athletes over the woman they raped. It couldn't end the same way."

Rich nodded. "Makes sense."

"I'm glad they're all gone," my father said. "I think a bunch more will follow."

"No doubt," I said. "Baker's probably gone whenever they lose a game. I think they'll broom all the cops out. Too many problems there. The county will probably have to take it over until they bring in new people."

"Maybe your buddy Gonzalez will end up running it," Rich said.

I chuckled. "He has enough problems."

A few minutes later, my mother brought in another round of food. This time, it was dueling plates of chicken tenders and scallops wrapped in bacon. "I need to watch more games over here," I said, putting a little of each onto my plate.

"Don't get used to it, dear," my mother said. "Your father's in charge of the menu and cooking for the next one."

"Pizza and wings sound good?" he said.

We all concurred. Tipoff took place at two-thirty sharp. Hanson deployed their three-guard lineup, and I remembered Coach Bowser educating me on "Nellie ball." So much happened since then it seemed like a long time ago. South Carolina won the tip, worked the ball to their center, and he dominated the smaller defenders for an easy bucket. Calvin led the offense, working a give-and-go with another player, then making an inside cut. He deked a defender and banked a layup in off the backboard.

"I think this is how they'll both play," Rich said. "Hanson

doesn't use their center much, and South Carolina has a good one."

"You must've watched the pregame show."

Rich grinned. "I may have read up on the matchup."

The first half continued the back-and-forth pace. Neither squad could build a big lead. Hanson went up by six at one point, then a cold spell from the floor caused them to trail by three a minute later. The Gamecocks enjoyed a lead for a while, but Calvin made a great pass before the halftime whistle, and a last-second three sent the teams into the locker room with JHC trailing by a single point.

"What was the line?" my father asked.

"Hanson is a seven-point underdog," I said. "They were last night, at least. I don't know if everything happening earlier affected it."

"It's nice to watch the team and not wonder if they're trying to hold down the score," Rich said.

I nodded. "Now, we know they're trying to win. They're playing a good game."

Gloria looked up from her phone. "Calvin leads all scorers with sixteen points. I hope Iris is watching the game somewhere."

"Me, too," I said. "Someone needs to record it for her. It might be her dad's last college game, and she's too young to remember it."

"Nothing's come out about the point shaving?" Rich said.

"Not yet."

"You think it will?"

"I don't know. The administrators are dealing with enough at the moment. Some of them will be charged, I'm sure. If the emails get released to the public, it could come out."

"What happens to Calvin, then?" my father said.

"No one knows. It should hurt his draft stock, but considering everything else going on at Hanson, plus his daughter getting kidnapped. I wonder if it would even damage him."

I brought everyone fresh beverages from the kitchen and went back to fill up the snack bowls. My mother disappeared somewhere. Sports didn't interest her, and I knew she'd be happy to cede the family room to the basketball crowd. The second half continued the give and take of the first half. None of us got off the couch except for quick bathroom breaks at TV timeouts. The Presidents, despite being a smaller school engulfed by scandal, were hanging with the much larger program.

A few seconds remained. South Carolina enjoyed a one-point lead, 86-85. Hanson inbounded the ball. Calvin dumped it off and moved up the floor. Eddie Robinson brought the ball up for Hanson. He'd been their second best player all game. Robinson faked a pass to the left side. Calvin made a sharp inside cut, took a perfect bounce pass, and laid it in for the lead. South Carolina called an immediate time-out, and the actual end of the game dragged on some more.

They got the ball in. "They'll look for the center," Rich said, and he proved right when the ball headed toward the big man. Calvin jumped in the way, however, and dribbled away the final second. The Hanson players raised their arms in victory and ran around the court. Coach Baker and his staff congratulated their counterparts, then joined in the merriment. For this evening at least, John Hanson College experienced something to smile about.

In the fracas on the court, cameras found Calvin. He cried tears of joy.

END of Novel #7

HI THERE,

I hope you enjoyed this book.

When pretty blonde girls start disappearing across Maryland, C.T. realizes his next case might just overwhelm him. You can read it today at https://books2read.com/thenextgirl.

THE END

Do you like free books? You can get the prequel novella to the C.T. Ferguson mystery series for free. This is unavailable for sale and is exclusive to my readers. Visit https://bit.ly/CTprequel to get your book!

If you enjoyed this novel, I hope you'll leave a review. Even a short writeup makes a difference. Reviews help independent authors get their books discovered by more readers and qualify for promotions. To leave a review, go to the book's sales page, select a star rating, and enter your comments. If you read this book on a tablet or phone, your reading app will likely prompt you to leave a review at the end.

The C.T. Ferguson Crime Novels:

1. The Reluctant Detective
2. The Unknown Devil
3. The Workers of Iniquity
4. Already Guilty
5. Daughters and Sons
6. A March from Innocence

7. Inside Cut
8. The Next Girl
9. In the Blood

While this is the suggested reading sequence, the books can be enjoyed in whatever order you happen upon them.

Connect with me:

For the many ways of finding and reaching me online, please visit https://tomfowlerwrites.com/contact. I'm always happy to talk to readers.

This is a work of fiction. Characters and places are either fictitious or used in a fictitious manner.

"Self-publishing" is something of a misnomer. This book would not have been possible without the contributions of many people.

- The cover design team at 100 Covers.
- My editor extraordinaire, Chase Nottingham.
- My wonderful advance reader team, the Fell Street Irregulars.

CPSIA information can be obtained
at www.ICGtesting.com
Printed in the USA
BVHW081800200521
607794BV00003B/297